BETWEEN
GOOD
AND
EVIL

R. MICHAEL PHILLIPS

Mechanicsburg, PA USA

Published by Sunbury Press, Inc.
105 South Market Street
Mechanicsburg, Pennsylvania 17055

SUNBURY
PRESS

www.sunburypress.com

For information about special discounts for bulk purchases, please contact Sunbury Press Orders Dept. at (855) 338-8359 or orders@sunburypress.com.

To request one of our authors for speaking engagements or book signings, please contact Sunbury Press Publicity Dept. at publicity@sunburypress.com.

ISBN: 978-1-62006-660-7 (Hard cover)
ISBN: 978-1-62006-729-1 (Trade Paperback)
ISBN: 978-1-62006-661-4 (Mobipocket)

Library of Congress Control Number: 2015957947

FIRST SUNBURY PRESS EDITION: January 2016

Product of the United States of America
0 1 1 2 3 5 8 13 21 34 55

Set in Bookman Old Style
Designed by Crystal Devine
Cover by Amber Rendon
Edited by Janice Rhayem

Continue the Enlightenment!

To Janice and Christopher –
There would be no story to tell without you.

CHAPTER ONE

"Why are we b–back here? I hate this p–place. Why here?"

There was no answer. Glaring back in the reflection of the broken pane of glass in front of him was the dismissive, malevolent smile he received for most of his objections.

"S–say something!"

Nothing. Just a nod towards the task waiting behind him.

He lowered his head, leaning against the peeling, brown trim, tapping his knife against the shard remains of a windowpane. He cupped his neck with his hand, slowly rubbing the back of his neck, trying to calm his escalating nervousness. He looked over his shoulder and then at his watch, the second hand clicking past each of the illuminated dots above the hours. He couldn't put it off any longer. The pale sliver of the moon resting just below the dense, gray storm clouds drifting to the east cast enough light to illuminate the second-floor room. It was a room best left in the dark. A room the innocence of day would find disturbing. A room long past its time for being of comfort to anyone. It was time.

In the center of the room a metal gurney rose up from the dust, its white paint yellowed and chipped with age, the leather straps and dark-brown stains hinting at a more sinister than assistive medical use. The large, thin-spoke, back wheels and angle iron frame attested to its pre-war age. Like the building it remained in, the medical conveyance for the mentally insane was abandoned decades before the young woman strapped to its cold surface entered into this world.

The young woman's attempts to call out were futile, muffled by the cloth gag she franticly tried to bite through. Her clenched fists struggled against the coarse leather, her head rolling from side to side looking for any sign of a sympathetic face.

He ignored the desperate rattling of the old gurney, turning his attention back to the night sky.

"It's not like you haven't done this before."

"S–stop it. Just stop it. I'll d–do it when I'm ready."

"You say that now, but you're acting just like you did in Chicago. Sniffling coward."

"S–stop calling me that! Th–that was different. She was a c–cop."

"Was? So you think she's dead? Maybe, maybe not."

Just beyond the tree line that defined the outer perimeter of the graveled parking area, the diffused light of Auburn Notch's nightlife filled the sky. It added a welcome infusion of vibrant color to the usual pale glow of the streetlamps along Main Street as the third and final night of the annual Spring Arts Festival drew to a close. The youth of the town were shaking off the drowsiness of winter, gathering once again at their favorite watering holes, comparing notes to substantiate or challenge the rumors and innuendos that had cluttered up their social media pages over the past few months. Traffic, blithe voices, and the hint of brass instruments synthesized into a high-pitched drone, hitching a ride on the lazy, late-evening breeze.

The surrounding forest bristled in the cool, night air, waking from its winter slumber. A fresh pine scent wafted through the rusted ornamental front gates, up the stone path and through the shattered panes of glass. The otherwise soothing aroma met bitter defeat as it entered the room, struggling against the pungent, musty, and foul odors left behind by the four-legged inhabitants who took refuge in the dark corners inside the abandoned hospital to avoid the harsh winter.

The upper casement of the window had slipped down at some point during the building's decay. Through the opening the gnarled, sinewy branches of a Japanese Wisteria reached into the room, securing itself in the varicose vein-like cracks of the damp, peeling plaster wall. Small, green buds along the tendrils were visible in the dim light near the window, but quickly disappeared into the shadows.

The sudden appearance of headlights rounding the curve in the road in front of the building broke his concentration. "I s–see them," Bob snapped. The car continued slowly toward the large, rusted gates. He tightened his grip on the knife. Any interruption now could mean abandonment of the plan. That suited him just fine. "We should l–leave. We can't go th–through with it now." It didn't take a genius to figure out adventitious collateral damage could easily give a strategically orchestrated plan the appearance of a random and senseless act. "D–damn it, answer me."

"You're done, I'll take it from here. GO! I'll see you in the car."

Bob didn't reply. He just stood quietly in deviance.

"Go!"

Bob fought back, trying to gain the upper hand in the decision to remain or flee. He understood the reason for choosing that night. The festivities going on in town would offer just the right distraction. It would increase the odds of success. An unexpected intrusion like this never entered into the equation. This wasn't good, Bob thought to himself. This wasn't good at all. With other parts of the plan already in motion, he resigned himself to the fact changing the plan now wasn't an option. He determined he could only try to avoid or minimize the collateral damage.

"Th–they'll leave. Just give it a few m–minutes."

He stepped away slowly from the window, resting against the wall. His wool coat snagged and popped against the cracked paint, his boots settling into a pile of wet leaves and dirt on the linoleum floor.

The car continued toward the gate. His heart began to race. He could hear sounds now. There were voices. Young voices. He inched his way along the wall toward the second window. The years of decay and abandonment crackled beneath his feet threatening to give him away. A faded tapestry curtain clung in ragged shreds to a bent, brass rod on the side of the window closest to him. With the tip of his knife, he slowly pushed the curtain aside enough to peer out with one eye. He could see the headlights.

"Kids, I th–think. Just kids. L–leave them alone. We'll be c–caught for sure."

"Shut up. You're pathetic. I'll take care of this. It's time for you to leave. I'll be done here in a few minutes."

Without another word, he took a deep breath and turned back toward the window.

The car slowed as the headlights washed across the gray, stone façade of the building. It was close enough to make out a couple in the front seats. The bright-yellow, two-door convertible stood out against the deep-green pines running parallel with the road. You would expect to see it cruising by the dunes at a swanky, Southern beach resort. Inching along a winding stretch of mountainous road in New England made it that much more conspicuous, intensifying its presence.

A young girl in the passenger seat was pointing up at the building, the cool breeze tousling her soft, brown curls. The young boy driving—his first venture out with a new license and the keys to Mom's car—appeared more interested in his date's playful ass than what her petite finger was endeavoring to draw his attention to. The car slowed as it approached the gate, pulling off onto the gravel.

He looked over at the gurney, then again at his watch, followed closely by a petulant exhale. Bob had abandoned his protests. It was up to him now. A faint smile drew up the ends of his lips. "You'll just need to wait a few minutes more," he whispered.

The young woman strapped to the gurney was lucid enough to realize something outside had caught her captors' attention. While she struggled to free herself, she caught bits and pieces of someone talking, but this voice was different. It lacked the panicky pitch of before. The deeper, grittier, more controlled voice intensified the terror she felt. It came from behind her, his actions playing out in silhouette on the wall in front of her like Plato's Cave. Her pulse quickened, her breathing fast and shallow. She tried biting through the thick, cloth gag. It was no use. Her jaw was numb from the pain. Frantically, she tried kicking her feet. Anything to attract attention. The withered, leather straps securing her ankles and wrists were tight. Too tight. Two wider straps were over her upper and lower torso. Another thin strap secured her head flush to the gurney, the rusted buckle digging into her temple. Looking up, she could make out what looked like an old ceiling fixture. The edges were soft, diffused. Some type of plastic cover had been assembled over her, about a foot above her head. Perspiration had darkened her wavy, light-brown hair, her cheeks wet with tears flowing from innocent, green eyes.

He turned back, peering through a tear in the heavy tapestry curtain. A perverse amusement came over him when he realized the car had stopped. His breaths became short bursts, keeping time with his pounding heart. The young girl in the front seat remained animated, still pointing up at the building. She pointed directly at the window and the tattered curtain he concealed himself behind. *You don't want to come in here*, he thought smugly to himself, turning away from the window for a moment. Bob's warning echoed in his thoughts, sharply replacing the amusement with apprehension. He looked over at the gurney, and then back through the tear in the curtain. The sweat burned his eyes as it rolled down from his forehead. "Go away, we don't have time for this." He mumbled softly, wiping at his eyes with the coarse, wool sleeve of his coat. "We have work to do. There's a long, enjoyable life waiting for you down the road. Get the hell outta here." He rolled back against the wall, blinking uncontrollably, trying to clear his eyes.

The sound of car doors closing, followed by the rattle of the chain that was left unsecured on the front gate, turned him back towards the window. He drew the curtain aside slightly once more with his knife.

4

The kids were close enough now to make out what they were saying. The handsome, young boy dared his date to go inside, making ghoulish noises followed by childish clucking to intensify the dare. She just laughed, throwing the same dare back at him. They continued to goad each other for a few minutes. The level of volume and cowardice escalated with each volley. They pushed each other closer to the marble steps. Closer. Their eyes darted from one window to the next. The young man took her hands. He stepped backwards up the first step, pulling her along with him. "Come on," he griped. "Just some old building." She dug the heels of her Pro Keds into the gravel, playfully shaking her head.

His heart continued to pound as he watched the antics of the young couple. He squeezed his eyes tighter as if that would make the whole situation go away. "Get out of here," he snarled through clenched teeth, leaning back against the wall. "Get out of here." He patted the pocket holding his gun. He only needed ten more minutes alone, and it would be over. Just ten minutes. Adding two more murders would ruin everything. But he will.

Suddenly, a metallic crash broke the silence. His eyes abruptly opened. The young woman strapped to the gurney had twisted her body enough to tear away the leather strap on her lower torso. With a violent shake she knocked the metal pan next to her left hip off the gurney and onto the linoleum floor. The weight of the metal pan and its contents was enough to tear away the corner of the plastic tent secured over her with clamps.

Before he could react, the slamming of car doors and screeching of tires arrested his attention—he wasn't the only one startled by the crash. Peering back through the window, he caught a quick flash of the red taillights on the fishtailing convertible. It disappeared into a tan cloud of dust and leaves, speeding down the road leading to that long, enjoyable life. The not-so-brave kids were heading back to town as quickly as Mom's car could get them there.

He shook his head and breathed a deep sigh of relief. He took a couple more deep breaths and walked over to the gurney. "If we see those two again," he said, wiping at the sweat from his eyes and picking up the tray, "I'll make it a point to explain how close they came to joining you this evening."

His breathing returned to normal, but he knew it might not be the end of it. If he's lucky, they'll convince themselves it was the ghostly presence of old man Willis roaming the halls, rattling a few bedpans along the way. The thought produced an amusing grunt. The task at hand quickly wiped the slight amusement from his face. "It appears your foolish attempt to get their attention scared the little shits off for now," he mumbled under his breath. Another possible scenario muscled its way into his head. If they exaggerate the story to their friends in town, he could soon find himself overrun with young ghost hunters looking to prove their manhood and scaring the shit out of their girlfriends. This more than slightly conceivable outcome refocused him, producing an added urgency.

He put his gloves back on, protecting his hands from the freezing effect of the dry ice, and replaced the tray on the gurney next to her hip. The young woman's sobbing fell on deaf ears. After reattaching the loose corner flap of the plastic tent assembled over her, he resumed his post by the window, looking back at the gurney every few minutes.

The young woman continued her struggle. The remaining straps held tightly. They were stronger than her depleted strength could fight. Hypercapnia was taking hold. Her heart pounded, her muscles twitched uncontrollably. A lethargic limpness began setting in. With a final burst of consciousness, she made a last desperate attempt to save herself. It wasn't to be. Within ten minutes the silence of the grave had absorbed her last cries, her last breath. The fear in her eyes melted into an inconsolable stare. The once-soft blush on her cheeks hardened into a pale blue. Her struggle to understand what was happening and why was over.

"I'm s–sorry," Bob said softly as he paused by the gurney, leaning down close to her ear. "I tried to s–stop him."

He placed a small table he brought in from another room in front of the window. From a canvas bag on the floor he retrieved a thick, black candle and a chipped plate, taking care to position them just right on the table in front of the few remaining panes of glass. He pulled a matchbook from his pocket—a souvenir from a cheap motel outside of Seattle he kept with him. There were only a few matches left in the book. He tore one off. With a single strike the room filled with a soft glow as he lit the wick.

The room felt as cold and quiet as charity. Bob methodically disassembled the small plastic tent secured to the gurney, stuffing it into the canvas bag on the floor. He took the metal tray back to the outer hall where he found it, taking care not to disturb the pile of debris too much while carefully burying it. He returned to the room. From a cloth bag tied to his belt he tossed handfuls of soot and ash around the gurney, obscuring his footsteps, blending his presence back into the years of neglect.

Bob took one last look around the room, assuring himself the scene was staged exactly the way it needed to be. Satisfied, he took a few more handfuls from the cloth bag, releasing the soot and ash into the air with repeated sweeping motions. The grey clouds drifted down over the body of the young woman and onto the floor; the murderous act dissolving into the shadows. The ash filled the room with a fresh layer of neglect, almost snuffing out the candle he left by the window. He put his arm through the handles of the canvas bag, tossing it over one shoulder. Backing out of the room and down the stairs, he exhausted the last handfuls of soot and ash, covering his footsteps as he made his way out to the back of the building where the car remained hidden from view.

"Th–this was your idea," Bob grumbled, placing the black canvas bag and the empty bag of soot and ash in the trunk. "But once again I'm l–left to do all the w–work."

He got in the car and turned the key in the ignition. With the lights off, the car slowly made its way around to the front of the building, stopping at the gate leading to the main road. Looking up, he could see the light from the candle illuminating the second-floor window, the last remnants of ash producing an angelic halo around the elongated flame.

"Th–this has to s–stop. I won't d–do it any more. Do you hear me?" Bob looked in the rearview mirror. Staring back at him were the cold, dark eyes of his stepbrother. He clapped his palms over his ears, gripping his head as he pinched his eyes shut as hard as he could. "I'm not l–listening to you any m–more."

"Protest all you want, you have no choice in the matter."

"What is it?" Hugh Calder grunted, putting his phone on speaker. He recognized the name on the screen. "Shit. Do you know what time it is? I was sleeping."

"Where the hell are you?"

"Brooklyn . . . but I think you already knew that. I had a few vacation days coming. I thought I might take in the sights. This shithole's beautiful this time of year. All the graffiti's in bloom."

"Always a smartass. How's that reputation of yours doing?" He waited. There was no reply, only short, determined breaths. "You caused you're own problems with all that crap you were making up. I'm surprised your editor didn't can your ass for almost getting that cop killed."

The last statement struck a nerve. "I didn't almost get anyone killed. She's alive, thanks to me."

"I wonder if she sees it that way?"

"If you're done—"

"If I find out you're withholding evidence," MacGregor interrupted, "or manipulating facts to resurrect you're shaky credibility, you won't be able to get a job reporting on potato futures for the *Prairie City Iowa Gazetteer*. Do we understand each other?"

Calder laughed. "You woke me up just to insult me? You need'a get a life, Mac." He paused. "Look, I've told you everything I know."

"Except what you're doing in Brooklyn. Those four murders took place in Manhattan, so why are you there?"

"So you *do* think it's all related." Calder waited for a reply. Nothing. About what he expected. "Look, MacGregor, I'm not taking notes. Just asking. That's all."

"I don't know what to think yet, but I'm sure as hell not telling you once I figure it out. If you want to get back to sleep, answer the question. What are you doing in Brooklyn?"

"Look. I was chasing down a story lead in Manhattan when I got an anonymous tip to show up at a bar here in Brooklyn. Just some ass-wipe yanking my chain I guess. I wasted a whole night. Nothing. I'm heading back to Chicago in the morning."

"What was the tip about?"

"Don't know. Like I said, I waited all night. Nothing happened. I'm tired, and I'm going back to sleep. Good night, Mac."

Calder tapped the red button. Call ended. 1:17 a.m. replaced MacGregor's name on the screen. With a grumble, he turned, took another sip of scotch, and went back to sifting through the photos and newspaper clippings cluttering the desk in front of him.

◆ ◆ ◆

The festivities in town were slowly petering out as the eleven o'clock hour approached. The earlier-packed sidewalks along the main drag, crowded with assorted craft and food vendors, were opening back up in ten-foot sections at a time as booths were disassembled. The trendy watering holes were still flush with business. The locals shuffled through the crowds grumbling about quieter times, while the newly of-age drinkers were busy testing the waters and carving out a space for themselves at the bar. The clusters gathered around family activities had diminished proportionately with the ages of the children attached to the extended arms of their parents. Cafés and eateries were cleaning up after a long day of serving sandwiches, dinners, sweets, and coffee to an overwhelming flock of locals and out-of-towners in for the festival. The assortment of local college students hired for the event were busy wiping down tables, eagerly anticipating a second wave of good tips. About another thirty minutes they figured, as soon as the parents washed the cotton candy and ice cream off all the little faces and they were nestled snugly beneath their covers.

"Promise," a shrill voice called out from one of the tables on the sidewalk in front of the Auburn Coffee House. "Sheriff Flynn, do you have a minute?"

As Sheriff Flynn approached the coffee house, she couldn't help but notice Mrs. Johnson seated at one of the tables on the sidewalk. Policing the festival activities and the swelling of the population proved a long and tiring three days. Chitchat remained at the bottom of her list of things to do at that moment. She had hoped her hastened step, lowered head, and obvious intention of ignoring any recognition of her would give the impression of being off on police business. She paused, looking over the tops of the crowd, hoping to see some sort of minor criminal activity going on. Nothing major, she thought to herself. Public urination would work. Littering. A dog walker not scooping. Anything? Her thoughts eventually drifted to the possibility of a shootout in front of the bank as not being such a bad option at that moment. It wasn't to be. She caught a glimpse of Mrs. Johnson out of the corner of her eye still waving. Not a distraction in sight. This town is too damn law abiding.

"Sheriff Promise Mary Flynn," called out Mrs. Johnson, as if addressing a petulant child. "I've got a matter we need to discuss."

Sheriff Flynn tucked her hopes of a shootout away and walked over to the table. She took a deep breath and forced a smile. "I'm sorry, Mrs. Johnson, I didn't see you there. You see, I'm on my way—"

"Nonsense," replied Mrs. Johnson cordially but firmly. "There is always a moment for two civil servants to compare notes. Besides, you have a whole department to handle the day-to-day policing of this fine town." Mrs. Johnson paused, looked out over her reading glasses at the sheriff, giving the attractive, tall blond the onceover. "You know, it wouldn't break any laws if you did something with your hair other than stuffing it under that hat." She gave a petite snort to signal the end of her analyzing glance.

"With a little eye shadow, I would imagine some men might even find you attractive."

Sheriff Flynn clenched her teeth into what might be construed as a smile and groaned. Forget the bank, a shootout right here will work just fine. "If this is about the missing money from the swim club account, Hank has been quietly looking into it. I can assure you—"

"No. No. No!" Mrs. Johnson replied, looking around and making sure no one was listening. "Please keep your voice down. I don't want anyone to know I've asked you to look into that."

Promise bit her inside cheek, continuing the conversation through clenched teeth. "Is there something else on your mind, Alice?"

"Yes. There is something much more urgent I believe we need to discuss," said Alice Johnson. She pushed out the chair across from her with her foot, giving a nod of direction to the sheriff. "Have a seat, this will only take a minute. It's the well-being of our citizenry at stake, and I know it's as much a priority to you as it is to me."

There was no escape. Short of an actual crime being committed at that very moment right in front of them, Flynn had no choice but to sit, smile, and listen to what the councilwoman had on her mind. "Well-being of the citizenry? I'm not sure I understand."

The councilwoman pulled a green folder from her oversized canvas tote, placing it down on the table in front of Flynn. "As you can tell by these photos, I've made an extensive investigation of that dangerous curve out by the old asylum. This photo here," she continued, nudging one of the photos out from the pile, "is of particular interest. You see that guardrail? I kicked it a few times, and it broke clean away from the support going into the ground. It's that way along the entire length of the curve. It's a deathtrap. I know this is a highway department matter, but I can't stand by when a potential hazard to the fine people of this town is being ignored."

Sheriff Flynn picked up the photo, making a careful examination of the evidence. "Those temporary barricades should be just fine." She pointed to one in particular in the photo. "Like this one you had to move in order to get close enough to kick the guardrail. As long as no one moves them again, these will certainly protect the fine citizens of Auburn Notch." Promise paused for a moment. "I believe there is also a sign directing people to use the fire access road as an alternative. It's just up around the bend from that curve."

"Nobody is going to use that narrow, dirt road. I certainly wouldn't. Besides, most people don't even know it's there."

"Well, I'm not sure what else I can do. At this point it's a matter between you and the highway department."

"Luke Sanders said he has money appropriated to replace the old guardrail in the new budget, but his department has a few other matters higher on his priority list." Councilwoman Johnson tidied up the pile of photos and slipped them and the folder back into her tote. "Those wooden barricades might be fine to block off a parade route, but a speeding car will go right through them and over that embankment."

Sheriff Flynn rose from her seat, eyeing her deputy coming in her direction at a hastened pace. No matter what he wants, she thought to herself, it was going to be an important matter in need of my immediate attention. "Everyone knows how treacherous that stretch of road is. I can't image anyone speeding around that curve. If it will make you happy, I'll talk to Luke and see if we can't get a few more caution signs posted further down the road in both directions until his men can get out there. In the meantime, try not to kick it anymore."

Councilwoman Johnson's eyes narrowed at the insinuation. She responded with a grunt and a halfhearted smile. "Thank you, Promise, I knew I could count on your support."

Sheriff Flynn nodded. She felt a light tap on her shoulder.

"Sorry to interrupt, ladies."

"What is it, Hank?" replied the sheriff brightly; uncharacteristically appreciating his interruption whether or not it turned out to be his usual bellyaching about something he would have done differently.

"It may be nothing, Sheriff," replied Hank, turning the sheriff away from the table and speaking quietly, "but we got a report there's a lit candle in a second floor window of the old mental hospital. I'll take care of it, I just wanted to let you know I'm goin' up there."

Sheriff Flynn didn't respond. A quick gasp stole her voice. She glanced passed Hank, her eyes rolling upward following the tree line. There, perched on a granite crag a thousand or so feet in elevation above the town, were the weathered edges of slate gables piercing the silhouette of a tired length of pine trees. Where the spikes and dips clustered together were a fair representation of the past health of such a grand structure, the sharp drop-off to a flat, indigo tree line is deathly expressive of its sudden and tragic end. Little more than the discarded shell of how it once appeared, there remained a slight whisper of evil in its squalid halls. To Promise, this evil had a different voice. A voice she never wanted to hear again.

"It's those damn kids," moaned Mrs. Johnson, her hearing as acute as rumor had it. "You know, that group that walks around here dressed in black with those God-awful tattoos and piercings. Vampires, that's what I say they are. Black shirts. Black pants. Black boots. Skulking about at night. Always up to no good. What decent child has coal-black hair with a white streak running down the left side? Up to no good, that's what I say. I've a mind to call their parents in front of the next council meeting . . ."

"Are you okay, Sheriff?" Hank whispered under Mrs. Johnson's rant.

Sheriff Flynn's eyes remained fixed on the asylum. The chill running up her spine muffled any recognition of what her deputy was saying. She could feel a dull ache rising in her left shoulder. Not again. It can't be. It can't be.

"Did you hear me, Promise?" interrupted Councilwoman Johnson. "It's those kids. Those vampires. Those damn—"

Sheriff Flynn raised her hand, shaking off the panicked look she hoped went unnoticed. She took a deep breath, tempering her response. "We don't know anything yet, Alice. As for your vampires, I don't think this town has seen a bit of trouble from any of those kids. They just express themselves a little differently than you and I." She hesitated, trying to hold the words back. The next remark went off like the snap of a mousetrap. "And if dressing in black was a crime, they'd be sharing a cell with you. If you'll excuse me, I think I better go out and see what's going on. I'll make it a point to find you tomorrow after I speak to Luke. Nice seeing you, Alice."

Mrs. Johnson replied with a carping grunt. Before she could mount her rebuttal, Sheriff Flynn and Hank were in the patrol car heading out of town on Interstate 93 toward the abandoned mental hospital.

"What are you looking at?" asked Sheriff Flynn, giving a quick glance over at Hank.

"If dressing in black was a crime?"

"Yeah, I'm probably gonna regret that."

Hank paused, trying to get a read on the sheriff's expression. She actually looked spooked. They had been working together for two years. Two irritating years, according to Hank. Auburn Notch certainly isn't a hub of criminal activity, just the usual share of traffic tickets and the occasional dead body due to a house fire or accident. Nothing ever happened that would warrant the mayor appointing some out-of-town, big-city detective as sheriff instead of him. He had the town council's ear and wasn't bashful about letting them know he was suspicious about her past. Hank was convinced it was only a matter of time before he would uncover the information he needed to replace his boss behind the big desk in the sheriff's office. For the time being, she was sheriff, and he just had to deal with it.

Promise Flynn might be some out-of-town detective, but she spent many years vacationing in Auburn Notch with her family. One thing she learned back then, there are no secrets in a small New England town. She was very much aware of Hank's resentment from her first day on the job and decided to let him dig around all he wanted. Just to make it interesting, she also put him in charge of the swim club investigation. She already had a good read on what transpired, but giving the investigation to Hank would flush out his true character. If he's half the cop he tells people he is, he should have no problem putting the pieces together. It will also test his loyalty. Flynn had a feeling at least two prominent people might be involved with the missing money, and one of them is a close friend of Hanks. If he comes up empty, writing traffic tickets in a small town is going to be the extent of his law enforcement career. Until then, she'll just have to continue to ignore him tugging at the rug under her boots.

"So why are you tagging along? I said I'd handle it."

Flynn's mind was elsewhere. By the time she realized he was talking to her, Hank tried another approach to get an answer.

"Just kids. That's all," Hank huffed.

"What is?"

"The candle in the window of the asylum. I chase those damn kids outta there once a week. You didn't have to come along. It's probably nothing. Just a candle in the window of an old building."

Sheriff Flynn looked over at Hank, her lips drawn tightly closed. She shook her head and looked back through the windshield at the dark road ahead. "It's never just a candle."

CHAPTER TWO

"There you are," said Angela Pierce. "I wasn't sure you were going to show."

Angela Pierce was a bright, energetic twenty-something. Tall, athletic, and quick to laugh, she possessed an arresting smile. After graduating from Boston College she took a position as an aide to Lawrence Banks, State Treasurer. When not working on state business, she indulges her passion for photography by working Saturdays at the Gordon Photography Studio in town. Not a photographer herself by any definition of the term, just someone with an appreciation of seeing life captured in a single frame. She readily admits to being all thumbs around the simplest digital camera. Even without the admission, the dark, blurry object in the upper, left corner in most of her photos is a testimony to a wandering thumb and her lack of ability. Despite these shortcomings, she has an exceptional eye for the work of others.

"Are you alright," Angela repeated, with a slight edge. "You look a little wrung out. Where have you been?"

"I'm fine," Marty snapped back.

Angela took a step or two back. "Sorry, I was just concerned. That's all. I didn't see you all day yesterday when we were setting up, and when I went by your place on my way here, your truck was missing. This weekend is a big deal for the studio, and you're right in the center of it."

Marty took a deep breath. He looked around the studio at the people admiring his work. "You're right. I'm sorry. Some jerk wanted me to shoot a location for him. Background shots for some kind of lip balm product I think he said. I've been sitting in my truck waiting for two hours. He never showed."

"Where's the shoot?"

"Does it matter?" Marty paused for a moment. He could see Angela wasn't in the mood for his attitude. He didn't have many friends in town. Pissing her off would leave him with? Oh yeah, none. He managed a smile. "Horseshoe Pond. He said to meet him out at Horseshoe Pond. He never showed. No matter. I'm here now."

Angela didn't reply at first. She stood stoically with her arms folded high on her chest. She slowly lowered the eyebrow the first part of his answer had raised. For what it's worth, Angela had become accustomed to his brooding, more so than her friends thought she should put up with. To them, Marty was magazine-handsome . . . until he opened his mouth. "Well, I can see why that would be upsetting."

"I've been stood up before. That shit don't bother me. My apartment. I stopped there on my way here to drop off my equipment. I think someone was in there. The door was unlocked."

"Were you rushing around this afternoon? Maybe you just forgot to lock it? But just to be sure, why don't you tell the police?"

Marty gave a dismissing harrumph. "There's no need to get them involved." He followed with a pleasant smile resting just below his pale-blue, I'm-sorry eyes.

All was forgiven. Angela put her arm through Marty's. "Enough about that," Angela said as she walked him over to where his photographs were displayed. "You're right, you're here now, and that's what matters."

Angela hung most of the photographer's work the previous morning. There were ten photographers featured, most local with a few as far away as Massachusetts. She got an earlier-than-usual start. Her intention was to get the others out of the way early so she could devote that whole afternoon to Marty. His photographs were un-proportionally tall, high-contrast, black-and-white gelatin silver prints. They were double matted in matte white, forming a 6" border, with a 1" black gallery frame holding it all together. There were six in total—three random subjects Marty was especially pleased with, and three moody photographs of the Willis Asylum—hung on a flat-black, freestanding wall section at the front of the studio. The wide, V-shaped section spanned sixteen feet from edge to edge, and visible through the large plate glass window facing the street. Track lighting hung above with filters attached, so only the photographs were illuminated. To add to the dramatic presentation of his work, Angela had convinced Jack Gordon, the owner of the studio, to *borrow* a few pieces from the asylum. She and Jack went out the week before. They scrounged up an old, wooden wheelchair, an enamel-topped table, and a handful of old medicine bottles. These were arranged in the corner where the two black walls came together. The presentation of the work was exceptional, certainly enviable of any top New York gallery.

"Marty! There you are," exclaimed a comfortably dressed, older man walking over from a small crowd in the corner.

"Sorry, Jack, I was going to meet a new client and got stiffed." He looked over at Angela and then back. "I don't wanna talk about it."

Jack Gordon was a resident of the community for as far back as anyone could remember. His baby face, a full head of pure-white hair, and impish smile always sparked a jovial greeting from friend or stranger. In the 1860s his family established a shoe factory outside of town manufacturing fleece-lined moccasins and open-heel slippers. It afforded a comfortable and stable living for his family and a few generations of townspeople. Jack took over when his father retired, quickly gaining a reputation for generosity and devotion to the town of Auburn Notch. He supplied slippers to the Willis Asylum free of charge, also providing part-time work assignments for those patients at the asylum approved by the director. Despite the money generated by the business, Jack remained levelheaded and committed to giving back any way he could to the town he loved.

The real money came a few years back when Jack's health became an issue and he decided to retire. Not having any children to pass the business on to, he sold it to a rival shoe manufacturer in Maine. He made the announcement of his intentions at an all-company meeting. It was an emotional event, one he wished never to go through again. He begged their understanding. There was so much more to the deal he wanted to tell them, but there was a necessity to keep a portion of it private. Instead, he assured everyone he would personally guarantee a generous severance package in the event any jobs were lost—their regular wages for one year or until they found a new job, whichever came first. After the announcement, Jack opened the floor for questions. One factory worker, a quiet man with only three weeks on the assembly line, took the sale and loss of his job personally. He openly and boisterously pounded out his objection, going as far as to refuse the severance package generously offered. It took everyone by surprise. Jack assured the man he was included in the severance package promise and pressed him for a reason. The man stormed out. It was the last anyone saw of him.

Within a month the final papers were drawn up. Jack's nobody's fool. He saw through the handshakes and patronizing smiles from the potential new owners long before they sat across the settlement table. In the final deal, Jack sold them only the business with an option to rent the factory. They gave him some nonsense about building a new state-of-the-art facility outside of town, so just the business would be fine. They followed with the usual promises, signed the papers, and promptly moved all manufacturing to their state-of-the-art facility in Georgia as soon as the ink was dry. It put 187 good people out of work.

The second part of Jack's deal, the private part he was forced to keep from his employees, was working behind the scenes. Two days after the papers were signed for the business and the pink slips hit the mail, Jack sold the building and land to a retail outlet developer. As a result of his foresight, the lost factory jobs were going to turn into new retail and manufacturing positions. He signed the building and land deal with a stipulation that all his former employees were guaranteed jobs if they so desired, comparable in salary to their current wages, and appropriate to their skill levels. He personally vouched for each of them, and the deal was completed. Afterwards, Jack went door to door contacting each of his former employees personally. He invited them to a meeting at the town hall where he made the announcement. He went over the details of the retail development and manufacturing facility, the timeline, and, most importantly, renewed his promise to continue paying their salaries until they started their new jobs. The only person missing was the aggravated employee who stormed out of the initial meeting about the sale of the business. Jack had a name and an address, but both proved to be fictitious.

Jack and his wife Martha were in their mid-sixties when they cut the ribbon to open the outlet mall and food court less than a year later. It became a destination for shoppers from Maine to Connecticut, with additional revenue being realized by the shops and eateries in Auburn Notch. The plastic bin manufacturing plant, a new structure built in the southeast corner of the property close to the interstate, opened two months later. Within a year it had doubled its floor space and staff.

Despite the windfall of cash, Jack and Martha Gordon remained as active as ever. Money, according to Jack, was no excuse for an idle existence. They were part of the community and fully intended to contribute on a daily basis. It's what New Englanders do. Together, they took several photography courses at the local community college to fill the hours, quickly realizing they had quite a flare for it. It started out small—a few local weddings for close friends, a christening or two, etc. But when a vacant shop opened up on Main Street a few doors down from the Rocket Cafe, Jack had a sign over the door and was open for business before the listing hit the local paper. The Gordon Photography Studio was established.

Besides doing most of the wedding photography and high school yearbooks in a twenty-mile radius, the studio showcased local photographers. It quickly became a very popular venue for young photographers, generating a six-month-plus waiting list. Every two months a different photographer's work was hung. Opening receptions followed where patrons could meet the photographer and purchase the originals or smaller-framed prints. The studio has been enjoying quite a bit of attention due to positive publicity from a syndicated morning show it was featured on. The town was profiled, Sheriff Flynn and a few council members were interviewed, and a number of local photographer's work served as the backdrop. The recent events were drawing visitors in from as far away as Boston. If that wasn't enough to kick-start a young photographer's career, coinciding with the Spring Arts Festival was a lucky break for Sam Martin, or Marty, as Angela and Jack know him. Marty was the current featured photographer; something Angela had a hand in arranging.

"No matter, you're here now," replied Jack, patting Marty on the back. "And just in time. Your photographs have stirred quite a bit of colorful discussion, particularly the shots of the Willis Asylum."

The three turned the corner, facing into the structure holding Marty's photographs. He stopped short, his mouth agape.

"Well?" Angela asked. "What do you think?"

Incredible, Marty thought to himself. He looked over at the two smiling faces staring at him. His eyes darted about from photo to photo, then to the pieces from the asylum arranged in the corner. Angela had added a faded, antique quilt bunched on the seat of the wheelchair for just a hint of color. It took a moment before Marty could speak. "I don't know what to say."

"No need to say anything," Jack responded, giving Angela's shoulders a squeeze. "Someone wanted to make sure your photographs would linger on people's minds long after this opening reception."

"You know how much I love those asylum shots. You've really captured the eerie quality of the place."

"You know I didn't want to include those." Marty quietly protested. "People don't understand them. 'Depressing crap' I believe I heard one of your more outspoken council members say that day when I dropped off the work."

"Nonsense," Angela smartly interrupted. She took two glasses of wine from a passing server, handing one to Marty. "Don't judge the town by the opinions of a few narrow-minded blowhards."

"Exactly," Jack emphasized with a determined nod. "Your work is of extraordinary depth. You'll see. Those that appreciate the work will far outweigh the naysayers."

"A few?" Marty choked on his wine, still focused on Angela's remark. "Who else called them crap?"

"I didn't mean to imply—"

"Enough, you two." Jack smiled and shook his head. He turned the two young people back toward the walls where Marty's work hung. "We're here to celebrate these intriguing subjects and the brilliant, young photographer who has brought them to life in these photographs."

"Jack is right," said Angela. "Your work is remarkable. And these shots of the old mental hospital? I get goose pimples just looking at them."

"They've been the talk of the exhibit since I opened the doors," Jack added. He paused in reflection. "Just terrible what's happened to the old place. I made many trips out there, taking slippers to the patients. Oh well, what's done is done. As for you, I think once you start talking to people, you'll find I'm right; you're amongst admirers here, not critics. Now, take a good gulp of that fine wine Angela purchased for this event and get out there and mingle. This group is here looking to invest a few dollars in the work of a promising local photographer, so let's not disappoint them."

Marty was not well-known in town. He and his mother moved to town in the summer prior to his junior year of high school. It proved a tough adjustment for him. Shy kids in high school were never just shy to other students; they were labeled oddballs or loners. That was just fine with him. There was only one girl he liked. They shared a science table. Everyday he told himself that was the day he was going to ask her out, and everyday he found another reason why he couldn't.

After graduating he went off to Syracuse University, attaining a fine arts degree with a minor in photography. His mother died a few years after his return to Auburn Notch. It was a quiet funeral on a bitter Thursday evening in February at the local Episcopal Church where they were members. He never mentioned anything about his father. At twenty-eight, and relatively comfortable from an insurance payment received after his mother's death, there were only a handful of people in town who could add very little past describing him as, "that guy that lives in the cabin out by the lake." He had sandy-brown hair, always tousled, the tips directing your glance down toward determined, light-blue eyes that seemed to look through you. He had strength in his stature, but gentleness in his touch.

Angela remembered Sam Martin from their senior year. He didn't participate in any of the school functions she was active in, but they did share a class. Even then she could sense a possible attraction between them. Many times she caught him looking at her across the science table, or maybe it was just wishful thinking on her part. She viewed him as a challenge, and hoped one day to peel back the layers. Angela was actually the one who gave him the nickname Marty. They had graduated and were off to separate universities and back before they became anything more than a casual glance through the bubbling beakers and endless lengths of rubber hoses and clamps rising from the polished, black tabletops of a noisy science lab.

They met up again not long after they both returned to town; finally engaging in the conversations Angela bashfully admitted she secretly regretted never took place in the locker-lined halls of Auburn Notch High School. Marty laughed at the coincidence, reminding her how shy he was back then, with just an added hint of pessimism clinging to the edges. He did manage to profess the same regret through his surprise at the admission. This gentle side strengthened her resolve to renew her attempts to get to know the handsome, well-mannered, hunk resting just below the shaggy surface.

Marty inevitably became a prime element of every conversation Angela engaged in when out for cocktails with the girls from the State House. She quickly rebuffed any idea there might be more going on than she was willing to admit to, though not for a lack of trying. After a few months of well-orchestrated chance meetings, and dodging more than a few dozen subtle hints, his reluctance to commit to any type of relationship, including just the occasional coffee at the Rocket Café, slowly eroded her desire to delve any deeper below the surface. As time went on, his segment in her conversations over cocktails with the girls grew shorter. Eventually, any mention of Marty ended the same way with a long sigh and a determined pledge to stop pining over a hopeless cause.

For all outward appearances, Angela was never going to be anything more to Marty than an old classmate and the part-time manager of the Gordon Photography Studio. Angela assured her friends she had moved on, but there still remained the lingering hope a frayed edge of his coarse, outer surface might someday unravel and expose the true character lurking below. She had no idea someone else was already tugging at a different thread—a thread that would eventually put both of their lives in danger.

CHAPTER THREE

Hank raised his lantern. "Sheriff? You look like you've seen a ghost. If you're not up for this, I'll take you back to town and come back."

Sheriff Flynn only made it a few steps into the room. Her eyes were fixed on the young girl's body. With one hesitant step after another she approached the gurney, unconsciously rubbing her left shoulder.

This was far from being the first time she saw a dead body. This wasn't even the first time she found herself in an abandoned mental hospital. What took her breath away was the frightening similarity to a dark part of her past. It was a case tucked away in another life. A case she had hoped never to return to.

Hank raised an eyebrow of surprise over the sheriff's reaction to the crime scene. Regardless of his determination not to like her, he often remarked how calm she remained no matter what circumstances she faced. He stood quietly near the window, continuing to hold his lantern up. After a few moments Hank repeated his question.

Sheriff Flynn looked up slowly but without a response. Instead she scanned the room, taking in everything the dim light revealed. There was something unnerving about the setting; it seemed to be mocking her. The slight chill and dampness of the room, the musty smell, the long shadows stretching down the hall behind her. All this drew together into an eerie and all too familiar apparition—an apparition which would normally jolt her awake in a cold sweat in the small hours of the morning. This time it wasn't a dream. There would be no waking from this haunting image. Her muscles tensed with every step she took closer to the body. The shadows of her past, so painstakingly buried deep within her, were clawing their way to the surface. Everything she struggled so hard to forget now appeared laid out before her in a pale, blue-gray light. Her shoulder throbbed. Her whole body shivered. Those shadows will be ignored no longer.

Flynn's gun scraped against the gurney, breaking the silence in the room. She leaned over the body. The face on the young woman before her could easily have been a carved alabaster bust, her vacant eyes staring upward, her final pleas for mercy leaving her mouth agape. She knew that face.

Flynn closed her eyes. The image remained. A voice from the past drifted in on the cool night air through the broken panes. A gritty voice. A voice she had hoped never to hear again. The tattered curtain ruffled, the voice taunted her, attempting to provoke acknowledgement. She could make out the words clearly.

"This is your fault," it whispered. The familiar, abrading tone raised the hair on the back of her neck. "This is your fault. You've brought us here. You can't hide from us. *You* killed this woman."

"No!" Flynn jumped backward, refusing to succumb to the weight of the spectral impeachment.

"No, you're not okay?" Hank responded.

Flynn rebuffed the accusation with a shake of her head, turning over the facts in her mind. What might have appeared to be a hasty departure from the crime-infested streets and dark alleys of the big city had everything to do with recuperating, not hiding. She wanted to stay on the case. She had every intension of chasing down the bastards that killed three people and left her for dead. It was the department, and most assuredly at the insistence of their insurance carrier, that had other ideas. She was the victim of a horrendous act of violence they said. She was too close to the case to be objective was the foundation of their argument. What if she froze? What if her assailants tried to finish the job? That was crap as far as she was concerned. What stiffened her resolve even more were her critics, the handful of disgruntled officers she leaped over in her rise to detective who cackled like ruffled hens behind her back. They continued their backroom lambasting, boasting how the fearless Detective Flynn stared into the crimson eyes of death and had her confidence stripped away. Just a through-n-through, they would mock. It started more than one shoving match in the locker room, but that sort doesn't care.

Dr. Laura Dearing, the precinct's clinical psychologist and a close friend, finally began to chip away at the defiance Flynn had wrapped herself in. It was Dearing's suggestion for Promise to withdraw into the quiet, pleasant ambiance and familiarity of the small town where she and their families spent summers when they were young. Dearing had dealt with many victims who walked away from horrendous crimes over the years. She knew from experience what Promise went through wasn't something you shake off in a week and get right back out on the streets. It was going to take time. Three months of recuperating away from everything that reminded her of the event was the first step. This would jumpstart the healing process, helping to erase the mental and fiscal torture she was subjected to at the hands of these madmen. Dearing felt the fond memories and sharp contrast between Auburn Notch and Chicago could eventually help Flynn wrap her head around what happened. She needed to confront it and deal with the aftermath before it did any irreversible damage.

Promise Flynn refused the idea. She wasn't about to be run out of town. Outwardly, she professed to Dearing she didn't care what anybody thought, but in reality she did. In her mind, getting right back out on the street and bringing those monsters to justice would do a lot more for the healing process. That's the best therapy. That's what she needed. Her captain and Dr. Dearing stood their ground. The more Flynn protested, the more her resistance began to look like irrational ranting. Dearing finally drew a line in the sand, declaring Flynn mentally and physically unfit for duty at that time. Flynn left her with no other choice, but that's not how Flynn chose to view it. In her eyes, it was a betrayal.

Despite her thunderous objections, Flynn was removed from the case permanently—the investigation being continued by Williams, her partner. Until cleared for duty, she was left polishing a desk, interrupted only by the twice-weekly sessions with Dearing, until such time she was declared fit for duty.

A few weeks in the noisy, testosterone-soaked squad room began taking a toll on her nerves. The one-hour sessions with Dearing continued, affording little more than Flynn's admission to understanding why Dearing did what she did. Any attempts to scrape together the pieces of what she went through were brashly dismissed.

Flynn's decision to stay in Chicago was quickly deteriorating. With each day the leads in her case became fewer, eventually grinding to a halt. The murders had stopped almost as quickly as they started. Their chief suspect, Samuel Kaminski, vanished without a trace, without even a clue as to who his accomplice might have been. Even Williams, Flynn's partner on the case, was getting tired of her constant inquiries, peppered with what she claimed were just humorous overtones regarding how she would have had the case closed before this.

By the second month she had enough. The idea of replacing the idleness imposed on her by the department with the cleansing affect of a deep breath of New England air suddenly became very appealing. Dearing was pleased with the decision, remarking it would most likely get her back on the job quicker. Promise intended to hold her to her word.

By the end of the following week she had closed up her apartment in town and had settled very nicely into a small house on the shore of Lake Auburn. It was off-season, so she had her pick of rental units. The one she chose, being on the lake, was a little more expensive than the others, but figuring she would only be there a month or two, she could swing it.

She met Mayor Bob Olson in town one Saturday morning at the Rocket Café. They remembered each other from days at the lake when they were young. He was a skinny kid who followed her everywhere. Now he was charismatic and bigger than life. His friends called him Bear. He was also the local insurance agent, so he knew everybody and everything. Talking with Bear reminded her of conversations she had with her father in the local diner when she was a young girl. It was just the two of them. He was so easy to talk to, she could tell him anything. She missed that.

One conversation led to another. They laughed about old times, friends they missed, and how fickle life was. He was impressed with her position as a detective in the big city, though he noted a bit of apprehension on her part to talk about it in any detail. He let it go for a while. A few weeks had gone by when Bear abruptly threw a job offer out on the table during one of their conversations. It took Flynn by surprise. Bear smiled, but she could see he was serious. She felt comfortable enough at that point to tell him everything. She told him about Chicago, what she went through, what she left behind, and the reason she came to Auburn Notch. She finished with her intention to return to the force as soon as she was approved for duty. Accepting a job in Auburn Notch was out of the question, she had one waiting for her back in Chicago.

Dr. Dearing kept a regular appointment on Skype every Tuesday and Thursday to monitor Flynn's progress. In the beginning, Flynn told Dearing what she thought she wanted to hear. She was coming to terms with what happened and was eager to get back to Chicago. Neither of those claims were true, but it made Flynn feel better when she said it out loud. Dearing wasn't so easily fooled. As a result, two months turned into four, which turned into six.

Flynn and Bear had become a regular fixture in the café on Saturday mornings. At some point in the conversations every week he would pose the offer again. And every week she would change the subject.

Early one Saturday morning, Flynn rolled over onto her back. The night air was still, the faint sounds of the interstate wafted in on a slight summer breeze through her open bedroom window. She felt a warm breath by her ear. "Don't think we've forgotten about you." It sent shivers through her whole body.

Promise Flynn jerked herself out of bed, landing on her fuzzy slippers on the rug. She backed away on all fours, banging into the nightstand, and almost knocking over the lamp as she fumbled with the knob. She pulled the revolver she kept between the mattress and the box spring. Her hands were shaking as she waved the gun around the room. She was drenched in sweat, her breathing deep and deliberate. An intense thirty minutes went by before she convinced herself she was alone, but by then she had made a decision. Going back to Chicago was no longer an option. If Bear posed the same question that morning, it would be met with a different answer.

Flynn's eyes were still fixed on the face of the young woman. This is just a coincidence, she thought to herself. Some copycat trying to make a name for himself. Try as she might, her efforts to convince herself were falling slightly short of the mark. Flynn was too seasoned to believe in such nonsense, but for the moment it was all she had.

Hank walked over to where the sheriff stood. He lightly tapped on Flynn's arm. "Are you okay, Sheriff?"

Flynn abruptly grabbed Hank's wrist. It took a moment before she realized what she had done, and just as quickly released her grip. "S . . . sorry," she stammered. "What did you say?"

"Are you okay?"

Flynn looked up and smiled. "I'm fine, just thought I saw a ghost. That's all."

"You know her?"

Flynn turned towards the young woman again. She understood exactly what this innocent woman went through. The why still lingered on her face, as it did on Flynn's. She slowly shook her head. "No, I don't know her."

"Are you sure you're all right?"

"I'm fine," Flynn snapped. She took a deep breath, looked up at Hank, and smiled. "Sorry. I appreciate the concern. It's been a long day, that's all. I'll call the ME. Just hold that lamp up."

Hank did as he was told. Flynn dialed her cell phone and walked over to the window where the candle continued to flicker, the wax dripping down the side and pooling around the base.

Hank stepped closer to the gurney, getting a more straight-on view of the victim. "Damn," he finally said under his breath.

"What?" answered Promise, tucking her phone back into a pocket of her jacket.

"Nothing . . . but . . . it's just that—"

She walked over to the gurney and stood on the opposite side of the gurney from Hank. "What is it? Have you found something?"

Hank held his lantern up, looking from the lifeless body on the gurney to the sheriff. "She looks just like you."

CHAPTER FOUR

"So, how long will you be staying with us, Mr. Clayton?"

"Oh, I'm . . . I'm not s–sure," stammered Bob Clayton as he fumbled with his coat in an attempt to locate his wallet. His hands sifted through the layers like someone checking the pockets in a short, disheveled pile of laundry. He smiled through a day's worth of stubble, hinting at the need for a good oral hygienist. "You said I c–could have the room by the week f–for $109?"

"Yes, sir," replied the young girl behind the counter brightly. "It's off season, and we're just happy to have you here."

"Two weeks, probably," he replied, finally locating the elusive simulated leather wallet, "maybe th–three. Cash is okay?"

"Sure. I just need your license for our records and the first week in advance."

About twenty minutes later, with the transaction completed, Bob Clayton found himself settled into cabin number 4. The small, family-run motel broke the pine tree line along Route 93, about two miles out of town on the north side of Auburn Notch. Nothing fancy, just a row of small cabins outfitted with Pecky Cypress paneling, a sitting room, kitchenette, bedroom, and full bath. It had an envious view of the White Mountains wrapped in a fresh pine scent, the polar opposite of his dingy, one-room apartment in Brooklyn that faced an alley.

Bob Clayton stuffed the contents of his suitcase into a drawer in the dresser, pushed the suitcase under the bed, and flopped down on the sofa in the sitting room. From his briefcase he produced a half-full bottle of curiously expensive vodka, a bottle of Pepto-Bismol, and two well-worn, overstuffed folders. One folder held photocopies of police reports and copies of crime photos. The other was stuffed with computer printouts and photographs.

He smiled finding a full tray of ice in the freezer. With a fresh drink in hand, and everything from the two folders laid out on the coffee table in front of him, he rifled through the pile producing a photo taken at a crime scene in Brooklyn. A grease pen had circled one of the faces in the crowd. The name *S. Martin* had been scrawled on the back followed by a large question mark, below it *Auburn Notch, NH*. Bob rested back on the sofa staring at the photo and swishing the ice around in his glass.

A specific, young woman appeared to be the focus of a small, paper-clipped group of photo printouts and screen captures that spilled out from one of the folders. In the top photo, with her face circled with the same grease pencil, the young woman was sharply dressed and squeezed between two colleagues or friends out for an evening of drinks. In one hand she held up a large cocktail glass with an orange slice over the rim, with the other she held out her phone to snap the selfie for her Facebook page. The photo expressed the carefree lifestyle of a bright, successful, young woman, highlighted further by the Raymond Weil Othello watch visible on her left wrist and the Coach clutch resting on the bar in the foreground. It proved to be the last photo she would post on her page. She had no idea the next photos of her would be taken in a dark, unsightly, second-floor room 264 miles away.

CHAPTER FIVE

Before coming to Auburn Notch, Promise Flynn enjoyed a decorated career as a detective with the Chicago Major Crimes Unit. Backed by a degree in criminal law from the University of Delaware, and an irritating determination to be the first one through any door, she worked her way up through the ranks in only ten years. Her promotion to detective had mixed reviews. There were applauds for her ambition by half of the department, while the other half saw it as the mayor's way to secure the women's vote in what pollsters were calling a close political race that year. Either way, she became one of the youngest female officers to achieve the rank.

It wasn't all bang-bang-drag-the-bad-guy-in. Unlike the leg up it might give a woman in other professions, her runway looks worked against her on the force. Along the way Promise dealt with unwanted advances from slimy lawyers, slanderous gossip by officers she leaped over for promotions, and a series of partners who didn't like playing second fiddle to a woman who got more press coverage than the Cub's infield. Originally from New York, her Long Island accent intensified proportionately with the level of danger she faced. As a six-foot, no-nonsense blond, she stood out enough in the squad room, so keeping her well-toned body hidden beneath lose fitting blouses and jackets was always a priority with her. Life on the street encased her soft, gooey center with a hard outer shell, further enhanced by a string of Losers.com dates. All work, no play, and consistently ranking in the top ten in marksmanship, carved out a detective every bit as sharp as the crease in her black, wool trousers.

On those rare occasions when she let her guard down, Promise Flynn could be soft-spoken, articulate, and graceful. Shaking out her wavy, blond hair from the tight bun she wore on the job could stop a conversation, and her inviting, green eyes were deep enough to drown the sorrows of the string of lovesick men she denied a second date. She was every inch a woman who enjoyed the company of an interesting man, but always found a reason why *it just won't work*.

Everything changed the day she walked into the trap. Going alone was stupid, but her arrogance convinced her she was invincible. The events of that day were a sharp slap in the face, shattering her tough exterior and finally driving her from Chicago and the job she loved. Though she would never admit it, she knew the uncertainty of why it happened erased any desire she had to return. Still, she tried. The weekly meetings with Dr. Dearing were chipping away at the effects of the trauma, but the slow pace was also chipping away at her patience. Flynn was getting more and more frustrated regurgitating the same facts over and over, week after week with little progress in her mind. Dearing was an old friend. A friend she spent summers with talking about boys, hairstyles, and how dreamy Tom Selleck was. Flynn was having trouble separating that image from the clinical psychologist who was trying to help.

In the long run, the Saturday morning conversations with Bear did the most good. She was at peace finally with what happened. To her surprise, even the nightmares went away. Whether he was subconsciously the father figure missing in her life for so long or just a good friend, either way Flynn felt comfortable talking to him about anything. It also made her decision to stay and accept the position as Sheriff easier. Over waffles with fresh maple syrup, she had revealed all the skeletons in her closet, so he knew exactly whom he was hiring. Bear was not so forthcoming. He could talk endlessly about the old days, but was curiously tightlipped about his political dealings in town. She didn't give it much thought at first, but eventually she would hear the rattle of bones in his closet. Despite their renewed friendship, it was a noise she wasn't going to be able to ignore for long.

Once Flynn accepted the open sheriff's position, Bear explained it would be better to all concerned if certain aspects of her background were left between them. She didn't agree at first. His insistence it was only her decorated career in police work that would matter to the people of Auburn Notch finally persuaded her. He was right to a certain extent, the conspicuous exception was the deputy she was going to inherit with the job. Deputy Harris wasn't about to take anyone at face value, especially some out-of-towner who snaked the sheriff position right out from under him. He accepted the decision, but grumbled about her appointment to anyone who would listen.

After a swift and unanimous council approval of her appointment, Flynn resigned from the Chicago Police force and

clipped the Auburn Notch shield on her belt. She and Mayor
Olson remained close friends, joining him and his third wife for
most holiday and town celebrations. So when Bear called, she was
quick to respond, and this morning was no exception.

"Have a seat, Promise." Mayor Olson pointed his chubby finger
at a chair across the desk from him. "We need to talk about this
business out at the old asylum."

Sheriff Flynn shook her head, remaining by the door of his
office. She could tell by his tone he had his mayor's hat on, so
there was going to be more to the conversation than just a quick
update. "I've only got a few minutes, Bear. We're just getting into
the case, so maybe I'll have something to report later today. I'll get
back to you then."

Flynn turned to leave. The mayor wasn't about to be dismissed
so quickly. "This is important, Promise." He got up, walked over,
and closed the door to his office. He leaned back against the
cabinet by the door. "There's more at stake here than just solving
the murder of that poor, young girl."

"What do you mean?"

"I got a call a little while ago. Some reporter asking some
pretty pointed questions."

"What's the big deal? This type of crime always stirs up the
bottom feeders. There'll be more calls like that before we get to the
bottom of this. Pass them on to me, I'll—"

"You don't understand, Promise. This reporter was asking
about *you*."

"What about me?" Promise thought for a moment. A sudden
realization replaced her puzzled look with one of green rage. "That
meddling bastard. Look, I don't know what he told you, but—"

"Calm down, Promise," Mayor Olson replied, placing his hand
on her shoulder. "He didn't tell me anything I didn't already know
about your past. I'm just afraid of what else he might do with the
information. I like you, Promise, but if these people think you
brought a couple serial killers to town for revenge, I can't withhold
what I know. They'll hang me out to dry right next to you if I do.
I've taken flack before. As a result, I've had to roll a few heads to
appease the voters and stay ahead of the damage. I don't wanna
be backed into that corner with you. If you know something, tell
me now. If we get out in front of this, we can—"

"Look, Bear, I don't know what's going on here yet, but it's too
early to jump to that conclusion." Flynn smiled, taking his arm
and turning him back toward his chair. "If it comes to it, I'll
address the town meeting and explain how I withheld parts of my

past from you. I'll resign before I let any of my past jeopardize the people of Auburn Notch or affect your reputation in this town." Bear started to object, but was cut short by a playfully determined stare followed by a few pokes to his chest. "Don't make me shoot you, Mr. Mayor, Sarah would never forgive me. I'll take care of this reporter. Now, if you'll excuse me, I've got to get downstairs to the ME's office."

Bear nodded, and then held up his chubby finger once more. "Before you go—"

"Something else?"

"Carl over at the bank mentioned your deputy was poking around in the swim club account? I thought we put that business to rest when Sheriff Dunn passed away. Do you know what he was looking for?"

"Not really. I'll bet he was just tying up loose ends. You know how anal he is."

Mayor Olson smiled. "I'm sure you're right."

Sheriff Flynn left the office and turned the corner toward the stairs. She got halfway down the hall when a man coming in her direction brought her to an abrupt stop. "I knew it. I knew you were at the end of that call. What the hell are you doing here, Calder?"

CHAPTER SIX

Sheriff Flynn shook her head, giving a snort in reply to the shit-eating grin in front of her. Without waiting for an answer, she picked up a quick pace down the stairs, not stopping until she pushed through the swinging doors of the ME's lab.

Calder followed behind close on her heels. He wasn't about to be outpaced, until one of the doors swung back sharply catching his shoulder and just missing his head. "Ouch. What's wrong with you? Is this any way to treat an old friend?"

Flynn's abrupt entrance caught the ME by surprise, springing him from his chair by his desk. "Everything okay, Sheriff?"

Flynn ignored Dr. Abrams for the moment, choosing to clear up a few things with Calder first. "That's what you think we were? What I remember is a pain in the ass who managed to get in the way of my investigation in every way possible. I don't know what you're doing here, but it better be for the fishing."

There was an awkward silence as Calder glanced over at Dr. Abrams and shrugged his shoulders.

"Did you want something, Sheriff?" asked Abrams. "I was just on my way out, but I can certainly spare a few minutes."

Flynn continued to stare at Calder as she answered. "No. Nothing that can't wait."

"If you'll excuse me then," said Doctor Abrams, looking around on his desk for something to do. "I should get these results up to the DA. Good-bye, whoever you are. Nice to see you again, Sheriff."

Sheriff Flynn forced a smile as Doctor Abrams passed her on his way out. Calder didn't say a word. The door to the room squeaked on its hinges as it slowly swung to a stop. Calder sat down in the chair next to Abrams's desk, quietly watching Flynn pace back and forth in front of him.

Like an ache in an arthritic joint when you know it's going to rain, Flynn knew the sharp pain she felt in her shoulder earlier was surely a harbinger of things to come. She wasn't wrong. Calder's appearance was a lingering reminder of what drove her out of Chicago in the first place. He was a sharp pain she couldn't ignore. He was a mistake one night after the last sip of one too many bourbons. She's avoided him since then, but that wasn't a choice now. Ignoring him could unravel the new life she had established for herself and drag her back into the dark hole she escaped from.

Seeing him brought back a flood of memories. The weeks of therapy sessions before she even considered trying to understand the events that tipped the first domino. How hard she found it to ignore the dull ache in her shoulder left behind long after the wound was stitched. One by one, the dominos fell in front of her. Sessions with Dearing revealing her once indefatigable confidence being chipped away by the diluted uncertainty the abduction brought about. The admission that there might be some truth to what her critics were saying. Flynn explaining over and over again to Dearing the circumstances of why she followed up on that lead alone. Remembering each time coming to the same conclusion—she had acted appropriately—but each time fighting the nagging doubt scratching at her reasoning. And behind every bit of that doubt stood Hugh Calder.

No matter how you stack the evidence, what happened could never be construed as Calder's fault, but no amount of therapy will ever convince Promise Flynn of that. She allowed herself to be manipulated by his theories, which in her mind slowly dulled her senses, taking the edge off her concentration. In reality, this reasoning would certainly point more at Flynn than Calder, but she would have to be open to that possibility. Seeing him again reminded her she wasn't.

"You in a trance, *Detective?*"

Flynn paused, looking over at Calder, his notebook catching her attention. He sat quietly tapping a pencil on the familiar Merchant & Mills oilskin. It had a couple more years of wear along the edges, with new scraps of research stuffed into the pages amongst the yellowed remains of previous notes. The leather pencil loops, once used to hold the notebook closed, had been torn away years ago, no doubt stripped away with any moral character he might have processed at the time. For a moment it amused her to see he still carried it with him. She remembered the day he left it behind in a café. You would have thought he lost his only child in a crowd. He raced back, dodging traffic on Michigan Avenue, eventually disappearing into the swelling hoard of office workers departing their respective buildings. The plan was for him to accompany her to investigate a lead at an abandoned hospital on the outer edge of the city by the old stockyards. Calder said the tip came from an anonymous source. He passed it along to Flynn. She waited by her car for almost twenty minutes; finally getting a text from him indicating he needed to check in with his editor. He couldn't say how long it would take, but suggested she wait until after the call and they would go together. Already irritated over the wait, she dismissed that, deciding to proceed without him. He could meet her there when he was done, or not. She didn't care. She tucked the phone into a pocket, ignoring the series of calls and text messages from him that followed.

She shook off the flashback. The memory of the events that unfolded later that day at the abandoned hospital wiped away any lingering trace of amusement that oilskin gave her.

"How long are you going to blame me and hold this grudge?" He could see in her eyes, as she stared at his notebook, exactly what was going through her mind. "What happened wasn't my fault. How would I know they were laying in wait for you? This is shit. You should be thanking me. When you said you were going with or without me I knew it was trouble. Then you blow off my calls, so I called your partner. Lucky for you I did. Not real bright, *Detective.*"

She even hated the way he called her *Detective.* His smug indifference to her pain raised her blood from a simmer to a rolling boil. She had a decision to make—listen to whatever blatant nonsense slips out from his veneered smile about his unexpected appearance in Auburn Notch, or retrace her steps back up the stairs and forget she ever saw him. For a brief instance a third option came to mind, but she would never be able to justify shooting him.

Twice she appeared ready to speak, but twice she decided more thought might be required. Calder's irritating tapping with his pen on the cover of the oilskin became louder, resulting in the final deciding factor. Her mind was made up. Without any additional acknowledgement of his presence, she turned and stormed out of the office, continuing down the hall towards the staircase leading up to the main floor exit of the State House.

Hugh Calder caught up with her halfway up the steps. He grabbed her arm. "Hey! Did you hear me? I think a small thank you is in order. The only reason you're alive is because I mentioned to your partner what a stupid idea I thought it was for you to follow up on that anonymous tip alone."

"I wasn't alone until you bailed on me. Remove your hand, or I'll remove it for you, and you won't like where I'll put it."

Calder raised both hands and took a step back. "Fine. You wanna blame me? Go right ahead. Just remember, you dismissed that tip as a prank. I saw it as the threat it turned out to be."

"Well, maybe they should have put you in charge of the investigation."

"That's what this is all about, you, second-guessing yourself? You're a good cop, you just took one too many chances. You knew what those guys were capable of. Instead of treading cautiously, you dared them to come after you, and they did. Now they're here. So what do you intend to do this time?"

Flynn's nostrils flared. She took a step down, forcing Calder against the handrail and knocking his oilskin to the steps. "You think they're here to finish what they started, don't you? You're looking for a chance to say I told you so and maybe pen my obituary?"

"Whoa, where's that coming from?"

Flynn eased off a bit. "Look, I put certain parts of my past behind me. I don't need you getting this town all worked up with your harebrained theories and idle gossip about what did or didn't happen in Chicago."

Calder was pretty slick around the edges, so he was quick to pick up on the subtext in a conversation and know when he approached the line. "Look, Flynn, I don't know what you got going here, but I'm not here to hurt you. I'm just here for the story."

Calder just had a way of making an innocent referral to a job sound like you were some grifter on a score. "I'm the sheriff here. That's all."

"Okay, okay." Calder bent down and picked up his oilskin. "All I'm saying is I wanna be in on this when these guys show their faces. I've been right about this all along, and nobody's going to muscle in on my story."

The temperature of Flynn's blood was on the rise again. "There's NO STORY, period!"

"Says you, but you know as well as I do that murder over the weekend in the abandoned mental hospital is the work of our friends. I even heard there was an uncanny resemblance between you and the victim. That's how they left you years ago. I'll bet it was quite a shock when they found out you were still alive. So, here we are. They found you, and now they're playing with you."

Flynn poked her finger into Calder's chest, pushing him down another step. "You have no idea that's what's going on here. The last thing these people need is an arrogant headline whore filling their heads with talk of a serial killer lurking about town, stalking their family and friends. Your days as a big-time crime journalist ended with that false story you filed. Now you're nothing more than an instigator. Do us both a favor before your next tip really gets somebody killed, leave this town alone and crawl back into whatever crack you crawled out of."

Calder just rolled his eyes and smiled. He never met an insult he didn't like. "So finding the victim strapped to an old gurney is just a coincidence? That's what you're sayin'? Even that lanky Deputy Fife in your office wouldn't buy that one."

Flynn started up the steps, and then turned back. "The only coincidence I see is we have a murdered, young woman here, and you suddenly show up. It makes me wonder if there's another connection I'm missing between you and those other murders?"

"Come on, Flynn, it's them, and you know it," Calder replied smugly. He took his pencil and began to jot down a note.

Promise smacked the pencil from his hand. "I'm not going to tell you again. There is nothing to suggest this poor girl's murder has anything to do with those murders in Chicago. This is an isolated incident. Don't make anything more out of it. It wouldn't take much for some headline-seeking wannabe to pick up where those assholes left off and turn this into a killing spree."

"Come on, Flynn, look at the facts. You don't believe that. Abrams will confirm the details, unless he already did. You're putting the same pieces together that I am." Calder fumbled with his notebook looking for his recent notes. "Young girl. Unfamiliar to anyone in town. Asphyxiated with dry ice. No sexual assault. Not even robbery. That watch she had on had to be worth at least six grand. Looked like a Raymond Weil." He snapped his notebook shut. "With the exception of how the murder was committed, everything was just like his last victim in the Chicago case, right down to the black candle in the window."

"There's one big difference."

"And what might that be?"

"I was his last victim in Chicago, and I'm still alive."

"I'll give you that one." Calder lost the attitude. "Despite what you think of me, I was worried about you back then . . . and I still am. Leaving without as much as a phone call? That hurt. I got over it, but it still hurt. I even thought we might have a chance to . . . you know."

Flynn's expression softened, followed by a hearty laugh. "What planet do you live on?" She paused for a moment. "Lets get one thing straight, I made a huge mistake back in Chicago. There will never be an *us*."

Calder replied with a playful pout. He tucked his oilskin into his pocket. "You know, after you left Chicago the murders just stopped. No one could figure it out. Maybe those guys thought you were getting too close and decided to do something about it and move on? It made sense at the time. They never did find a clue to their identity. All they had was your description of a dark figure with a gritty voice arguing with another man. I'll even bet your crime scene here was devoid of any pertinent DNA, wasn't it?"

Flynn smiled, finally gaining the upper ground. "That's where you're wrong. We found something in the stairwell leading up to the second floor. Those guys in Chicago would never be that sloppy."

"You did?" Calder pulled his oilskin back out of his pocket and searched around on the steps for his pencil. "Let's hear it. If you rattled those guys, and they're here to finish the job, maybe they *are* getting sloppy. You might just have a chance to catch them this time."

"You know, now it makes sense. After they patched me up and I left Chicago, you had nobody feeding you insights from the case for your articles. If that's what you're here for now, forget it. You're just going to twist the facts around because you want this to be the work of the same guys, don't you? You're just looking to pull your reputation out of the gutter."

"Look, Flynn, I'm not trying to twist anything to suit a storyline. All I know, and even though it's been almost eight months, the circumstances with this murder are too similar to be coincidental."

"Eight months? I left Chicago almost two years ago."

"Yeah, yeah, that was your case. Get over it. These guys struck again in New York less than a year ago. At least I think it was the same guys."

Flynn put a little personal space between them while she digested Calder's last statement. "I didn't hear anything about similar murders in New York. What are you talking about?"

"Those cops chalked it up as a copycat. The victims were from different areas of the city, but at one point all worked for the same company. They narrowed it down to some guy with a health-food store and a history of mental problems. Revenge they concluded. I tried to set them straight. All I got was a pat on the head and a get-the-hell-outta-here for my trouble. They're still looking for the health-food nut. Chasin' their tails."

"And you think they're wrong?"

"What I think doesn't matter. What matters is the pattern. Those four people were left for dead on abandoned wharfs. They were very carefully laid out. No DNA. No clues. A black candle left next to the bodies. The cops get an anonymous tip after the last murder. They show up, but they're a little too late, the guy is gone. A little too convenient for my tastes."

"Were they all shot in the left shoulder?"

Calder paused. "Well, no. Anaphylaxis was the ME's conclusion in all those cases. They even found peanut oil residue in the victim's mouths."

Flynn laughed. "Oh yeah, exactly the same. What are the odds of stumbling across four individuals with peanut allergies?"

"That's what the NYPD said, too. That's when they made the connection with Roy Barnes."

"Roy Barnes?"

"Yeah. That's the guy the cops think committed the murders."

"The guy they can't find, right?"

Calder took a deep, frustrated inhale. "Think about it. Candle-boys pick five victims instead of four. From one of them they get all the information about the others. He kills the four, framing the fifth. Then he kills the fifth and disposes of the body. The cops spend all their time chasing their tails looking for number five, while the real killers skip town and start all over again."

"And that's why you're here? To hell with the facts, you're just connecting random dots for your next headline."

Flynn didn't move a muscle; the look on her face was enough to back Calder down a few steps.

"I'll admit it. If I'm right, and this does turn out to be the same guys, it would certainly go a long way to restore my credibility. But I'm not going to make anything up. Just the facts, that's all I'm here for. I swear." Calder paused for a moment struggling for a way to shift the conversation and the skeptical look on Flynn's face. "Abrams said you haven't identified her yet? Is that true?"

Flynn shook her head, turned, and continued up the stairs. "I'm sorry, but I can't divulge any information about an ongoing investigation. And just so we understand each other, I'll be instructing Doctor Abrams not to speak with you again about this case."

"I'll do a little digging on my own then. If it does turn out you're right, I'll pack my bags and leave this godforsaken backwoods town and head back to the big city and some real crime. You can go back to hiding out and judging the pie contest at the county fair."

Flynn stopped. Her face went flush. She looked back over her shoulder at Calder. "I'm not hiding."

"Well, maybe you should be."

Flynn didn't say another word. She took a deep breath, turned, and continued up the steps to the exit and the parking lot.

"Don't say I didn't warn you," Calder shouted out as Flynn slammed the door of her Ford Edge. "They just might be here to finish what they started. I saved you once, don't think I'll do it again with that kind of attitude."

CHAPTER SEVEN

The police station in Auburn Notch was in a central location in town next to Jack Hanson's Rocket Café. It sat across the street from the bowling alley near the end of Collier Avenue, the main street running through Auburn Notch, just off the corner before Maple Way. The Major Holloman Bridge spanned the cool, spring-fed lake that ran along Maple separating the north end of town from the south. The bridge itself had been blocked off to all traffic a month earlier to accommodate a county work crew. The council-approved, one-month painting project quickly turned into a two-year revitalization once cracks were discovered along the ornamental iron beams supporting the asphalt decking.

Following an outcry from the local businesses, the Auburn Rotary lead the charge at a boisterous town meeting, siting the economic hardship such a closure would cause.

Councilwoman Johnson leaped at the opportunity to take up the cause. She and her husband Steve were long-time residents of Auburn Notch. Steve owned a tax and accounting business in town, and Alice served on the town council after retiring from teaching tenth grade algebra. They raised three children, all of whom are grown and entrenched in lives and the local PTAs at least two hours away by plane. Since her husband's unexpected passing a few years back, she has turned her attention to, and has been a tireless champion for, the local businesses of Auburn Notch. With leaflets she distributed door to door, she vowed not to allow this unexpected event to, ". . . lay waste to the town she has served tirelessly for the past ten years." In the small print she blamed the Highway Department for failing at their duty to ensure the safety of the citizens of Auburn Notch, something she hoped to leverage with regard to the dangerous guardrail situation. The full-color photos of the cracks and excerpts from the engineers report included on the back page were also earmarked as exceptional fodder for her reelection campaign in the fall.

The Auburn Notch Small Business Association cheered her on, with the whole effort resulting in the construction of a pedestrian bridge over the lake on the east side of the bridge. It would allow for uninterrupted foot traffic for the businesses in town, leaving motorist the option to park on the south side of the lake in the lot behind Starlight Bowling, or drive the 1.8 miles around the perimeter of the lake to the public parking lot on North Maple Way. After about a month the dust settled, and the normal day-to-day business returned. Dealing with the anticipated tax increase the pedestrian bridge was expected to cause will be something Mrs. Johnson will carefully hang around the necks of her opponents during the fall candidate debates.

The slamming of the office door startled Hank. He was turned away in the other direction talking to someone as Sheriff Flynn entered.

"I'm glad you're back, Sheriff," said Hank, rising to his feet. This is Mr. Clayton. He's a private detective from New York."

Sheriff Flynn shook off the last remnants of her anger and greeted Mr. Clayton warmly. She stretched out her hand and said, "Very nice to meet you. What brings you all the way from New York to our little town?"

Mr. Clayton slowly stood up, stumbling out a response. "Yes . . . very n–nice to meet you, Sheriff." It took a moment before he realized her hand was stretched out in front of him. Finally, he reached out and shook it. "I'm s–sorry, you just look very f–familiar. Have we met?"

Sheriff Flynn smiled, directing Mr. Clayton back to his chair. "Please, have a seat. No, I don't believe we have." She walked around and took her seat in the well-seasoned oak chair behind her desk. "We get a lot of tourists through here in the summer, have you been here before?"

"No, ma'am, it's my f–first time." Clayton fished around in his pocket, produced a business card, and handed it to the sheriff.

"Well, welcome to Auburn Notch, Mr. Clayton. So, what can we do for you?"

Hank took the picture he held in his right hand and handed it to the sheriff.

There was no hiding the surprise on Flynn's face. "Where did you get this?" she remarked to Hank.

"I g–gave it to him," replied Mr. Clayton. He pulled a small, paper-clipped stack of additional photos from the pocket of his overcoat and handed them to the sheriff. "I have these t–too. I was hoping you c–could confirm if the young woman you f–found dead in the old hospital was this woman?" He pointed in the general direction of the blond woman circled on the top photo.

"What's your interest in this case?" asked Flynn. "And where did you get all of these photos?"

"I was hired b–by Mrs. Alice Newcomb to locate her d–daughter. She and Jane, that's her d–daughter's name, Jane Newcomb, meet every Sunday m–morning for brunch at Rockefeller Center. When she didn't sh–show up this past week, and she couldn't reach her b–by phone, Mrs. Newcomb called me. I met her at her home in Br–Brooklyn, that's when she gave me the photos." From another pocket he fished out a crumpled piece of paper that had been folded in quarters. After smoothing it out on his knee, he handed it to the sheriff. "That's a copy of the p–police report she filed last w–week."

Sheriff Flynn studied the photo Mr. Clayton handed her. It was a standard 5 x 7 photo. On the back the name Jane Newcomb was printed in pencil. She held it up, giving Hank another look. As she did, the glare from the light hinted at additional words that appeared to have been erased. Flynn ignored it for the moment and looked at the stack of additional images. They were certainly of the same young woman but in an assortment of sizes and printed out on copy paper. Something you would do off your home or office computer.

"It certainly looks like her," replied Hank.

Sheriff Flynn took one final look at the photo. "We'll have our ME give the final decision," she said to Mr. Clayton, "but as far as I'm concerned, this is the young woman we found in the hospital. Do you mind if I keep this for a day or two?" Flynn didn't give Clayton the opportunity to reply. Instead, she handed the photo to Hank. "Hank, would you run this over to the State House and give it to Dr. Abrams, please?"

Hank took the photo and left the office at a hastened pace, not giving Mr. Clayton the opportunity to mount any type of objection.

"I'm curious," Flynn continued, getting Clayton's attention off Hank and the photo, "what brought you here? Why did you think our body and your disappearance were connected? Auburn Notch is a long way from Brooklyn, and you say you've never been here."

Mr. Clayton fidgeted a bit in his chair. He stood a good six inches shorter than Hank, a little on the plump side, with an honest face. His gray eyes were in a perpetual squint, as if working out some intricate mathematical theorem in his head, and tucked neatly between high cheekbones and a furrowed brow. A bit frumpish in dress, most likely a byproduct of monotonous hours staking out cheating husbands or suspect employees from the front seat of his car, but nothing more particular to make him overly memorable in appearance. He's the type of guy who lives down the street, keeps to himself, and lends a hand when he sees an old lady needs help. We all know the type. You'd nod politely if he smiled as you walked by, but in a crowd you wouldn't give him a second look. In conversation he might stand out a bit more due to a slight stutter.

Mr. Clayton took a handkerchief from his pocket and wiped his brow. With one swipe a tempered smile replaced the puzzled look Flynn's actions and questions originally produced. With only a slight bit of additional maneuvering, he replaced the handkerchief in his pocket. "The I–Internet's an amazing thing," he said, taking short breaths between each sentence. "I don't kn– know how we got along years ago without it. Now we just type in a f–few key words and POOF. All the answers are at our f–fingertips. I'll get that photo b–back, right?"

Sheriff Flynn rested back in her chair studying her nervous detective friend. After a quiet and what probably came across as a somewhat judgmental moment, she returned the smile. "Of course. I just want it so our ME can make a positive identification. I know what you mean about the Internet. Everything is digital these days, even old cases, right there at your fingertips. It's an amazing world we live in. So, Jane Newcomb goes missing in Brooklyn, her mother picks your name from the phonebook and hires you to find her, you read a local news story on the web about an unidentified woman found dead in a town you've never been to, put the two incidents together, and POOF, here you are? You're some sharp PI, Mr. Clayton."

"Y . . . yes, ma'am," Clayton replied. "Well, n–no, not exactly."

"Not exactly? So you're not a sharp PI?" Flynn had him where she wanted him, rattled and nervous. She pushed the little man a step further. "Is there something I missed? I'm just a local sheriff. I can use all the help I can get."

"Well, nothing . . . really. I mean m–most of that is correct." Clayton paused, taking a moment to get his nervousness under control, and his story. He wiped the sweat off his brow once more, taking his time putting his handkerchief away.

Sheriff Flynn smiled innocently, acting very indifferent to his outward appearance. She waited patiently, taking a closer look at the small stack of photos in front of her. One in particular caught her attention. It was a photo of Jane and two other girls laughing and clinking their glasses together. With her forefinger, and a few inconspicuous movements, she shifted it out away from the stack. "You were saying?"

"Sh–she didn't exactly pick my name from the ph–phonebook," Clayton half-heartedly replied.

"Oh," said Flynn. "Family friend? Did work for her before?"

"You'll th–think me a bit of a leech," Clayton continued, "but on occasion I s–spend a little time in the squad room d–down at the 33rd Precinct. It's a quick w–way to drum up business when things are slow. That's wh–where I met Mrs. Newcomb."

"I see. So you approached her?"

"That's right. I overheard her c–conversation with one of the detectives. It was last S–Sunday when her and Jane were supposed to meet. She didn't s–seem happy with the answers she was g–getting from the detective." The short bursts of breath were back. "I met up with her outside. Told her my n–name and said I could help."

"That's when she hired you?"

"No. She said no th–thanks that day, but two days later she c–called. That's when I m–met her at her house, and she gave me the photos."

"So you scanned the Internet for crimes involving unidentified victims, and that's what brought you here?"

"Yes. I thought I owed it t–to my client to check it out."

Sheriff Flynn was less than convinced with his response, but she smiled and nodded just the same. There was something almost rehearsed about Clayton's details and final reply. This unassuming, little man was playing her, but to what end? Even his innocent smile at the end appeared drawn from a handy stash he keeps at the ready for just such an occasion.

He looked up and smiled at the sheriff, as if he just stepped aside at the last minute, allowing an oncoming train to race by him.

"So, what will you do now, Mr. Clayton?"

"I'll probably st–stick around for a few days. At l–least until you confirm the young girl's identity. You'll contact her m–mother, right?"

"Yes. If it turns out our victim is Jane Newcomb, I'll call the Brooklyn police and have them send someone to her home to deliver the news." She paused and leaned forward. "I'll caution you not to say a word to her in the event she contacts you before I have a positive ID. Despite our assumption of the victim's identity, it's not the type of thing you blurt out over the phone to a client."

Much to Flynn's surprise, Clayton actually appeared offended at the remark. "I can assure y–you, Sheriff, I'm not s–some insensitive, stereotypical gumshoe." Clayton stood up. "If you don't have any m–more questions, I'll just take my ph–photos and leave."

Mr. Clayton reached for the stack of photos. Sheriff Flynn put her hand up and then pointed back to his chair, suggesting the questions were not quite over. With reservation, Clayton sat back down on the edge of the chair, indicating his intention of staying not a moment longer than he absolutely had to.

Sheriff Flynn pushed the photo that had caught her attention in the pile toward Clayton. She pointed to the crowd in the background, looking toward the camera. "Do you know any of the other people in this photo?"

Clayton glanced at the photo barely long enough to identify any of the faces in the crowded bar. "No. Sh–should I?"

"No, I guess not. Do you mind if I hold onto this photo also?"

"Do I have a ch–choice?"

Flynn smiled. "Of course you do. I just thought in the interest of justice you would want to do all you could to help us find out what happened to this young girl?"

"Sure, fine . . . but, why th–that one? Is there someone in the background *you* know?"

Flynn ignored the question, and instead took her pencil and pointed to the television screen in the background above the heads of the crowd. "You see that? That's the Boston College vs. Syracuse game. I was having a late dinner at Horse Feathers down the road here on Saturday night. I worked that night. I'm not a big sports fan, but I watched parts of the game while I ate. The crowd was pretty loud, so I wanted to see what all the excitement was about. According to this photo, Jane Newcomb was alive and well Saturday night. She doesn't show up for brunch the next day, so these two girls she's with might be able to shed a little light on what happened between those two events. Once Mrs. Newcomb gets here, I'm hoping she can tell me their names. They might have information that could help solve this case." Flynn paused, turning the photo back towards herself. "I'm sure you know the names of these girls, right? No? I'm surprised, I would have thought they would have been the first two on your list."

Clayton stared at the photo. His face became red. He wasn't about to answer any more questions. He stood up. "Take any ph–photos you want. Anything else, Sh–Sheriff?"

"Just this one will be fine. Are you staying in town?" Flynn remarked casually.

"No, just outside. It's that l–little motel with all the cabins out on 93. Cabin 4. You can find me th–there if you need me."

Sheriff Flynn nodded. "Make sure you let me know before you leave town."

Mr. Clayton tugged on the lapels of his overcoat, as if the motion would instantly smooth out the years of hard-pressed wrinkles and reveal his indignation over the insinuation in her voice. He didn't see that train coming.

Sheriff Flynn had a few expressions of her own to draw from. She held up the photo and smiled. "I just want to make sure I get this back to you before you leave, that's all. Enjoy your stay here in Auburn Notch."

Following one last defiant tug on his lapels, Clayton gave a harrumph, tucked the remaining photos back in his pocket, and left the station. Sheriff Flynn watched out the window as he got into a relatively new, black Malibu. It was a rental, and she made a note of the license number.

Flynn sat back down at her desk and stared at the photo Clayton left behind. Taking out her cell phone, Flynn hit number 2 on her speed dial. She could hear the muffled ringing coming from the back room of the station. Before the second ring, Hank came through the door. He brought with him the original photo Clayton handed to him.

"I thought I saw the patrol car out there," said Sheriff Flynn. "I had a very interesting talk with our new friend, Mr. Clayton."

"Not as interesting as what the ME found on this photo I'll bet."

Flynn smiled. "I was hoping you two might find that. What did it say?"

Hank put the photo face down on Flynn's desk. There was a pinkish area below Jane Newcomb's name. You could make out the words *Auburn Notch, NH* in the smear of color.

"Why would he erase that?" asked Hank, pushing his hat back on this head.

"Why indeed?" whispered Flynn, running her finger over the words.

"Doc Abrams wiped some kind of chemical on there and it came up plain as day. He also confirmed Clayton was right." Hank turned the photo back over and pointed to a spot on Jane Newcomb's wrist. "See that? It's a small four-leaf clover tattoo. The girl in the morgue has the same one. It's Jane Newcomb." Hank paused, seeing the sheriff was lost in thought. "You okay, Sheriff?"

Flynn didn't answer right away. She looked at Hank then out the window overlooking Collier Avenue, tapping her pencil on the photo Clayton left behind. "There's something about that guy I don't like. Something that seems familiar."

"You think you met him before?"

"I can't place the face, but something about him is making me uneasy."

"How about I see what I can find out about him?"

Flynn swung back around in her chair and nodded. "I'm sure it's nothing, but it won't hurt to check. Thanks. See what you can find out about a string of related murders about a year ago in New York. Peanut allergies and some guy who owns a health-food store."

Hank was trying to understand the reasoning. "Is all that related to Jane Newcomb?"

"I don't know. Just see what you can find out, please."

Hank nodded, once again frustrated with the sheriff's all-too-often reluctance to read him in fully. "Will do. So, what else did Clayton have to say?"

"It's not what he said, it's what he didn't say." Hank sat down on the chair recently vacated by Mr. Clayton as the sheriff continued. She handed the other photo Clayton left behind to Hank. "See anyone we know?"

Hank scanned the photo, then his eyes lit up. "Hey, that's—"

"Yes it is," interrupted Sheriff Flynn.

"You think Clayton knows him?"

"I don't know whether he *knows* him or *knows of* him. It's something we need to figure out pretty quickly. I don't think locating a missing person is the only thing that brought Mr. Clayton to town. He could have identified her by the tattoo over the phone. He's staying out at Mitchell's place on I93. Why don't you give John a call out there and ask him to quietly keep an eye on his guest in Cabin 4."

"Will do. What are you going to do?"

"First, I'm going to call the Brooklyn police and tell them what's happened up here." Flynn tapped her finger on the photo. "Then, I'm going out to have a conversation with our friend in the photo." She paused for a moment then said, "How's that swim club investigation going? You're keeping a low profile, right?"

Hank nodded. "So far. I've got a new lead I'm going to follow up on." A slight smile broke the surface of his lips. If I'm right, he thought to himself, you're not going to like what I found. "It might piss a few people off, or it may not lead to anything."

"It doesn't matter, what matters is that you get to the bottom of it."

Hank stood up. "Will do."

CHAPTER EIGHT

A very cheerful fellow extended his hand, shaking the hand of the young man standing in front of him with a large camera bag. "You must be Sam Martin? I'm Mark Warren."

"Yes, I am. You got that giant billboard out on Route 10, don't you?"

"Yep. It's a bit big, but it does the trick. People go by and see that, so when it's time to develop some land, who do they call? That's right, Mark Warren, the real estate guy."

Marty had a tendency to be a bit gritty, but he promised himself to keep it under control as best he could. This was a new client, and they're not easy to come by. "You said you needed some photos taken for a development project?" asked Marty, pulling one of his cameras out of the case.

The two men were standing on a gravel road. The paved portion of the road, called 2½ Mile Road, ended about twenty yards behind where they were standing, just around a small bend. The gravel marked the spot where the last developer had progressed to before running out of backers, money, general interest, and an assortment of other reasons the banks used to deny funds for the project. Despite that, it was a nice stretch of land, certainly suitable for development in the mind of Mark Warren. It was a property he's had his eyes on for years, hoping the right person with vision would come knocking on his door. That day had finally arrived.

The main drawback, at least the one most often used in conversations regarding the prior defunct development attempts, was how far off the beaten path this parcel of land was. Most council members were certain it would take years before suburban development would venture out that far from town. Mark Warren laughed at the excuse, noting the shortsightedness of those who came before him looking for the quick return instead of the long-term return such an investment would be capable of producing. He had no intention of waiting for the people to discover his vision; he intended to bring his vision to the people.

Until that happens, the only practical use for the land remained a location for snowmobile racing all winter long.

Mark Warren put his arm around Marty and pointed out over the field. "Let me tell you something, Chief, this is going to be the second largest outlet shopping complex in the state. It will be the pinnacle of my real estate career. Not only will it have acres of the finest retail names, there will be restaurants, a theater complex, condominiums, and seasonal rental units." He stepped forward, raising his hands to God Almighty. "This will be my legacy to the fine people of New Hampshire. And when it's complete, I'll tear down that billboard on Route 10. There'll be no reason for me to explain who Mark Warren is, Mark Warren will be a household name." He turned back, winked at Marty, and smirked. "Those damn paintball jerks will just have to find another target."

When Warren turned back around to once more admire what would soon be his legacy, Marty shook his head and rolled his eyes. He didn't want to burst Warren's bubble, at least not until he was paid. This isn't the first time he was contracted to shoot this same parcel of land. He could have saved Warren a few hundred dollars by just giving him copies of the photos he took for the last guy who thought he was going to become a household name. But why step on another man's dream? Besides, he could certainly use the money.

Marty followed behind Warren into the open field. He took with him his Nikon D5200 with the monopod attached to the bottom, leaving the case behind on the hood of his car. He handed the lens cap to Warren and began to shoot each spot Warren pointed to. They spent the better part of two hours shooting every corner of the site. As they walked through the tall grass and brush, Mark Warren explained every aspect of the project to Marty, starting with how a chance meeting got the ball rolling.

Just four days earlier, Mark Warren had been down at a real estate convention near Waltham, Massachusetts. After dinner on the second evening, he sat enjoying a quiet drink in the bar when a stout, yet dignified, gentleman approached him. The gentleman introduced himself as Ronald Habberset, asking if he might take the seat next to him. A conversation commenced. After a few pleasantries, Habberset divulged his appearance at the convention, and subsequent introduction to Warren was not the coincidence it might seem. Habberset expounded in more detail of his position as a broker for a well-respected, New England developer. His purpose in meeting with Mark Warren was with regard to his employer's interest in acquiring a parcel of land outside Auburn Notch.

While he was not at liberty to divulge the name of the developer he represented, Habberset was very forthcoming in explaining his employer's wish for Mark Warren to handle the transaction. They had spent a few months investigating many sites throughout Vermont and New Hampshire, finally settling on the parcel located off 2½ Mile Road. Mr. Smith, as Habberset referred to his employer in the conversation, had personally investigated that particular site. They spent a few days quietly assessing every corner of the land, comparing it against the other two properties under consideration. Habberset remarked how in the process they came across Warren's billboard on their way out of town.

The conversation already had Warren's attention, but the last statement brought a large grin to his face. I'm a marketing genius, he thought to himself. He ordered another round of drinks as Habberset continued.

Much like the imposturous way Disney purchased the land in Orlando before announcing his intensions to build a second Magic Kingdom, Habberset explained how Mr. Smith felt obliged to follow the same route. Any time a big name gets associated with a speculative land deal, the price of the land skyrockets. If this project was to see the light of day, it was essential the name of the buyer remained a secret until all parcels of land were purchased.

Mark Warren listened in earnest, making copious notes of all the major aspects of the proposal. The land adjoining 2½ Mile Road was one of several parcels needed for the project, and it was also the largest. Securing this first parcel was essential to the success of the development. If word leaked out after that deal was finalized, it would have very limited impact on any further purchases. The remaining two parcels were much smaller and weren't essential to the development. They would only be included if they could be purchased at a reasonable price. The initial purchase would secure enough land for phases one and two of the project, also allowing 2½ Mile Road to be widened and extended in both directions to connect Route 93 with Route 4. The project was a monumental undertaking, including a turn-of-the-century-style bridge spanning the Merrimack River, complete with a River Walk outfitted with cafés and upscale boutiques.

Mark Warren couldn't write fast enough. The whole proposal blossomed beyond anything he could ever imagine being involved with. But there he sat, sharing a drink and sitting opposite the man who had the power to catapult his limited local real estate name into a nationally recognized brand. Warren's vanity interrupted the conversation, inquiring exactly how Habberset knew he was in Waltham. Habberset responded with a smile and an explanation of how he had phoned his office a day earlier, being informed by his secretary of the conference. Rather than wait the few days until the conference concluded, he decided it prudent to make the trip himself to Waltham—noting the handsome image on the billboard made it easy for him to spot him in the hotel.

A flattered Warren quickly jumped back into the details about the project inquiring about the location of the remaining two parcels. Habberset dismissed discussing them until a deal was finalized on the 2½ Mile Road land. His reasoning being they were going to have enough to do within the short span of time between acquiring the land and pushing the first shovel into the dirt. That was enough to satisfy Warren. The two men shook hands and finished their drinks.

"That's pretty impressive," Marty said. His tone was less than enthusiastic, but Warren was too consumed with his recitation of the facts to notice or care.

Warren forged ahead as the two men made there way through the brush to the east bank of the Merrimack River. He stopped at a weathered wooden stake with a faded orange plastic strip tied to the top sticking up through the tall weeds. "You see that?" he said, pointing it out to Marty. "Whoever the developer was who drove that marker into the dirt will be kicking himself when I'm done with this property. They had their chance and blew it."

Marty stumbled along behind Warren as the two men continued towards the river. Warren paused when they reached the large, granite boulders along the embankment, taking in a deep breath of satisfaction. After a moment he turned his attention back to Marty. "Of course, everything I've just told you is privileged information. I've been sworn to secrecy, and if you want to continue as the official photographer on this project, I will expect the same from you." He smiled, giving Marty a friendly slap on the back. "There's a lot of money to be made here, Chief. Do we understand each other?"

Mark Warren took a check from his pocket and handed it to Marty. It was almost twice the amount Marty quoted him over the phone.

"Absolutely, Mr. Warren. You have my word." Marty smiled, staring at the amount. There remained a lingering remnant of doubt in Marty's mind, but a final glance at the check before stuffing it into his pocket was enough to plaster an enthusiastic smile on his face.

The two men shook hands and walked back to where their cars were parked. Warren continued to elaborate on the confidential details he shouldn't be talking about. Marty smiled and nodded each time Warren looked back at him, returning to a skeptical shake of his head when he turned away. Once they reached the area where they left their cars, Warren shook Marty's hand again, once more reminding him of the secrecy of the project. With a wave over his shoulder, Warren walked over to his car still mumbling details to himself.

As Marty detached the monopod from the camera, a thought came to mind. He called over to Mark Warren.

Warren's black sedan rolled slowly towards Marty. He lowered the window as the car came to stop next to the car where Marty was putting his equipment away in the trunk. "What is it?"

"I was wondering," Marty asked, "what made you pick me for the photographs?"

"Oddly enough, it was Ronald Habberset who suggested you. He said he and his employer saw your work on display somewhere. Once he realized you lived here in Auburn Notch, he insisted I call you and sign you onto the project. He wanted to keep everything local. It looks like we both have a new admirer." Warren put his sunglasses on and smiled. "Let me know when the pictures are ready."

The window went up, and Mark Warren disappeared around the bend onto 2½ Mile Road.

Marty shook his head. Maybe this time it might work, he thought to himself. Nah. He finished packing up his camera equipment, zipped the bag, and tossed it into the trunk of his car. Marty headed into the grayish-brown dust thrown up by Warren's car as he followed down the gravel road. Up ahead, he saw the red taillights of the Mercedes turn left onto Route 93. At the stop sign Marty did the same, heading back toward his cabin at the lake.

"Is th–that him?" asked Bob Clayton. He watched out the windshield of his car as Mark Warren's black Mercedes came into view.

Clayton's car was tucked back between a small convenience store and a roadside, self-serve vegetable stand that had not yet opened for the season. The faded, white building blocked the view to his right—the direction of 2½ Mile Road—and a small grove of trees flanking a makeshift sign touting the weekly specials restricted the view to the left. From where he sat, Clayton had a clear view of Route 93 for seventy-five feet, enough to accomplish what was needed. He thought about inching up closer to the front of the building. The idea was met with a stern look in the rearview mirror and quickly rejected. Any closer and the front of the car would be in view of anybody turning east onto Route 93, or going in or out of the convenience store.

Mark Warren was focused on the road ahead, singing along to one of his favorite country songs. He paid very little attention to anything going on along the sides of the roads he traveled, other than a glance and a big thumbs-up on the occasions when his travels brought him passed his billboard. As a result, he was well into the chorus of a twangy, Merle Haggard favorite as he passed by the convenience store and the boarded-up vegetable stand, unaware he was being observed as he made his way down the road.

CHAPTER NINE

"So. What do you have there?" asked the sheriff, entering the office and taking her seat behind the desk.

She caught her deputy a little by surprise. Hank quickly drew his hand back from the pile of papers he was fingering through in the IN box on Sheriff Flynn's desk. He quickly held out the folder he carried in his other hand. "It's the info on those murders in New York you wanted."

Sheriff Flynn took the folder and thumbed through the papers. After a moment she put the folder down and leaned back in her chair. "Why don't you give me the highlights?"

Hank bit his tongue and did as he was told. "Most of that is the police report. The NYPD figured the same person committed all four murders within a two-week period. One was on Monday, two was on Thursday, and three and four were on the following Tuesday. They're looking for a guy named—"

"Roy Barnes?"

Flynn's knowledge of the name gave Hank pause for a second. He continued. "Yeah . . . yeah that's who it all points to. All four victims were found on abandoned wharfs along the Hudson down around lower Manhattan. Three women, one guy. All four appeared to have been wacked over the head, murdered at other locations, and then laid out on the wharfs. They found a black candle next to the body at three of the four locations."

Sheriff Flynn sat forward. "Only three?"

"Yeah. One, three, and four. Number two was found after a major rainstorm. There could have been a candle, but they figured anything that small would have been blown into the Hudson during the storm."

"So, why Roy Barnes?"

"All four people shopped at his store. He specialized in peanut-free products. According to neighbors of the victims, this guy Barnes made frequent deliveries to their apartments. One neighbor recalled an argument Barnes and number three had in the parking garage about a week before she ended up dead."

"Did they say what the argument was about?"

"Nope, just saw they were arguing."

"Anything else?"

"They all had phone calls from Roy Barnes the day before they were killed." Hank sat down in the chair across the desk from the sheriff. "You think Roy Barnes is in Auburn Notch?"

Sheriff Flynn ignored the question. "Could the NYPD link Barnes to a similar series of murders in Chicago?"

Hank was dumbfounded. It was like the sheriff already read the report, but that wasn't possible, he thought. "Nope. Four Chicago murders were mentioned in one of the reports, but they have nothing to indicate Barnes was ever in Chicago. That's why they didn't like the FBI's theory about the murders being connected. But how did you—"

"Let's just say I'm not the burned-out, big-city detective I'm portrayed to be."

Hank took a quick breath and held it. That's the exact phrase he used during his last bitching session with the town council.

"Was he working with anybody?" Flynn continued with her line of questions, choosing to ignore Hank's astonished stare.

It took Hank a moment before he could stutter out a response. "Well . . . well, the report doesn't mention anything about an accomplice. Why would you think there were two?"

"No reason, just asking. Did Barnes have an alibi for any of the murders?"

"That's just it, by the time the NYPD figured out it was Barnes, he disappeared. Not a trace." Hank tried once more to get a little more clarity on the sheriff's line of thinking. "So, you think this Barnes guy killed Jane Newcomb and dumped her here?"

"If he did," replied the sheriff, standing up, "he might have had to come back from the dead to do it."

CHAPTER TEN

Bob Clayton looked up from his newspaper. "Do I know y–you?" he said in as innocent a tone as he could muster, which did little to mask his obvious recognition of the man standing before him.

"Bob Clayton, isn't it?" replied Hugh Calder. He pulled out the chair across the table from Clayton and sat down. "Catching an early dinner?"

"Yes, but I r–really don't want any company. I just w–want to read my paper."

"How long's it been? About eight months, I'd say." Calder leaned forward knitting his fingers together below his chin. He quietly continued. "It was after that third abduction in New York, a day before that poor woman turned up dead out in the old maintenance shed on the waterfront. You were at the station trolling for victims . . . uh . . . I mean clients if I remember correctly. You seem to have put on a few pounds, Bob. I also remember you being a bit more friendly."

"I'm s–sorry, but I don't r–remember m–meeting you at all."

"Are you sure I don't look familiar? I thought I saw you hanging around one of the police stations. You are Bob Clayton, right?"

"N–no . . . I mean, yes. If you d–don't mind—"

"Do you live in Manhattan?"

"N–no. I'm a PI from Brooklyn." Clayton abruptly folded his paper, putting it down next to his plate. "Do you w–want something?"

"Oh, well, my mistake. I guess we didn't meet. I just thought you looked familiar."

Bob Clayton forced a smile and shook his head. He made a casual glance around the café and tapped on the newspaper with his fork indicating his desire to be left alone.

The Rocket Café was a little quiet after the lunch hour, staying that way until around four o'clock when the early birds arrived for the dinner special. It sat in the old Buster Brown shoe store that closed up in the early 1980s. A number of people tried to make a go of it there with everything from a hair salon to an eBay

58

storefront. Nothing caught on until Burt and Lily Anderson opened the Rocket Café. It was a hit from the start with the older set, and it didn't hurt having the police station right next door and the State House at the other end of the block. Always a steady flow of hungry customers.

During the quiet time between the lunch and dinner hours, the seniors of Auburn Notch would saunter in for coffee and to catch up on the latest gossip. Murder at the Willis Asylum had everybody's jaw working overtime in the café all week. Most conversations started the same way. There hasn't been a suspicious death in Auburn Notch since '97 when old man Morris was found dead in his truck out by the lake. Most said it was that woman he had taken up with over the summer. She came to Auburn Notch from Las Vegas, a bit too flashy for most people's taste. You know how that type is. No one took the trouble to acknowledge she was eighty-seven and used a walker. Others said old man Morris had a ghost from the past finally catch up with him to settle an old debt. Miserable men like that usually do, was the reasoning. The coroner said the old fool had an exhaust leak in that crappy pickup he used to drive. His unofficial cause of death was stupidity—sitting out by the lake in the winter with the engine running, the windows up, eating a sandwich. This, too, was glazed over in the conversations, noting that the young coroner recently hired then wouldn't know a suspicious death if it bit him on the ass. The bottom line now is old man Morris could finally rest in peace; there was a new suspicious death to take his place.

"I'll bet the pie is great here," said Hugh Calder, ignoring Clayton's hint. He waved at the waitress, making hand gestures like they were playing charades to indicate his desire for a cup of coffee. He followed with a smile, pointing in the direction of the covered pie plate on the counter and nodded. "Nothing like a hot cup of coffee and a slice of homemade apple pie. You do like pie, don't you, Bob? Can I get you one?"

Mr. Clayton shook his head. He made the decision to return to his paper, paying no further attention to Calder's attempts to engage him in conversation.

Lucy, Lily's daughter, brought over the aforementioned pie and coffee, placing them down in front of Calder. She went to top off Clayton's cup but he was quick to wave her off. "Just a ch–check, please."

"I was right," Calder said, taking his first bite, "this pie is excellent." He continued his commentary of the local fare, ignoring the fact he was being ignored. With exaggerated movements, he added four packets of sugar to his coffee, a little cream, and a pat of butter he took from the plate Clayton's half-eaten roll sat on. He concluded with the delicate finesse of a magician as he rattled the spoon against the sides of his cup, stirring the odd concoction. Each morsel of pie brought about some sort of gastronomical moaning of delight, followed by a childhood recollection of dinner with granny. It was incredibly annoying, so it did the trick.

The gastronomical review of each bite and the rattle of metal against ceramic was a solid indication Calder was not about to be blown off so quickly.

"I guess the only w–way to get rid of you is to hear wh–what you have to say, Calder," said Clayton, folding his paper and slapping it down on the table this time. "You're that reporter f–from Chicago, aren't you?"

"I knew you recognized me."

Clayton ignored the remark. "I saw your p–picture in the paper, that's all. You're here about th–that girl they found in the asylum, r–right?"

"It seems we both admire my work, but I guess for different reasons. Such a tragedy. I can't imagine what her parents must be going through, and so far away from home. It's a real shame about—" Calder paused, as if trying to recall the victim's name.

Clayton wasn't about to bite. He smiled and shook his head. "You don't know her n–name, do you?"

Hugh Calder returned the smile. "No, but I know the rest of the details. I'm just wondering why you're here? So what is it? Missing person, I'll bet. Yes, just like New York." He waited, looking for some indication of an affirmation on the furrowed brow of Bob Clayton. It became obvious there would be no voluntary information coming any time soon. Instead, he chose to continue acknowledging his own assumptions whether or not he got a confirming facial tic from Clayton. "Ah, there it is. I'm right. So the young girl was from Brooklyn. If you're here, that means Sheriff Flynn probably has the information, too. Don't trouble yourself, I'll get the name from her."

"I wouldn't c–count on it," replied Clayton. "She's a tough one, p–pretty slick, too."

Calder laughed. "I'll take my chances." He leaned back in his chair and gave Clayton a long, dissecting look. "I guess you'll be going back to Brooklyn now, right? Or are you going to stick around and try to figure this all out? You think there are similarities with this murder and the cases in New York, am I right? I thought so. I put those same pieces together. There's a reward offered, you know, for the whereabouts of that Barnes guy. That's why I showed up in New York, and that's why I'm here now. Did you know there were also similar murders in Seattle and Chicago?"

Calder rattled off the questions without any regard for an attempt on Clayton's part for an answer, he already knew them. He was just trying to get a rise out of Clayton. The last question did the trick, and Calder knew it.

"You th–think this is the work of those two guys you k–keep writing about in your articles, running around the country k–killing people?" asked Clayton through a wry face. "You r–really have a wild imagination."

"So, you're a fan of my work?" Calder leaned back in his chair quite satisfied. "Surely you read about how similar the four murders were? Well, three really, the forth victim—" Calder paused, recalculating the amount of information he was willing to share. "Let's just say the fourth victim was a little more special than the rest. That's part of the reason why I'm here."

"I don't know anything about m–murders in Seattle. I read about the k–killings in Chicago. They s–said it was some doctor who went off his m–meds. Said he would just p–pick random people from the phonebook, stalk th–them, and then abduct and kill them."

"That's the official report." Calder leaned in close and continued in a whisper, as if about to reveal the identity of who actually killed Kennedy. "About six months after the murders stopped in Seattle, four similar abductions happened in Chicago over a two-week period. They were drugged, taken to abandoned buildings in the area, and then shot in the shoulder and left to bleed out. Four victims shot and left for dead."

"That doesn't s–sound anything at all like the m–murders in New York." A flush came over Clayton's face. "They said the New York m–murders were from peanut allergies. Anaphylaxis I think they c–called it. You said it. They're l–looking for some guy n–named Barnes. The police don't th–think any of this, do they? You're m–making all this up. You're m–making all this up just to g–get a headline out of it."

"I'm not making anything up," Calder snapped back. "These are the facts. If the police are too stupid to see the connection, it's my duty to the public to bring it to their attention."

"You're full of sh–shit, Calder."

Lucy Anderson had returned, handing Bob Clayton his bill. She removed his plate, refilled Calder's coffee, smiled, and returned to the conversation she and her boyfriend were having at the counter by the register.

"Think what you want," replied Calder, resting back in his chair, "but there's a connection. It all comes down to the black candles in the windows. Sure the murders were different, but everything else was the same. No clues. No DNA. Just three random people murdered, just like Seattle and New York."

"That's the s–second time you said th–three. I thought there were four p–people murdered in Chicago."

Calder waited in anticipation of the light going on in Bob's attic to indicate he had put two and two together. Nothing. There was even a note of innocence in his eyes. "You don't know, do you?"

Bob Clayton stopped fidgeting in his seat trying to retrieve his wallet from his back pocket and looked at Calder. "Know wh–what?"

Calder snatched the bill from Clayton's hand. "That last victim in Chicago was Sheriff Flynn. She was a detective with the Metro Police back then. Her hair was dark and a little shorter. She was a few pounds heavier, too, but don't tell her I said that. She looks great now though. She was the lead detective on those Chicago murders." Calder waved Clayton's bill in front of him. "I'll take care of this, Bob."

Clayton stared at Calder as if he had just seen a ghost. "N–no."

"No?"

"N . . . no, I'll buy my own d–dinner."

"Don't be an ass." Calder looked over at the counter and got Lucy's attention with a wave. Before Bob Clayton could mount another refusal, Calder had handed Lucy twenty-five dollars and Bob's bill. "This should take care of that and mine. The rest is for you, sweetheart. Thanks."

"So that w–was her? How can that be? I read about the Ch–Chicago murders, but I remember them saying all f–four victims died. They said the lead detective was a twenty-five-year v–veteran of the force. Williams, I think his n–name was."

"That was her partner. He's the one that found her, thanks to me really."

"Th–thanks to you?"

"It's a long story, but the short version is we had a thing going on, Flynn and me. I was supposed to go with her to follow up on a lead, but my editor changed my plans. She went alone. The

Candle-boys were there waiting for her. When I figured out she was going out there without backup I let Williams know. The best the cops figured at the time was their plans got interrupted. Williams heard a gunshot from inside the abandoned hospital when he pulled up. He had to make a choice: chase the shooter or save his partner. Another few minutes she could have bled out. The Candle-boys were pretty smart. Williams figured they heard him pull up outside. Shooting her gave them the time they needed to escape. No way Williams would leave her there to die. That was it. That was the last anybody in Chicago heard from the Candle-boys."

"Stop calling him that," Clayton demanded, his voice deeper and coarse. He pounded his fist on the table. The abrupt action brought every conversation at the surrounding tables to a halt, turning all eyes in their direction.

Calder smiled, looked over at the guys at the counter staring at them, and waved his hand. "Sorry, guys, just struck a nerve. Go back to your conversations." He waited a moment until the tension in the room dissolved and then turned back toward Clayton. "What's wrong with you?"

"Stop calling him that." Clayton repeated, leaning in and speaking in a hushed but coarse voice. "This isn't funny. He's out there killing innocent people, and you give him some kind of comic-book name."

Calder took a moment before he responded. "Easy there, Bob. You're taking this a little too personally aren't you? What's with the *him*? What aren't you telling me?"

"Nothing. I meant *them*. And you got your facts screwed up, Calder. That's all. The paper said all four victims died. The paper said they were well-planned and diabolical in there execution. The paper said—"

"That's right," Calder interrupted, "but that doesn't mean any of it's true. I should know, I wrote that story." Calder felt a slight pang of regret after the last statement slipped out. There was no retrieving the words. He rested back in his seat and addressed the confused look on Clayton's face. "The Metro Police thought it best to have the murderer believe he had succeeded. They also thought it best for Flynn. Despite my insistence about the murders being connected to the Seattle murders, the police were focusing on a retired doctor, Kaminski I believe his name was. Those shits had their man. They dismissed my theory completely. Then Kaminski just drops off the grid. The police had what they thought was a pretty good lead on him, but—"

"What?" Clayton grumbled.

"You know you don't stutter when you're mad?"

Clayton took a quick breath. His narrowed eyes widened. "I've g–got to go." Without another word Bob Clayton picked up his paper and walked out the front door.

Calder sat motionless, his mouth agape in mid-word. By the time he was able to shake a few words loose, Bob Clayton was across the street, disappearing into the alley leading to the parking area behind Starlight Bowling.

CHAPTER ELEVEN

The Starlight parking lot was half full. Normally early Friday afternoon would find the lot empty. The bowling ally didn't open until 4:30 in the afternoon when the after school crowd gathered at the front door waiting for Jack Stanton to open up. The local leagues, getting in a few practice games to loosen up, followed them at 5:00. League play started at 7:05 sharp, leaving just enough time for a quick sandwich and a beer for those lucky enough to get out of work on time.

The bridge situation changed the daily routine for the time being. Cars were going in and out all hours of the day and night. The people loitering around the lot went about their business, paying little if no attention to the stranger as he walked in and out between the cars across the lot to where he left his car parked. He got in, not saying a word, just snorting.

"Stop l–laughing. It isn't f–funny. We're going to g–get caught." Bob Clayton's chest heaved up and down between every sentence. The red in his face rose like a thermometer. He pounded on the dashboard, his fist knocking the rearview mirror off the windshield with one of the upward strokes. "That damn C–Calder is here. We have to l–leave. He knows s–something, I know it."

"Calm down. He knows nothing."

"He knows th–that girl in Chicago didn't d–die."

"I'm very much aware she didn't die. Why do you think we're here?"

Clayton took a few deep breaths; his tantrum was diminishing. His blood pressure was returning to a less elevated and more life-sustaining pace. He picked the mirror up off the floorboards and put it on the dash. No one in the parking lot noticed anything. The car slowly made its way to the exit on Maple Avenue. Clayton remained quiet. He turned onto Collier Avenue, making his way north towards Route 93 and the motel.

About a mile out of town he decided to return to the conversation. He also decided he was not going to be pushed around. Not again. There was too much at stake now.

"What do you m–mean, that's why we're here?" Clayton asked.

"It would seem we have some unfinished business . . . or at least you do."

Clayton shook his head. "No. I'll have no p–part of that. If we g–go after her again, we'll be c–caught for sure. Do what you w–want, but you're on your own with th–that sheriff."

"Perhaps you're right. We'll talk about it later. Right now we have another pressing matter. We can't allow Calder and what you think he might know interrupt our schedule. We need to hurry. You've got a lot to do."

"All r–right," Clayton barked. "Stop t–telling me what to do." Clayton paused as he stopped to check traffic before turning onto Route 93. "And this is it. When we're d–done here, I'm not d–doing this anymore. Do y–you hear me, John? I'm not d–doing this anymore."

There was no response.

CHAPTER TWELVE

"Who are you?" Marty called out from his car window. Marty turned off the ignition. He got out of his car, trying to make out the features of the man approaching him from the porch. The afternoon sun was dropping slowly behind the house, leaving the man's face in shadow. "What do you want? What were you doing on my porch?"

"Are you Sam Martin?"

Marty clenched his fist. "What's it to you?"

"Calm down, son, I'm not here to hurt you." He held out his ID. "I'm with the FBI. I think we can be of service to each other."

"What do you mean?"

The agent held out an enlarged photo, pointing with his forefinger to a face in the crowd. "That's you, isn't it?" Without pausing for an answer, he pointed to another less obvious face in the background. "That's Hugh Calder. He's here in town, and I believe he knows something about the death of that girl they found in the asylum last weekend."

"What does that have to do with me?"

"Maybe nothing, but I believe you might be in danger. Can we go inside to talk?"

The bell above the door of Gordon's Photography announced Sheriff Flynn's arrival. Jack looked over and smiled. He held up his index finger and nodded, indicating he would only be another minute or two.

Promise nodded, walking slowly down along the wall where the latest photographers were featured. She came back up towards the front, stopping in front of the main instillation. An intensely contrasted shot of the second-floor hall of the Willis Asylum caught her attention. It looked down the hall through the doorway towards the pile of plaster and rubbish. Next to that hung a large photo of the room where the body of the young woman was found. A chill shot up her spine.

"Remarkable, aren't they?"

Sheriff Flynn gave a start.

"I'm sorry, Sheriff," said Angela Pierce. "I didn't mean to scare you."

Sheriff Flynn's face flushed with a tinge of embarrassment. "Not a good sign when you can sneak up on the sheriff."

Angela wasn't sure how to respond.

Sheriff Flynn followed quickly with a smile, letting Angela off the hook. "No problem, I just didn't see you there." She looked down at the name on the white card tucked into the lower, right corner of the frame. "This is Sam Martin's work?"

"Yes, it is. He has an incredible way of presenting the macabre. It's some of his best work." Angela abruptly stopped her sales pitch, putting the look on Flynn's face and the photograph together. "I'm sorry. How insensitive of me. That's where that poor girl was found, isn't it?"

Flynn nodded thoughtfully. "Is he around?"

"Who, Marty?"

Sheriff Flynn nodded again.

"I haven't seen him at all today. Did you try his place out by the lake?"

"I stopped by there a little while ago. It didn't look like anybody was home. His car was gone, too." She stepped closer to the photographs. "When were these taken? Do you know?"

"I believe he said last December. Early in the month I think, just before that big snowfall. I remember him saying something about being out at the old asylum when we talked at the town Christmas Parade. *The Chronicle* asked him to take the photos of the festivities for their Sunday supplement. I met up with him at Horse Feathers afterwards. We had a drink together before my friends showed up. Marty said in all the years he lived in Auburn Notch, he never once went inside the old asylum until that day. He said he took a few photos, but the place gave him the creeps, so he left. I told him I would love to see the photos. He agreed, but he never got around to showing me. When Jack decided to feature his work, I badgered him until he agreed to include them in the show. I figured if they were anything like the other work of his I've seen, I was sure they would be a big hit."

"And you think that's when he took these photos?"

"Pretty sure. Why?"

Sheriff Flynn pointed at the pile of plaster and debris in the one photo. "See that pile of trash? About two weeks ago Hank was patrolling out by the asylum. He noticed what looked like flashlight beams in the upper floor. When he went in to investigate, he found a group of teenagers partying it up. The place was bad enough to begin with, but they proceeded to trash it even more. Hank knew most of the kids, and their parents. He made a deal with them. If they showed up the following morning with brooms and trash bags, he wouldn't charge them with criminal trespassing. They did, and at the end of the day, they hauled away forty bags of trash. The big pieces they swept into that corner. So you see, this photo had to have been taken in the last ten days."

The implication drew all the color from Angel's face. She didn't know how to respond, and it didn't go unnoticed by Flynn.

"If you see or hear from Marty," Flynn continued, "please tell him I have a few questions for him."

"How are we doing here?" asked Jack Gordon, walking up to the two women, his arms outstretched. "Sheriff, always nice to see you." He looked at the photograph on the wall behind Sheriff Flynn and then back at her. "Terrible tragedy, just terrible. Are you any closer to catching who did it?"

"We've got a few leads, but nothing solid yet." Flynn patted Jack on his arm. "I've got to go, Jack. Give Martha my best. Thanks, Angela."

Jack walked the sheriff to the front door and said good-bye. The bell above the door echoed the salutation.

"What was that all about?" asked Jack, walking back to where he left Angela standing, straightening one of the frames along the way.

"I'm not sure," Angela replied, studying the photo Sheriff Flynn was referring to. "She was asking about Marty. She has questions for him about that girl's murder."

Jack stopped what he was doing and turned around. "Surely she doesn't think he had anything to do with that terrible business out at the old Willis asylum? I know Marty has a tendency to rub some folk the wrong way, but I don't think he's capable of anything like that."

"I wouldn't think so either. He does seem a little distracted. Do you think he's been acting strange lately?"

"Nonsense. I'm sure the sheriff will get to the bottom of it."

Angela didn't answer. She continued to study the photo on the wall.

CHAPTER THIRTEEN

The sun had set over the lake, raising a rich, pinkish-orange hue up from behind the deep-purple tree line and dissolving into a starry, indigo night sky. This was Mark Warren's favorite time of day. Summer. Winter. The season didn't matter. Each evening, with a glass of his favorite Merlot in hand, he walked down the flagstone path leading to his beach area along the shore to watch the brilliant show nature put on. After a few sips and a long sigh, he blocked everything else out, including the dilapidated boathouse resting against his property line.

Because of the curvature of the shoreline, the boathouse remained in his peripheral vision no matter how much he concentrated on the distant horizon. In the summer months he would wade out to his knees just for a few solitary moments to be free from the distraction. His hope was to one day turn and be surprised by its conspicuous absence, but no such luck yet. It was an eyesore, and Mark Warren had no problem explaining his displeasure to the owner of the property it sat on with monthly letters and threats of council action.

Always the optimist, he knew other forces were working in his favor. As the first flakes fell with each winter storm, he would giggle like a schoolgirl, his nose pressed against the cold glass, watching the snow pile up on the roof of his nemesis. Two inches. Ten inches. Fifteen inches. As the heavy snow layered onto the sagging roof of the boathouse, he clung to the expectation that maybe one more inch would be enough to bring about its ultimate demise. Then the morning would break, and there it stood, thumbing its warped and splintered nose at him. His only satisfaction was each year the boathouse seemed to lean a little closer to the lake, a little closer to disappearing into the murky waters of Lake Auburn. With another deep sigh, and his wine in hand, Mark Warren faced away from his source of irritation, choosing instead to reflect upon his good fortune that night.

The wind had kicked up slightly, so lines of miniature whitecaps were rhythmically breaking on the sandy shore in front of him. It was mesmerizing, enough that he didn't notice the figure approaching him from behind.

Mark checked his watch, remembering it was the third Friday of the month. He couldn't linger too long at the lake. The small group of local relators he meets with once a month would be there in about two hours or so. He had mushrooms to stuff and crab dip to prepare. The group washed it all down with a mango-infused vodka punch. The punch was not so much a favorite with the group, but Warren liked it, so he had no problem convincing himself the group did, too.

Finishing the last of his wine in a single gulp he turned. The dark figure standing an arms-length away caught him by surprise. His final gulp was in a quandary as to which direction it would go. He swallowed hard, taking a step backwards. "Jesus, you scared the shit out of me." Warren took a moment to compose himself. He smiled once he recognized the chubby face before him. "Pardon my language, I just wasn't expecting you."

"No need to apologize, I should have called first. I've got some exciting news. We've decided to move ahead somewhat quicker than expected, so I thought we should meet as soon as possible."

"This is exciting." Warren looked over Habberset's shoulder towards his parking area. "Are you alone? Is your employer with you? I'm really excited about meeting him. Well, I assume it's a him?"

"He'll be stopping by shortly. He's excited about meeting you also."

Warren wrung his hands together. "Excellent. Let's go up to the house, we can talk while I prepare the hors d'oeuvres for my relator group. You'll stay, of course?"

"Do you think that's wise? One slip about what we're doing, and it could cost my employer millions."

Warren took Habberset's arm and pulled him along the path towards the house. "Not a problem, Chief. I haven't told a soul about our plans. I'm so delighted you're here. I've drawn up a few ideas I wanted to propose to you and your employer. I'm sure you'll love them. I'll cut my group meeting short, and we can concentrate on my ideas after they leave. I'll just introduce you as out of town clients here to look over a few properties. They know it's always clients first with me. Where did you say you were from?"

"Seattle. Are you sure we won't be in the way?"

"Not at all."

"When did you say your group would be arriving?"

Warren checked his watch, holding his wrist up to catch one of the last glimmers of sunlight before it disappeared for the evening. "Not for a couple hours. And between you and me, they're usually late."

"That should work out just fine. We'd be delighted to stay."

CHAPTER FOURTEEN

The pale-green walls and antiseptic scent of the long corridors of Willis Mercy Hospital were in complete contrast to the decay and stench of the asylum also carrying the Willis name. At the turn of the century, Dr. Arthur Willis had established himself as a celebrated surgeon and internationally known speaker on the new practice of neurosurgery. He attended Harvard Medical School alongside Harvey Cushing, maintaining a lifelong friendship. Fascinated by Cushing's numerous monographs on brain and spinal surgery, he followed a similar path into the new surgical discipline.

Willis was the youngest of three children from a well-respected New Hampshire family. Benjamin Willis, a Scottish immigrant and great-grandfather to Arthur, was one of the first to understand the relevance of, and capitalize on, the introduction of the power loom to New England in the early part of the nineteenth century. By 1828 he had six factories, employing just fewer than three hundred workers—mostly farm girls from the surrounding counties looking to financially assist their families.

As the Industrial Revolution charged ahead at full speed, the urban landscape was quickly changing in its wake. Cities grew, and more opportunities opened for young women to fill the need for cheap labor. The mills replaced their local workforce with young Irish and French immigrants mostly through attrition. The massive increase in production of cotton textiles, establishment of rail lines, increases in agricultural output, and technological advancements all combined to help a struggling, young nation distance itself from dependency on imported British products.

As the family business flourished, Benjamin turned his attention to the improvement and manufacture of power looms. He established Willis Manufacturing in 1834. The Willis C543-RC Shuttle Loom set the standard of excellence for woolen production, maintaining that distinction well into the twentieth century.

Benjamin had one son, Francis. Upon reaching adulthood, he took over running the mills. Francis was sickly as a child, something he never fully grew out of. He married a woman he met in one of his mills—Ester Stevens. She was a lovely woman, strong-willed with a good head for business. They had two children, Harrison and Arthur. The boys were inseparable as children, but their youngest, Arthur, died after a tragic accident at one of the mills. The two boys had been running around playing hide-n-seek on a hot summer day. Ester, noticing the boys had not been heard from for about a half hour, went looking for them. She found them in one of the cloth storerooms on the second floor. Arthur had ingested a glass of cleaning fluid he mistook for water. He died in his brother's arms.

Harrison never got over the effect of his brother's death, refusing to step foot in any of the mills again. He went off to boarding school, eventually becoming a doctor. He returned to Auburn Notch and married a local girl he knew from childhood. Together, they had one son, who they named Arthur in honor of Harrison's departed brother.

Harrison's father died relatively young, but his mother continued to run all the mills. Arthur followed in his father's footsteps, himself becoming a doctor. He also shared his father's indifference to the family mills. Upon Ester's death, a board of directors was assembled to run the mills with the intension to sell them off either as a group or individually. Within a year, all six were sold. Slowly, over the next thirty years, production in the mills ceased. All but one of the buildings had been torn down or crumbled due to neglect, returning the land for use by the next generation.

Arthur received a substantial inheritance after the death of his mother. This, combined with his lucrative surgical practice, afforded him the means to establish a hospital bearing his family's name just outside of town on Route 4. He never married, so the hospital would be the legacy he would leave behind as a thank you to the town he and his family cherished. A large medical group later acquired the hospital. To honor his legacy, it was stated in the agreement the family name was to be retained. The following summer it became Willis Mercy General.

The Willis Asylum, also founded by Dr. Willis and considered part of the hospital facilities, was not included with the sale of the hospital due to its dilapidated condition. Dr. Willis established the facility to better understand and treat mental disorders. It flourished during his lifetime, but quickly became enveloped in questionable practices after his death. The final nail in the coffin came following a series of suspicious deaths attributed to a one-time orderly at the facility. The asylum abruptly closed, the staff dispersed, and the investigation into the allegations faded away after the suicide of their main suspect. It was a dark period for the Willis name.

Councilwoman Johnson, as one of her first official acts after her appointment, put fourth a bill to condemn the property, ". . . thus relieving any undeserved association between the fine name of Dr. Willis and the actions of one delusional orderly." The town took control of the property after the passage of the bill with the intention to sell it and the adjoining six acres to a developer. That was in 2005. Mark Warren, the realtor of record for the property, has shown the property eight times since, but has yet to ink a deal.

The automatic doors closed behind Sheriff Flynn. She walked at a determined pace past the large portrait of Dr. Willis, her countenance more severe than one would expect from a person known for her compassion. The horseshoe-shaped reception desk was ahead, flanked by glass doors on either side. The wing on the left went to Trauma, the right to Surgery and Maternity. A very cheery receptionist looked up as Flynn approached.

"Good morning, Sheriff," said Marjory. "What brings you out here?"

Sheriff Flynn didn't return the smile, and it didn't go unnoticed. "I believe you had a man admitted last night with a concussion? Hank would have followed him in. I believe he was assaulted—"

"Oh, yes," interrupted Marjory, hastily flipping through her log. She nervously rattled off what she knew while she located the name. "Terrible crack on the head, Doc Waters said. Here it is. He's in observation. Down that hall, room 123."

Marjory was a very young nineteen-year-old, but very eager to do a good job. She had short, blond hair pulled back with a light, peach ribbon. Soft, blue eyes, the very definition of innocence, looked up at the sheriff hoping she was pleased with the response.

Sheriff Flynn was quick to see what affect her mood had on Marjory. Her harsh stare quickly dissolved into a mushy smile. "I'm sorry, Marjory. Thank you. That's exactly who I'm looking for."

Marjory brightened up.

"How is your mom?" Flynn continued. "I bought her pecan pie at the festival the other day. I'm embarrassed to say I've almost eaten the whole thing. She makes the best pecan pie I've ever tasted."

"Oh, she'll be so happy to hear that. It's my favorite, too."

"Tell her I said hi." Flynn started toward the glass doors. "Room 123, you said?"

"Yes, 123."

Flynn waved her hand in the air as the automatic doors opened. A bustle of activities ran down the length of the hall. Breakfast was concluding. Morning rounds were underway. Visiting hours were just starting. The walk down the corridor was just the right length to get her irritation back up to pre-Marjory levels. She paused at the door, allowing a nurse to pass, and then walked over to the side of the bed.

Hugh Calder was lying there under the covers, his upper body slightly elevated, his eyes closed. A slight pinkish-brown discoloration stained the left side of the white gauze bandage wrapped around his head, probably from his blood. He stirred, wincing as he turned his head, then opening his eyes slightly.

"Before you say anything," started Hugh Calder as Sheriff Flynn came into focus, "I was minding my own business having a few drinks at the bar. I'm unlocking my car door when *Whack!* He came out of nowhere. Whacked me on the back of the head with a pipe I think. The next thing I know, your deputy's helping me up from the pavement. I didn't want to come here. Deputy Fife insisted. Not too gently either."

"Serves you right," Sheriff Flynn grunted. "Any head injury, even one to a pigheaded jackass, gets a free ride to the hospital in this town. It's my rule, and Hank is the best at enforcing it."

"Why are you so pissed? I'm the victim here." Calder pulled himself up to a more seated position. He was certain the slight smile he noticed on Flynn's lips was a direct result of his wincing from the pain.

"Do you blame me? This is a quiet, little town. Then you show up. Now I've had an endless stream of bazaar events to deal with. I have a dead body out at the old asylum. A private dick from out of town who's lying to me about what, I don't know? A person of interest I can't locate. A realtor whose gone missing, or so his little group of minions says. And now I find you in a hospital bed with your skull bashed in."

"Yeah, like that's all my fault?"

Sheriff Flynn paced back and forth along the length of the bed trying to regain her composure. After a minute she stopped, pulled a small photo from her pocket, and held it out. "Does this guy look familiar?"

"Yeah, he was in the bar last night." Calder moved around, still looking for that right comfort spot. "I remember he was eyeballin' me every time I looked over. Gave me the creeps. I finally went over to see what his problem was, but he got up and took off."

"You didn't say anything to provoke him?"

"I had a few drinks," protested Calder. "That's all. None of this shit is my fault, so stop acting like it is."

"Maybe not your fault," responded a man standing in the doorway, "but it certainly raises a few questions about you're possible involvement with other matters."

"Who's there?" Calder shouted, followed by a grunt. He couldn't see the doorway due to the privacy curtain.

Flynn swung her head around abruptly to put a face to the voice. He didn't look familiar. "This is a private police matter," she said, holding up her left hand to stop the advancement of the man at the door. The man didn't stop. She unsnapped the leather strap securing her Sig Sauer with her right thumb. "I'll have to ask you to leave."

Realizing she meant business, the man stopped. "I'm going to very slowly reach into my jacket and get my ID, Sheriff. I would appreciate it if you didn't shoot me." He retrieved a leather billfold from his inside pocket and handed it to Flynn.

Flynn opened the billfold, shook her head, and handed it back to him.

"I'm Agent Harry MacGregor with the FBI, but you can call me Mac." He stepped forward into Calder's line of sight.

"I should have known," said Calder, crossing his arms. "It wouldn't surprise me at all if you were the shit that whacked me over the head. Ask him where he was last night, Flynn. Go ahead, ask him."

"You two know each other?" said Flynn to MacGregor, ignoring Calder completely.

"You could say that," replied Mac. "We became acquainted in New York."

"Did it have anything to do with a string of murders?"

"It had everything to do with them. I received an anonymous tip on a serial killer I've been tracking. I was told he had picked four new victims in New York, and if I hurried I just might catch him. The tip came in right after they found the body of the third victim. The NYPD said I was wasting my time, and the tip was a hoax. They had a suspect and a motive. I didn't care. I was convinced it was the same person who committed similar crimes in Chicago."

"Chicago?" replied Flynn.

MacGregor was sharp, and one of the bureau's best at reading body language. He could see the concern flash in Flynn's eyes when he mentioned Chicago. "I know what happened," said MacGregor in a hushed tone. "You and I can talk about it later if you want. If you don't, that's okay, too."

Flynn responded with an appreciative nod.

"If I was right," MacGregor continued, "his next victim was going to be the fourth and last until the next town. If there was a chance at stopping this guy, I had to take it, otherwise he would disappear again, show up in another town, and start all over. I had to follow it up even if New York's finest were right. I've profiled a lot of killers, but I can't seem to get a read on this one."

"Yeah, yeah, yeah. Tell her what happened next." Calder winced again, trying to get himself closer to the conversation.

"We staked out the location, an alley on the Lower East Side. A guy fitting the description we were given showed up dressed in dark clothes, black skullcap, and gloves. He settled back into the alley and just waited. A woman approached the alley. One of New York's finest got spooked. Next thing I knew all hell brakes loose. Calder's on the ground in cuffs, and the woman's screaming. Your boy here claimed he was in New York conducting his own investigation. He claims one of the serial killers contacted him and wanted to turn himself in. Instead of calling us, he's in the alley waiting for the guy to show. He never did. About two hours later, while we were babysitting this one, I got word the fourth victim was found dead at an abandoned wharf near Battery Park."

"So what do I get for trying to help?" Calder added abruptly. "Two days and nights in a detention facility until they could confirm my alibies for all the murders." He paused for a moment, took a deep breath, and moved about in another attempt to find a more comfortable position. It wasn't to be. Instead it just stoked his anger. "All the murders! Including the ones in Chicago."

Sheriff Flynn looked at agent MacGregor and broke her silence with a cleansing laugh. "I think you and I are going to get along just fine, Mac."

"Sure, you think it's funny now, but this shit was talking major jail time. He threatened to charge me for the murders if just one of my alibies didn't check out."

"Stop being such a baby," MacGregor snorted. "My boss wanted to charge you with obstruction. He thinks you're the accomplice you keep alluding to in those articles you've been dreaming up about there being two serial killers. Spending a couple days in that holding cell was my idea. I convinced my boss you weren't bright enough to commit those crimes. Just teaching you a lesson. You should be thanking me."

"I haven't made anything up!" Calder barked, collapsing back onto the pillows with a groan. He rubbed his forehead and took a deep breath, continuing in soft, short breaths. "Tell him, Detective, tell him. They're here to finish the job. They're here for you."

"I'm not a detective, and stop calling me that."

"Whatever. Just tell him."

MacGregor took Sheriff Flynn's arm and leaned in close. "Why don't we speak privately?"

Flynn looked over at Calder. "Sure, I think we're done here."

"Done here?" Calder shouted out grabbing Flynn's other arm. His eyes welled up from the shooting pains that followed each word. He swallowed hard and continued in a calmer tone. "What about this crack on the head? What about my statement? I deserve justice, too, you know."

Mac started for the door. "I'll be in the hall, Sheriff."

Sheriff Flynn nodded, then looked back at Calder. "Hank told me you gave him a statement last night. If you want to add to it, I'll send Hank around. The way I see it, he found you, so you're *his* problem." She tried pulling her arm away, but he wasn't ready to let go yet.

"You know there are two of them." Calder closed his eyes, taking deep breaths between remarks. "Tell him. If they're here, you better tell him before they figure out who you are."

CHAPTER FIFTEEN

Mac quietly paced back and forth in the hall, waiting for Sheriff Flynn. When she joined him he pointed down the hall towards one of the waiting rooms. They quietly made their way through the activities in the busy hall. The room was empty.

"What do you make of all this, Sheriff?" said Mac, taking a seat across from the window overlooking the back courtyard.

"Well, you're right," agreed Flynn. She sat down in the next chair, a small, round table separating them. "Calder's a baby, and he's certainly not capable of orchestrating a series of murders."

Mac smiled. "No, I mean about the young woman you found out at the old asylum? Do you think there's a connection to the murders in Chicago and New York? You did read about the New York murders, didn't you?"

"I hadn't really given it any thought."

Mac waited, hoping his silence might nudge Flynn into some kind of admittance of a connection. Turning more in her direction, he looked over his glasses at Flynn, raising an eyebrow in disbelief. "You're too good a cop to not have put those together."

"I used to be."

Mac shook his head. "Look, I know what happened to you, and I know the last thing you expected was all this crap showing up unexpectedly on your doorstep in your new town. Hell, I don't blame you for wanting to put a little distance between you and that killer."

"I didn't run away, if that's what you think."

"I didn't say you did."

Flynn paused for a moment to get her thoughts together and her emotional baggage in check. "Calder thinks they're here to correct their mistake. He thinks they're playing with me. He thinks they're going through the motions just to get me in the right place to finish what they started in Chicago."

"You two still think we're dealing with two killers acting together to commit the murders, don't you?"

"I know what I heard, Mac." Promise paused for a moment to collect her thoughts. "I may not have been fully conscience, but I heard arguing. One voice was gritty, I'll never forget that, but I'm not sure about the other. They were too far away, and I had a burlap bag over my head. There were two, damn it. Let's just leave it at that."

"We don't have anything to suggest we're dealing with two killers. You said it yourself, you weren't fully conscience. You could have imagined the conversation." Mac paused for a moment. "Lets put that part aside for now. What about this guy in New York, Roy Barnes? The NYPD seem to think he's responsible for those crimes. Owns a health-food store in Soho. All four victims shopped there. He even has a peanut allergy. I'll be honest with you, the threads I'm clinging to are slim. I'm beginning to think my boss might be right about me chasing after something that isn't there."

"And have they found him yet?" interrupted Flynn.

Mac just pursed his lips.

"Well, there you go," Flynn continued. "Look, I don't know what to make of this yet. The only similarity between this case and the ones in Chicago and New York are the black candles left at the scenes. Even the way the victims were killed was different in those cities."

"Exactly!" boasted Mac. "That's the pattern. Don't you see it?"

"I see what you see, but I don't know whether I'm ready to believe it yet. And what about Seattle?"

"Yes, Seattle. Calder told me all about that. I was going out there before your murder at the asylum came across my radar. I sent one of my men out there to chase down the facts and see if Calder's claims hold water."

Flynn stood up. She walked over to the window that overlooked the courtyard. "What if you're wrong, Mac? What if this murder is totally unrelated to those other crimes? I'm afraid what the news of a serial killer loose in this town will do to these people."

"I get it, Promise, but what if I'm right?" Mac waited, but there was no response. "You think I'm wasting my time here. You think this is just a copycat. He'll slip up, you'll catch him, and that will be the end of it. I'm hoping that is the case, because I don't like the possible outcome of the other scenario."

Sheriff Flynn paced in front of the window for a minute or two, digesting Mac's assessment of her situation. She finally returned to her seat. "You haven't told me what *you* think of all this. Do you think Calder's right?"

MacGregor sat forward. He spoke in a hushed tone. "I think Calder's full of shit. I think if someone came here to correct a mistake and finish the job, we wouldn't be having this conversation. You'd be in the morgue, not that poor, young girl."

"That's the conclusion I finally came to." Flynn perked up, getting a little more animated in her response. "At one point I thought Calder might be right. I put all the pieces together, and it did sort of add up to that. But why that young girl and not me? That part didn't make sense. Part of me knows it's possible, but the other part just doesn't want to believe it's happening to me all over again. I hate to say this, but unless there's another victim, I have to believe this is an isolated incident."

"Be careful what you wish for."

"What do you mean?"

"I only think Calder's thought process was wrong. Let's say for the sake of argument I agree with those other crimes being committed by a duo. I would also believe these guys didn't come here with the intention of tracking you down and finishing the job. It's more likely they picked this town for their next group of killings for some other reason or totally at random. Imagine how surprised they're going to be when *they* put the pieces together and realize who you are. That's if they're who you think they are." Mac sat back. "That's why I'm here."

Flynn was stunned by this revelation.

Mac gave her a moment to get her head around it, and then continued. "I didn't tell you this to stress you out. That whole theory could be totally off base, and I hope it is. I would rather spend the next couple weeks fishing while you chase after some jilted lover who chased that poor girl to your quiet, little town and killed her."

"That would go a long way to explain the events, but I'm so afraid that's not what's going on here. I can't go through that again, Mac."

Mac took an indirect route for his response. "You have a deputy, right?"

Flynn nodded her head, waning in enthusiasm.

"What?"

"He's got this bug up his ass about how he should be the sheriff."

"Do you trust him to watch your back?"

Flynn didn't hesitate in her response. "Despite his indifference to the mayor appointing me sheriff, Hank is a first-rate cop. Yeah, I trust him completely.

"Good. Does he know about your past?"

Flynn rolled her eyes. "Probably. I just don't know how much of it."

"I think it's in your best interest to fill him in."

Flynn sat back down. "I'll think about it."

"Okay. Now, for the moment let's assume I agree with you. This woman's death is totally unrelated to the others. What's your next move?"

"I have a person of interest I'm looking to question. Bit of a loner with a temper."

"What put him on the top of your list?"

"I have a photo of the girl taken the night she disappeared. She's with a group of friends at a bar. This guy is in the background."

"Well, that can't be too incriminating for a small town like this," replied Mac. "How many places are there for young people to blow off a little steam?"

"That's just it. The photo was taken in Brooklyn."

"Well, that changes things. Who is he?"

"Sam Martin. He's a photographer here in town. I've got the word out I'm looking for him."

Mac stood up and extended his hand. "I'll leave you to your manhunt then."

Sheriff Flynn stood up and shook Mac's hand. "What will you do now?"

"Well, I'm here now, so I think I'll stick around for a week or so and see if the fish are biting." He finished the statement with a wink and walked off down the hall.

Sheriff Flynn stayed behind. Her look of contentment quickly vibrated into a grumbling under her breath as her thoughts slowly drifted back to the problem at hand. As much as she didn't want to, she couldn't ignore Hugh Calder and the circumstances around his attack. He probably said something fresh to one of the locals' girlfriends, and the guy decided to express his displeasure in the parking lot. No matter what, she at least owed him her attention. She took a cleansing breath and stood up. Just as she was about to walk back to his room, Hank appeared in the doorway.

"Boy, am I glad to see you," Flynn said. "I need you to—"

"There's been a development, Sheriff," interrupted Hank. He was a little out of breath.

"What is it?"

"Mark Warren. He's dead."

CHAPTER SIXTEEN

The long shadows of morning were receding up Collier Avenue, taking with it the slight chill the night air left behind. Early risers were starting to mill about, bundled in light jackets in anticipation of what they were sure would be a pleasant start to the weekend. The OPEN sign at the Rocket had been turned outward a couple hours earlier. The grill was already working on its second pound of bacon, complimented with an assortment of eggs, sausage, and flapjacks. Miller's farm, just out of town, supplied most of the items on the menu, including the salted butter most fancy restaurants would die for. Heavy on butterfat and flavor, it's a meal in itself according to Bill Miller. People in town will tell you they're health conscious, but through a big smile and not until after they've enjoyed the breakfast special at the Rocket.

It was a week past the festival, but the town was still buzzing with tourists and activities. All the shops along Collier Avenue opened precisely at nine, and Gordon Photography was no exception. After a week of shuffling through documents, briefs, and assorted state matters for Lawrence Banks, Angela looked forward to spending the day in the gallery meeting new people and discussing the work of the local photographers. The large schoolhouse clock at the far end of the gallery wall had just struck 8:45. Angela looked over. Through an opening on the same wall she could see the backdoor. Someone waving out on the back steps caught her attention. It was Marty. He tapped lightly with his finger on the glass. She looked around. Jack Gordon stood at the opposite side of the gallery over by the counter refilling and straightening the notecards and assorted town-inspired souvenirs. She walked into the backroom, unlocked the door, and opened it just enough to have a conversation.

"Where have you been?" she said in a hushed but concerned tone. "The sheriff's looking for you."

"I know, she thinks I know something about that murder out at the old asylum."

Angela waited, hoping there was going to be a disclaimer added at some point.

"No," Marty grunted in response to her look. "I wasn't anywhere near that place last week. I never seen that girl before in my life." Marty paused, remembering the photo the agent showed him.

"What is it?"

"Nothing. You have to believe me. I didn't have anything to do with that."

"I believe you, but the sheriff's another story."

"Why? Because she has a photo of me in a crowd?"

Angela was confused. "What photo of you? She came by yesterday afternoon asking if I had seen you. She didn't say anything about a photo of you, but she was pretty interested in one of your photographs of the asylum. It's the large portrait of the hall. The one with the pile of trash over in the corner by the steps."

Marty thought for a moment. "Why would she be interested in that?"

"I told her you said you took that six months ago, but she said it couldn't have been then. She said it had to be taken a week or so ago. Just before the murder."

"Shit. Why did you tell her that?"

Angela started to close the door. Her sympathy and concern were only going so far.

Marty reached out his hand, shoving it between the door and the sill. "I'm sorry, I'm sorry. I'm just upset with all this shit going on."

Angela eased the door open again, looking back over her shoulder and listening for Jack. She hadn't decided yet how she was feeling about the whole conversation, but at least she was willing to continue listening. "I thought you took that photo with the others. You know, you told me at the bar after the Christmas party about being up there."

Marty managed a slight smile. "You're right. I did take a lot of photos out at the old asylum six months ago. We haven't really talked all that much since that night at the bar. About two weeks ago I was coming back from Concord. I forgot to send in my car registration. It was late afternoon when I was passing by the asylum. The light was perfect. The old place really looked creepy. I stopped, hopped the gate, and started to shoot some photos. I don't know why, but I decided to go inside. The light was fading, so I ran in and took a couple shots on the second floor. Then the sun sets, and suddenly I'm in darkness. Scared the shit out of me. I ran out, hopped back over the gate, and went home. It was the following day when I looked at the photos. The outside shots were shit, but those two shots inside were great."

"That's why you included them in the show, isn't it?"

"Well, yeah. That, and you were so excited about me including the other asylum shots, I figured you'd really like that one."

Angela's stern countenance softened. "I do like it. I like it a lot, but I think the sheriff sees it as incriminating."

"Incriminating?"

"Shhhh." Angela put her finger to her lips, checking once again for Jack. "Calm down."

"Sorry. What do you mean incriminating? I know she's looking for me, but it's no big deal. It's just to answer a few questions about why I was in New York a week ago."

Angela stepped outside, quietly closing the door behind her. "I think it's more than that. You have to turn yourself in to the sheriff and explain all this. I think she thinks you had something to do with that girl's death. This isn't good, Marty. You have to go straighten this out before it gets worse."

Marty looked around nervously, even though they were sheltered from view by a tall, wooden fence. "I'm not suppose to say anything, but an FBI guy was waiting at my house last night."

"What FBI guy?"

"He said his name was MacGregor. A dumpy, little, fat guy. The complete opposite of what you see in the movies, but he seemed to know his stuff. Said he's working with the sheriff." Marty pulled a flip phone from his pocket. "He gave me this. Said I should use it instead of my iPhone. He said he's pretty sure he knows who killed that girl, but he needed my help."

"What kind of help?"

"There's this guy, Hugh Calder. He's some kind of journalist from Chicago. MacGregor followed him here to town. He was in New York. He was in the bar where that girl was the night she disappeared. MacGregor had a photo of her with two friends. You can see me in the background, and that guy Calder is there, too. What are the odds?"

"What were *you* doing there?"

"I had Nick's tickets. I met up with a friend of mine from college. We had been planning it for a while. That bar's a pretty cool place. We go there every time I go to see him. We stopped at the bar after the game that night, and then I crashed at his place."

"Okay, so what's the deal with Calder?" Before Marty could answer, Angela held up her hand and turned towards the door. "Hold on, that's Jack calling me."

Marty stepped over to the side, out of the line of sight from inside. Angela went in, returning after only a minute. "Jack's going for donuts. I have to go in and open, but I have a couple more minutes. So, what's the deal with this guy Calder?"

"I don't know, he was there, too, that night, but I didn't see him. I just know MacGregor followed him here. MacGregor spotted me by accident yesterday and tracked me down. He showed me the photo. Once I explained what I was doing there, he asked if I would help him. All I had to do was keep an eye on Calder last night while he chased down a lead. MacGregor called me around eight thirty and said Calder was at the bar at Horse Feathers. I went over, sat in the back, and just kept an eye on him like I was told."

"That's it?"

"Well, no, not really. At one point Calder noticed me watching him. I took off when he started walking over to where I was sitting. I waited outside in my car, but he didn't come out. A little after one, MacGregor called and said he would take over. I was tired, so I went home."

"So why does the sheriff think you know something about the girl's murder? Your friend can verify you were together all night right? Just give the sheriff his contact info and get this over with."

"MacGregor says he doesn't want to read the locals in yet. He says Sheriff Flynn knows Calder. They got history, so he doesn't want to take a chance. Flynn saw me in the photo. I'm sort of keeping her busy looking for me so Calder doesn't suspect this FBI guy is closing in on him. I'm not supposed to say anything to anybody. You have to swear not to say anything."

"I won't, I promise."

"You know, I'm not too happy about any of this. The more Sheriff Flynn asks around about me, the more I'm gonna look like a real shit to everyone in town." Marty paused. "I just don't want you to think . . . well . . . you know."

"Are you sure about this FBI guy?"

"Oh yeah. He knew all about me. Everything I've done in the last month or so. I guess those conspiracy guys are right about that big brother stuff."

"It sounds dangerous. Are you sure you want to do this?"

"It's not right what happened to that girl. If doing this helps catch her killer, then I guess I can look like a shit for a little while. Hey, it won't be the first time. Besides, she at least deserves that."

Angela smiled, taking a step to close the distance between them. She took Marty's arm, pulled him in closer, and kissed him. "I don't care what anyone thinks, I think you're wonderful."

Marty's face flushed with color. "What was that for?"

"Don't be such a jerk. I'll be dead in my grave before *you* make the first move."

"I . . . I didn't think—"

"That's your problem, you don't think." Angela turned and opened the door, pausing before she went back inside. "Go do what you have to do. Stay safe. We'll talk about this later when you're off the most-wanted list."

Marty smiled, tucking the phone back in his pocket. "I'll call you when I can and let you know what's up."

Angela nodded her head.

Marty took her arm as she started through the door. "Maybe we can go out for pizza when all this is done?"

Angela rolled her eyes. "Sure, now you ask me out. Just don't get yourself killed, jerk."

Marty nodded. "Remember, if you see MacGregor or the sheriff, you haven't seen me."

"I don't like this," the voice at the other end of the phone stated bluntly. There was a pause. "Did you hear me? They're starting to ask questions again about—"

"Calm down. You start acting like you're guilty, and that's exactly what they're going to think."

"Easy for you to say, they can't trace any of this back to you. I'm not taking the fall for all this. Do you hear me? You better do something or—"

"Or what? They can't trace any of this back to you either. Did he find the signature card?"

"Yeah, I think he found it."

"Did you transfer the money into her account?"

"Yeah, and I back dated the transaction in the computer."

"That should do it then. You just give him anything he asks for . . . and stop calling me every time you get nervous and jerky."

"And what about the sheriff?"

"Don't worry about her. I'll take care of that. She owes me."

"Okay. Just get your girl to stop that deputy from sniffing around, and I'll be fine."

The phone went dead.

CHAPTER SEVENTEEN

For the first few hours the traffic had been slow in the gallery. Not at all odd for the morning, most people save art and the more refined pursuits for the afternoons after more important matters are tended to. Knowing wine is served at the gallery after four o'clock also lends itself to the reasoning. Jack had gone home for lunch, promising to bring Angela back one of Martha's meatloaf sandwiches and a slice of whatever pie she had baked that morning.

The bell over the door clanged. Angela looked up and smiled at the friendly looking man entering. She nodded, continuing to sweep the hardwood floors by the counter, giving him a few minutes to browse.

He was about mid-fifties, with a strong chin and course, salt-and-pepper hair. A bit on the portly side, but carried himself with the look of a man who could handle the rough stuff if he had to. He slowly made his way down the left side of the gallery where the photographs were arranged in groups, a cluster of four for each photographer. He meandered over to the right side where the featured photographer exhibit was hung; his hands folded behind his back, and giving Angela a smile as he passed. He stood back taking in all the photographs at once, then stepped forward to study one particular photo. It was the same photograph of the asylum the sheriff found so interesting. Angela put the broom down and approached him.

"Is that place around here?" he said, turning his attention toward another of Marty's photographs—pointing at the shot of the front gates of the asylum. "Exceptional framing and great contrast. A very haunting image."

"Yes," replied Angela. "It's the abandoned Willis Asylum just outside of town."

"Willis? Like the hospital?"

"Correct. The same man put the money up for both. The hospital has grown unbelievably since the days when it was just a three-story Victorian house Dr. Willis used for his home and office. There's an old photo in the lobby showing him standing next to his horse-drawn carriage about to make his rounds. His house was in the background with a sign on the porch that said HOSPITAL. The house was torn down years ago, and the hospital was built on the same site. It was recently purchased by one of those big medical groups, but still retains the Willis name."

"I was just there as a matter of fact. It's rather an impressive institution." He moved along to the next photo. A shot of a lower-floor window, the glass long gone, the wrought-iron bars dangling by the rusted remains of a single-carriage bolt in the upper corner. "And the asylum?"

"Well, that's a completely different story, and not one that ends well. At this point, it's hard to separate fact from fiction, but not long after Dr. Willis passed away, there were a series of suspicious deaths at the asylum. There was an investigation. The person they felt responsible was found in a motel in Vermont. He hung himself. It was ruled a suicide, but some of the better storytellers around these parts say the ghosts of his victims saved the town the trouble of hanging him. Either way, the state had already stepped in and closed the facility a few months earlier. They never did get to the truth."

"Never?" he said, moving farther down the wall.

Angela shrugged her shoulders. "I don't think anybody knows for sure what happened in there. All we know is it never reopened."

As she spoke, the bell above the front door announced a young couple. They waved, indicating their intension to have a look around the gallery. Angela smiled, turning her attention back to the friendly gentleman and their conversation.

"Well, these photos certainly tell an eerie tale." He took another few steps, stopping in front of the photo of the second-floor room. "Is this the room where the body of that young woman was found?"

The question took Angela by surprise, something that didn't go unnoticed, but was certainly intended.

"I'm sorry," he said, holding out his hand. "I should have told you who I am. My name is Harry MacGregor. I'm with the FBI, and I'm here helping Sheriff Flynn with this case. I hope I haven't upset you?"

"It's all right. Your question just surprised me, that's all." Angela shook his hand. She recognized the name from her conversation with Marty, but didn't acknowledge the fact. "Very nice to meet you, Agent MacGregor. Yes, that's the room."

"Mac. Please call me Mac." He took a couple steps backward, scanning all the photos as a group again. "Pretty scary looking place. I would imagine it's a real hoot around Halloween."

"It is that. Nobody really goes out there the rest of the year. The town took it over. They've been trying to sell it, but no takers yet. I think the whole town will be relieved when it's finally torn down and some positive use made of the property. It's a shame. There's a wonderful view of the town from up there, especially in the fall. Nobody's willing to go up and enjoy it anymore."

"I'm sure that will change soon enough." MacGregor smiled. "These were taken by a local photographer, right? Sam Martin, I believe?"

"Yes. You met—" Angela caught herself, but not before it raised one of Mac's eyebrows. "I mean, you can meet him, he's our featured photographer. Will you be in town long?"

"Well, I'm not sure. It all depends on what we find out about this young woman's death. So you know Sam?"

"Marty? I call him Marty. Yes, we've been friends for years."

"Have you spoken with him lately?" Mac's interest in her answer was apparent by the look on his face.

"Um . . . no. We haven't spoken since the opening the other night."

Mac smiled, apparently pleased with the answer. "I know the sheriff's looking for him, and he probably does, too. If you should see him, or he should call, tell him it's more important that he speaks to me first . . . only me. If you have any questions, you can find me at the Fairfield here in town, room 316."

That's a little unnerving, Angela thought to herself. She forced a smile, responding with a wave as MacGregor walked away. "I sure will."

CHAPTER EIGHTEEN

"What do you think, Sheriff?" asked Hank, prying some of the planks off one of the windows to allow a little light in.

The boathouse had a cedar, post-and-beam frame. It looked like hell on the outside, the weathered planks missing here and there and leaning slightly towards the water. The door on the north side stood rusted open on its hinges. The windows on each side were mostly in tact; probably because of how isolated it was tucked into the woods by the water. Mischievous kids are drawn to windows in abandoned buildings like moths to a flame, but this one was only accessible by water. Even the Auburn High star pitcher would have a problem hitting those windows with a rock standing in a shaky boat.

An easy restoration project for anyone with a little time on their hands. At least that's the argument Mark Warren presented to his neighbors any time he saw them out by the lake. They would smile at the notion, even giving the slight illusion they might consider it. The boathouse sat on the property line of Frank and Mary Henderson, but looking more like it rested on Warren's property than on their own. The Henderson's were older, and not at all interested in any restoration projects, no matter how easy they might be. Leave it for the next owners, they would quip to each other when Mark Warren walked away. Warren wasn't fooled. At least he had time and gravity on his side.

The inside of the boathouse had a free-floating, U-shaped dock, which bobbed gently up and down. It could accommodate a sixteen-foot motorboat, or two smaller rowboats. Metal rings at each corner of the dock wrapped around steel poles, allowing it to rise and fall freely with the water level of the lake. The far end leading out to the lake had a set of double doors that rode on tracks, sliding open to the left and right like barn doors. It would take some doing before any use could be made of them again; one door was off the track, the other nailed in place. Sitting in the slip was a partially submerged runabout. The mahogany deck was grey with age, a yellowed and chipped stripe separating it from the faded, red lower section. All the chrome was pitted, the sweeping windshield cracked and covered with a thick layer of age. Quite an eye catcher in its day, now just a receptacle for any trash floating in beneath the rotted planks of the structure.

Resting on the dock, in the back corner opposite the door, was a six-by-four-foot float—wooden planks on a frame—resting on four rusted and dented oil drums. It spent many summers moored out in the lake for the kids to swim out to. The Henderson's had no children of their own, but three young nieces on Martha's side made ample use of the lake. When the chill of autumn drew the season to a close, the float was reeled in and stored until the warm, summer days returned. As time went by, the children turned their attentions to other activities, reducing their once summer-long stays to just a couple weekend visits. Eventually, they reeled the float into the boathouse for the last time, hoisted it onto the dock, and secured it with the algae-stained rope that once moored it in place on the lake.

Just above the float, on the back wall, was a small, square window. It had a sill deeper than the other windows, because it didn't open. On the sill was a black candle resting in a chipped dish, the flickering light reflecting off the glass and illuminating the lifeless body of Mark Warren resting just below it on the float.

Mark Warren's face showed the same signs of asphyxiation as Jane Newcomb's—pale, blue cheeks and lips, petechial hemorrhages in the eyes. Hardened blood caked a clump of hair behind his left ear, but there were no other obvious signs of a struggle or defensive wounds on the body. He was dressed in a crisp, white shirt with his initials on the cuff, tan slacks, and a pair of British tan, Cole Haan oxfords without socks. Flynn paid particular attention to the shoes, as they had no visible sign of being worn on anything but carpet. They were new and fresh from the box. With this and the lack of blood on the boards beneath his head, it became apparent Mark Warren did not make his way out to the boathouse under his own power.

"Sheriff?" Hank repeated.

Hank walked over to where the sheriff stood gazing at the body. There was enough light now to expose the details of the scene.

"This can't be happening again," Sheriff Flynn mumbled quietly to herself. "Not here."

"You think this is the same guy that killed Jane Newcomb?"

"Yes, I think so."

Hank paused. "The same guy that committed those murders in New York and Chicago?"

Hank's last observation caught Flynn by surprise. It was cautiously transparent. She drew out a slight smile. Not one of amusement, but one of displaced pride. Hank was sharp, but she didn't realize how sharp until then. She heard from a few people in town he was a magician with a computer. Any problems with a laptop, everybody ran right to Hank. It was apparent his expertise ran deeper than just software issues. She had Hank dig up information on the New York murders, but never mentioned anything about Chicago, and certainly never shared her own involvement. He must have put the pieces together on his own at some point. The smile faded as she wondered how much of the story he actually knew.

"I don't wanna tie these two murders together with those other cities, at least not yet. The last thing this town needs is a panic." She raised her hand, stopping whatever objection Hank's deep breath was about to raise. "You need to keep what you know about those other cases between us. Are we clear on that?"

Hank nodded, followed by a long exhale.

"Call the ME and tell him what we've got. I'll call MacGregor and get him and his men out here."

Sheriff Flynn made her call and explained the situation to Mac, staring at the black candle on the sill as she spoke. After finishing, she turned her attention to a closer examination of the body. There were indications of redness and hair torn off the wrists, probably from duck tape, she figured. From what she could tell without moving the head, there was a two-inch gash on the side of the skull behind the left ear. It was hard to tell in the shadows, but a trail of blood looked like it streamed down his neck and under his collar. The blow probably didn't kill him, just rendered him unconscious long enough for the carbon dioxide to do its job. A dark patch of blistering was visible through his shirt on his chest.

Flynn knelt down next to the float, rubbing her finger across the boards. She sniffed the dust on her finger, and then touched it to her tongue. "Ash," she whispered.

"ME's on the way," said Hank.

"Thanks." Flynn stood up, rubbing her finger on her pants.

"What is it?" asked Hank.

"What's what?"

"On your finger," Hank replied, holding up his own. "I saw you do that out at the asylum, too. Thought it was kinda strange, but I figured you had your reasons."

"Ash. It's ash."

"Ash? Why would there be ash on the floor?"

"They put it there. Walking around disturbs the dust. They tossed handfuls of ash over the floorboards to cover their tracks. It makes it harder to tell how many people were involved."

"They?"

Sheriff Flynn smiled, patting Hank on his arm. "I know you don't like me, and I'm pretty sure you're the source of the distorted information about my past making its way around the town council. I can live with that, but don't lie to me. I don't know how much of my past you know about, but it's still a little hard for me to talk about. Anyone else know?"

Hank dropped his head, genuinely embarrassed. "Maybe a few in town are a bit suspicious, but they think they know everything. No one pays them any mind. No one's business but yours, I figure. Everyone's entitled to their secrets. Look, Sheriff, I didn't mean to—"

Sheriff Flynn shook her head and raised her hand. "Like I said, I can live with that. You're a good cop, Hank. That's all that matters. Whether it makes a difference or not, I had no idea you wanted the job. And I have no idea why your buddy the mayor gave it to me instead of you. All I know is I should have said something to you about my past before this. You deserve to know what kind of person you're working with. How can I expect you to be up front with me if I start out lying to you?"

"I didn't think you were lying. Like I said, secrets. I figured you'd tell me one day." Hank gave a childish grin. "I was going to act surprised when you did."

Flynn smiled. She turned and looked out the side door toward the house. "Let's take a look inside. Warren didn't die here, so there has to be another crime scene somewhere."

"Shouldn't we wait for MacGregor?"

"I have a feeling he'll be taking this case over when he gets here. If there's something to learn in there, this could be our only chance. The feds play real nice at first with the local LEOs, then the next thing you know we're fifty feet away from the crime scene behind the yellow tape in charge of crowd control." Flynn jerked her head toward the door. "We better hurry."

Hank laughed. "Yep, I think I'm beginning to see why he gave the job to you."

CHAPTER NINETEEN

The back door of Warren's house leading into the mudroom was
unlocked. Everything glistened with a shade of white for as far as
the eye could see. The wainscoting, the plate rail circling the room
at eye level, the plastered walls above, and the ceiling were all
white. The same motif followed into the kitchen, down the hall,
and beyond. In sharp contrast were the random-shaped and
colored slates of the floor, which seemed to run through the house
like an exposed riverbed. The current led you into a great room
with a cathedral-inspired kitchen at one end and a living area at
the other; a room that could easily have been torn out of
Architectural Digest that morning. Running the length of the room
were fluted, wooden columns rising up from the slate at six-foot
intervals, joined together high above with carved, transverse ribs.
A thick ridge beam tied it all together, set into a stone fireplace at
the far end and disappearing into the white plaster wall at the
other. Two white, leather sofas flanked the fireplace, separated by
a restored baggage trolley with an assortment of trendy magazines
stacked neatly in the center. Tasteful reproductions of modern art
hung between the columns braking up the monotony of the white
walls, highlighted with an intricate track-lighting system
suspended from delicate stainless-steel cables.

State of the art, stainless-steel appliances were tucked neatly
beneath the long expanses of polished Travertine marble
countertops, flanked by hickory lower cabinets inlaid with black,
walnut squares marking the corners of the doors. Pickled upper
cabinets with glass doors, softly illuminated from within, stood
proud above the white, tiled backsplash. Cast copper twigs,
chemically aged to a pleasing patina, were utilized for the lower
drawer and cabinet pulls. White oak trim glistening with amber
shellac framed large casement windows, directing the bright
sunlight bouncing off the lake into every corner of the space. An
archway at the end of the counter invited you down two steps
leading to a long hallway. The north side was lined with thin six-
panel doors, and floor to ceiling windows looking out over a stone
patio ran the length of the south side.

The aesthetics of the space were lost on Hank; it was just a crime scene to him. He walked through the kitchen, following the riverbed down the hallway, poking his head in each of the rooms. He joined Sheriff Flynn in the kitchen a few minutes later, shaking his head. "No sign of forced entry anywhere."

Sheriff Flynn handed Hank a pair of latex gloves she brought along. A quick look around the room gave no indication of a struggle. Nothing looked out of place except the long center island. The tall stools, which you would expect to find neatly concealed beneath the counter, were lined up along the opposite length of cabinets like naughty children along a schoolyard fence. The placement of the coffeemaker and blender caught Flynn's attention.

"It was here," Flynn said. "Those two appliances should be down at this end. The outlets are here."

Hank snapped his second latex glove in place. "Maybe he just left them on the counter and got interrupted before he could do anything with them?"

"Warren has his little group of realtors in for a pep talk the third Friday of every month. That was last night. No, he plans everything days in advance. There isn't a shop owner in town that doesn't look forward to the third week of the month. Warren makes his rounds from the florist shop right down the block to Fall's Bakery, bouncing from shop to shop like a pinball, spending a few hundred along the way. Yesterday he would have spent the day staging this place like it was going to be on the cover of House Beautiful. That blender and coffeemaker would have been plugged in and ready, I'll put my badge on that. Someone needed this end of the counter for something."

Flynn bent down, slowly moving her head from side to side, catching the light reflecting on the edge of the marble countertop. She ran her hand along the underside of the marble, then sat down underneath to get a better look. She shined a small flashlight she pulled from her pocket up at the underside. "There are scratches along this edge. Something was clamped down around this far end. Plastic of some kind, I'd bet."

Hank held out his hand to help Flynn up from the floor. "Like a drop cloth or a tarp?"

"Probably. They needed some way to concentrate the carbon dioxide close to the victim. Whatever it was, I'm sure it was used on the girl also." She took Hank's hand, but pulled him down instead. "Do you smell that?"

Hank put his nose close to the slate. "Yeah. Bleach?"

"Bleach." Flynn ran her hand over the slate. "I'll bet this discoloration in the grout is from Warren's blood. They probably scrubbed and cleaned this area, but the grout may still hold some particles of blood."

They both stood up. Through the window over the sink they could see a tan cloud of FBI dust wafting up behind the tree line, making its way up the long driveway.

"Let's take one more look around before they get here," said Flynn, walking towards the fireplace.

"I saw a datebook on the table in the hall," replied Hank. "I'll check that out." He stopped by the opening leading to the hallway. "You said 'they.' You think there's more than one person committing these murders? Those guys that . . . well—"

"We can talk about it later. Right now, it's more important we see what else this place has to tell us before our friends get here." Flynn shooed Hank away with her hand. She looked back out the window at the beige storm closing in on them. "Looks like Mac's bringing all his fishing buddies this time."

CHAPTER TWENTY

With all the grace of a herd of stampeding antelopes in aviator sunglasses, MacGregor and his boys rolled up the gravel driveway in their stereotypical black sedans. A half dozen agents in blue jackets with bright-yellow letters on the backs emerged, huddling in front of MacGregor's car, awaiting instructions. Flynn watched out the kitchen window as MacGregor pointed here and there, gesturing with his hands like a choirmaster giving the final instructions before the curtain goes up. His attention was particularly focused on the boathouse as he directed the herd. He finished with a clap of his hands, and they dispersed. Mac looked up toward the house. He saw Flynn in the window but didn't acknowledge her. Instead, he followed his men down to the boathouse.

Flynn continued to watch out the window at the flurry of activity going on in and around the weathered building. Some of the agents dispersed into the woods around the boathouse, while others walked down along the water's edge. MacGregor disappeared inside. It wasn't until their ME arrived and rolled a stretcher down to the boathouse that MacGregor emerged.

He made his way across the lawn toward the house. Two agents followed behind but remained outside on the flagstone patio when Mac entered.

Sheriff Flynn was resting against the country sink with her arms folded. "So, how's the fishing, Mac?"

Agent MacGregor's determined stare confirmed he left his congenial self in the car, his countenance further proved more the hardened FBI agent than a collaborating law enforcement officer. "This is officially an FBI matter now, Sheriff." He looked over as Hank walked up the steps from the hallway. "What do you have there?"

Hank walked over, holding a spiral-bound book at arm's length. "It's his day-timer. I found it on the table in the hall."

"I'll take that," Mac snapped, holding out his hand.

Hank looked at the sheriff, who responded with a nod of her head, and then handed the book to Mac.

"Thank you. Now, if you don't mind, Deputy, I'd like to have a private word with the sheriff."

"I'll wait outside," replied Hank, peeling the latex gloves from his hands.

Agent MacGregor waited until he heard the backdoor close. He relaxed only slightly; toning down the authoritative way he charged in. "So what do we have here, Promise?"

"More murders in one week than Auburn Notch has seen in the last hundred years."

Mac took Sheriff Flynn by the arm and led her over to the far end of the room by the fireplace. Flynn rolled her eyes, seeing the effort as his overly dramatic way to underscore the seriousness and sensitive nature of the intended direction of the conversation. "This has become everything we were afraid it had the potential of becoming. Whether *you* choose to believe it or not, I believe you're in grave danger. I don't know why these guys decided to set up shop in your little postcard town, but my feeling is they're here for a reason far beyond these two murders. You keep believing they don't know who you are, and that gives them the upper hand."

"You're starting to sound like that shit Calder. I guess you think I brought these murderers to town, don't you? There has to be another reason. There has to."

MacGregor eased off the authoritative tone. "So you're saying this murder and that candle down there in the boathouse is just some big coincidence? You're too bright for that." Mac paused, looking back toward the windows in the kitchen area overlooking the activity in the backyard. "I'm open for suggestions, Promise, but with this murder, it's looking like your jilted lover theory for Newcomb's death isn't going to cut it anymore. I'm afraid there's a more sinister link. I don't know how, and I don't know why yet, but we need to find out, and we need to find out pretty quickly before they get to victim number three."

"Are we at least in agreement there are two of them involved?"

MacGregor nodded his head. "Let's say for the time being I'll go along with your theory. Look, for what it's worth, I don't believe you started out being the target. Let's assume we're dealing with the same guys, and they haven't figured out who you are. If they follow their old pattern, there are two more people in greater danger than you at this point. That's where we need to concentrate our efforts. If by chance they have figured out you're still alive, well—"

"Except we don't know who those potential victims are."

MacGregor nodded once again. "I have a plan in motion. When I can, I will fill you in on the details, but at this point I'm not able to disclose anything."

"Not able to disclose, or not willing to?"

Mac ignored the question. "We don't know what these guys know about what we know. Let's say Calder's right and all those murders in all those cities are tied to these two guys. They proved themselves experts in misdirection, so there's no reason to believe they're going to divert from whatever plan they have for your little town just because they stumbled across you. If you're lucky, you'll just be an afterthought. It's business first, then they'll take care of you."

Flynn shook her head, giving a slight sarcastic snicker. "Well, that makes me feel better."

"Don't be so quick to dismiss the advantage here. As long as they don't perceive you as a threat, they have no reason to deviate from their plan."

"And you believe that plan includes the murder of two more people here in town?"

MacGregor's authoritative tone returned. "Let's hope it doesn't come to that. All I'm saying is, if we tip our hand too soon, we could accelerate their timetable here, driving them on to the next city and the next four victims. We have a chance to put a stop to this once and for all, but it all depends on what we do next. For now, I'm going to ask you to stand down."

"Stand down?" said Flynn, making no attempt to hold her voice down to a civil tone. "By the time this hits the morning papers, I'll have a full-blown panic on my hands."

"Not necessarily, Sheriff," replied Mac in a more reassuring tone. "I would suggest you get a firm grip on the flow of information and take advantage of the power of the press. You're in a position to stabilize this situation by carefully choosing what information you release."

"What do you mean? If you're suggesting I lie to these people, that's not going to happen." Flynn's voice began to rise again to an agitated growl. "I won't do it. Eventually, this will all be over. You'll be gone, and I'll be left with a hole in my reputation big enough to drive that ME's truck through."

"I wouldn't think of allowing that to happen to you."

"Then what do you mean?"

"Technically, this crime scene and the other investigation related to this are now under my jurisdiction. You'll find the paperwork on your desk—I dropped it off on my way out here."

Mac leaned in close and whispered the rest in Flynn's ear. "Not to put too fine a point on this, but you'll tell the press what I say you can tell them."

There was no mistaking the anger being held back behind Flynn's clenched teeth and guttural groan. Her cheeks were flush, her breathing deep and determined through her nose.

"I expect your full cooperation, Sheriff," Mac finished with a fatherly smile, after giving Flynn a moment to process the information and calm down. "Whether you like it or not, and until I can determine otherwise, I have to consider both of these murders a continuation of the murders committed by the same men in Seattle, Chicago, and New York. As your job is to protect the citizens of this quaint, little town, my job is to protect the citizens in *all* the quaint little towns from here to Oregon. Do we understand each other?"

"I'm perfectly fine with that," Flynn lied, loosening her jaw enough to get the words out without choking on them. "What happens now?"

Mac responded in a tone more suited to suggesting rather than demanding. "I'm not sure what type of press coverage to expect here in Auburn Notch, but if you're approached, the official story is you believe the murder of Jane Newcomb is a crime of passion, perpetrated as a result of unwanted advances by someone she met at a bar in Brooklyn and dumped here by the murderer. Hinting this guy Martin might be involved will help sell it, too. The death of Mark Warren is the unfortunate result of stumbling into a home invasion at his property on the lake. That should be enough to corroborate your tentative understanding of the facts to date and tie this up in a tidy, little bow for the time being." Mac waited for a response from Flynn, but she bit her inside lip and just nodded her head. He continued, "I'm sorry, Promise, but until we figure out another approach, it has to be this way. We can stop them, you just have to work with me a little."

"And what about Martin and the next two victims? Withholding facts from the press and deceiving the public isn't something I'm comfortable with," replied Flynn, not at all ready to climb into bed with MacGregor's reasoning.

"No, withholding facts from the *police* is a crime. Withholding facts from the press is akin to finding out your mother-in-law has postponed her visit; you know you'll have to deal with her eventually, but for now your life is headache free. As far as deceiving the public, their safety trumps their curiosity."

Flynn's breathing returned to normal, summing up her final opinion with a decisive grunt. Despite her feelings about Mac bullying his way into the case, they were still on the same side. "Okay, we'll try it your way for now."

"That's the spirit. It's not personal, Promise, at least not for me."

"Can I make a suggestion?"

"Absolutely."

"You and your boys come thundering onto a crime scene in your agent mobiles like you're invading Normandy. You may want to tone that down a bit if your intention is not to tip your hand."

MacGregor looked out the window again at the cluster of agents milling around the property. His lips curled to a slight chagrin. "You got a point there. I'll keep a few agents here in town and get rid of the agent mobiles. We're close, Promise, I can feel it. My gut tells me this is the best chance we've had to stop these guys. The last thing I want is to see another one of your citizens fall prey to these psychos. I'll figure this out, and you'll be there with me to bring them in."

"So you already have suspects in mind?"

Mac leaned in close. "As a matter of fact I do. Well, I'll not keep you any longer. I'm sure you have important things to do in town. I'll get you a copy of my report when we're done here."

"Don't you want to know what I found here?"

"Let me guess. Mark Warren was asphyxiated, probably with homemade dry ice. He was laid out on that island over there, unconscious with the dry ice in some kind of container on his chest. A plastic tent was clamped to the counter over his body. He was dead within ten minutes, and carried out to the boathouse. Did I miss anything?"

"No, that about sums it up," Flynn grumbled. "So, what do you want me to do now? I can't sit on my hands with a killer on the loose."

Mac gave a nod for Flynn to follow him over to the window in the kitchen. "I think it's important you continue on the course you've set."

"You mean about Sam Martin?"

"Correct." Mac could see the disappointment in her face. "It may not seem it now, but it's important, Promise. If it weren't, I wouldn't ask. As long as he appears a suspect, he's still of use to them. Keep poking around. Try to locate Sam, but don't try too hard."

"Okay."

"And don't worry, I've had a man keeping an eye on you since I hit town. I have every intension of you being there at the end when we reel these nuts in. Let's leave it at that for now." Mac knocked on the window, motioning for his agents to join him inside. "If you need me, I'm down at that little motel on 16, right by the fork. Good day, Sheriff."

Sheriff Flynn nodded and left the house without another word. She passed the two agents in the mudroom on her way out and found Hank sitting on the hood of their squad car.

"I guess we're in charge of crowd control, right?" Hank asked, nodding toward the house.

"Don't be a smartass." Flynn smiled and tossed the keys to Hank. "I'll tell you back at the station. Have you said anything to anybody about these two murders?"

"No. Why?"

"For the time being, refer all questions to me. And whatever you do, don't go running to the town council when I lie my ass off about what's going on here."

Hank smiled. It wasn't difficult to detect where the source of her motivation was coming from. He let the last remark go, knowing she would fill him in with the details when she could. They got in the car without another word. Hank drove, snaking his way through the collection of black sedans.

Deputy Henry (Hank) Harris spent his youth in Auburn Notch in and out of trouble, but straightened out when he discovered girls. He's tall and lanky, and considers himself quite the ladies man, though he hasn't quite convinced them yet. He's been with the Sheriff's Department for almost eight years. Sheriff Flynn was the third sheriff he's worked for. Despite his irritation at her appointment, he considered her the best of the lot, though he wasn't about to admit that in public. Together with Deputies Margie Jenkins, Frank Stamper, and two part-time officers, they represent the law in Auburn Notch.

"When we get back," said Flynn, breaking the silence as they turned onto Oak Lane, "would you find out who Mark Warren's next of kin is please? I need to tell them what's happened."

"Sure—" Hank began, but stopped and looked over at Promise. "Exactly what did happen?"

"Mark Warren was killed by an intruder when he came home unexpectedly."

"Really?"

"No, but that's what we're going to say."

"No problem, Sheriff." Hank pulled his cell phone from his shirt pocket, handing it to Flynn. "Here, take this."

"What's this?" Flynn asked, looking at the picture on Hank's screen. There was a name scribbled across the page.

"It's a picture of a page in Warren's day-timer. I took it in the hallway before Mac and his boys showed up."

Flynn looked at the name and smiled. "This is interesting. Agent MacGregor has enough on his plate at the moment. He'll send Warren's day-timer back to the lab to be scrutinized. That could take a while. Why don't we help him out and see what we can find out about this guy."

CHAPTER TWENTY-ONE

"I've got the preliminary report from MacGregor," Flynn said, waving a few pieces of paper as Hank entered the office. "How about I buy us both an early dinner and we'll have a long talk about the past, the present, and the future?"

"Sounds good, I'm starving. Horse Feathers?"

"I'm thinking the Black Parka Pub," replied Flynn. She knew it was Hank's favorite hangout. "It shouldn't be crowded yet, so we won't have to worry about being overheard."

"But you don't like that place. Noisy little shits, I think you refer to the patrons."

"Yeah, but you like it. I'll drive."

On the way out of town, Sheriff Flynn gave Hank the details in MacGregor's report of Warren's death. Same blistering on the body as Jane Newcomb; blunt force trauma to the back of the head rendered him unconscious; asphyxiated from carbon dioxide. Nothing they hadn't already noticed. TOD was between six and eight the night before. No signs of a break-in or a struggle. MacGregor believes Warren probably knew his attacker, not intimately, but enough to invite him into the house. One wine glass with Warren's prints was in the sink. A second glass, a rocks tumbler with a slight trace of scotch in the bottom, was found in pieces in the trashcan. Wiped clean of prints. MacGregor is hoping for a DNA match from the fluid, but it isn't hopeful.

"So what's the latest with the swim club investigation," Flynn asked.

"It's not making any sense."

"What do you mean?"

"I found a money trail that leads back to Alice Johnson. Alice Johnson! She's the one that asked you to take a second look into the embezzlement of the money. That case closed the same day Dunn's coffin did. If she was in on it with him, why would she ask you to look into it again?"

Sheriff Flynn smiled as she pulled into a parking spot near the side door of the Black Parka. "She was on the pool board when the missing money was discovered. She didn't make a big stink then, because she was being questioned along with Dunn and the rest of the board. If it wasn't for Dunn admitting to a gambling problem and taking the money, it could have dragged all their names through the mud for months. Then Dunn has a stroke. Case closed."

"So what should I do now?"

"Alice wouldn't be asking for this if she didn't have a few suspicions of her own. They tell me you're pretty sharp with a computer. If that money trail seems suspicious, it probably is. Keep digging. There's $40,000 unaccounted for. The speculation was that Dunn blew it at the casino, but I don't buy it. That was just a real convenient way to make an ugly blemish on the town go away. I think it might be time to ask a favor from our local FBI agent and his forensic accounting team. Someone knows what happened to that money."

The Pub, as the locals know it, was enjoying a lazy Saturday afternoon between lunch and dinner. It was nestled in a grove of scrub pines on the main road about two miles before the next town west of Auburn Notch. A little young and a little loud for Flynn's taste, but the food made it well worth the effort. A fair clutch of locals were at the bar swapping tales taller than the previous week's, getting an early start on the evening before the afternoon draft special stopped at five. The first chattering of tourists were rounding off their day of antiquing and exploring with an early dinner, filling in the open tables here and there that radiated out from the music stage in the restaurant portion. A young staff kept the tables prepped with red and white-checkered tablecloths, silverware wrapped in heavy cotton napkins, a small, tin bucket of fresh peanuts flanked by condiments, and the tent-card beer specials for the night. Chalkboards on the walls touted the dinner specials alongside the lineup of the music that would start precisely at nine o'clock, competing with the televised sporting events on the flat screens lining the upper walls in the bar area. The dining room appeared swept clean earlier, ready for a fresh layer of peanut shells.

Hank was a regular. He's had a tall mug with his name on it hanging above the bar since he turned twenty-one and ventured out for his first legal beer. Being one of the first, it was ceramic, had the original logo, and the faded remains of HENRY below it. It hung above the register, a place of honor among the hundreds of newer glass mugs that clinked and tinkled all weekend long. It was in easy reach of Jake the bartender, who reached up and gave Hank a wave as he and Flynn entered. Hank gave his head a quick shake, tapping his badge with his finger to indicate they were on duty.

"It's not too bad yet," said Flynn, looking over the crowd and following behind the hostess.

"It won't get noisy until after dinner and the band starts," replied Hank, acknowledging some of the locals at the bar with a nod as they maneuvered their way between the stools pushed out in the aisle.

A wood-planked wall covered in vanity license plates from every corner of the country, assorted skiing artifacts, and neon beer signs separated the bar from the dinner area. It was a theme carried out throughout the pub. The hostess stopped at a table near the small stage, but Flynn smiled, pointing towards a table nestled more into the back corner away from any distractions and prying eyes. The simulated, brown, leather booth was more suited for a party of six, but it was early, so the hostess obliged, giving Hank a wink.

Flynn looked over the menu; Hank could probably recite it from memory. An attractive, young girl named Rebecca, as the nametag attached to a black, cotton apron stated, walked over. She patted Hank on the shoulder. "I see you have company today, Deputy. I'll give you a few minutes to look over the menu. Can I get you something to drink, Sheriff?"

"Iced tea with lemon, please," replied Flynn with a smile.

"I'll have the same, Becca."

"Well, Hank," said Flynn as the waitress walked away, "I see you're quite the celebrity here."

"I don't know about that," Hank stated sheepishly through a large grin. "But I love this place. The food's great. I can try something different every time. I know just about everybody." He paused and looked back toward the bar area, giving a few final nods of recognition. The noise level returned to its previous state as the surly crowd at the bar returned to their conversations. Hank looked over at the sheriff. He was ready to hear what she had to say. "So, you said something about past, present, and future?"

"Yeah. It's probably something I should've done before this. Like I said, I just wasn't ready to talk about it. I spent so much time trying to forget what happened I was starting to convince myself it never did. Then that poor, young girl shows up dead, and now Mark Warren. There's no way I can ignore what happened now."

"I figured you had your reasons. I didn't take it personally."

Flynn smiled. "You're a good man, Hank."

Hank grabbed a fistful of peanuts, placing them on the table between them both. "Are you sure you want to tell me all this?"

"I might be the sheriff, but we're partners. You deserve to know whose back you have, and who has your back."

Hank didn't reply. He just nodded picking at a peanut shell.

Flynn looked down the aisle. "And I'll tell you all about it right after we order."

Rebecca had returned with the iced teas in large mason jars, a small bowl of fresh lemon slices, and a cutting board with black bread and a cup of whipped butter all balanced on an oversized tray. She tossed a handful of sugar packets she dug out of her left apron pocket in front of the bucket of peanuts. "Ready to order?"

Sheriff Flynn had decided on the clam chowder, with the stuffed haddock for an entrée. Hank, more a creature of habit despite his allusion to trying something different every visit, ordered the sirloin burger. He liked it topped with bacon, cheddar cheese, and cole slaw, the latter not being a menu choice but kept on hand just for him. Rebecca had written Hank's order down while she waited at the bar for the iced teas. The idea of soup did catch his attention, so he added a cup of chowder to the order just to change things up a bit. Rebecca was impressed. She took the menus and disappeared around the crowded tables and into the kitchen.

Flynn pushed the cutting board with the fresh loaf of bread closer to Hank. "First things first. Where are we with Sam Martin?"

"Nothing. It's like he packed up and left town." Hank tore off a hunk of bread and buttered it as he continued. "No sign of him out at the lake. Angela over at Gordon's says she still hasn't heard from him, but—"

"You think she's covering for him?"

Hank hesitated with his answer. "No. I think she knows more than she's saying, but I don't think she knows where he is. You still think he might have something to do with this?"

Flynn didn't answer at first. "If he does, it's not because he's a willing participant. I'm a little more concerned about *why* he's missing."

Hank's brow lowered, his head cocked like a beagle trying to figure out its master's command.

With her elbows on the table, her hands together with knitted fingers, Flynn lightly tapped at her chin contemplating where to begin. With the decision made, she settled back in her chair.

Rebecca returned with salads, an assortment of dressing packets in a basket, and two cups of chowder. This time she drew out a handful of Saltine packets from her right pocket and tossed them on the table next to the sugar packets. She made a hasty retreat, acknowledging an older couple waving to get her attention.

"Sam Martin's the present," Flynn started. "Let me fill in a few of the holes in my past first. Before coming to Auburn Notch I was a detective with the Metro Police in Chicago. You knew that part. To hear some of my fellow officers tell it, I was out of control. Always taking chances. I'll admit they might have been right about the taking chances part, but I was in control. I inched my way past them and up the ranks following hunches with solid police work. It irritated some cops, but too bad. I finally made detective and settled in with a partner I could trust."

"That was Williams?"

Flynn smirked like a proud mother. "Yes. You seem to know a bit more of my early bio than I thought, so I'll just give you a few case highlights then skip to the scary shit."

Hank nodded, tearing off another hunk of bread and dipping it into his soup. At Flynn's suggestion, they both started on their soup, no sense eating something that smelled that good cold. She filled in small bits of her cases in Chicago while they enjoyed the chowder. When they got around to picking at their salads, Flynn shifted to the scary shit.

"Yeah, I took a lot of chances back then, and one finally bit me in the ass. It all has to do with this Chicago investigation Mac's going on about. The first murder was on a Monday, Jack Morton. It had some odd circumstances, but nothing that stood out as anything more than a random murder. Maybe a mob hit; a jealous boyfriend; a business deal gone bad, hard to say. My partner and I were assigned to the case after the second victim, Mary Walsh, was found. At that point it quickly became evident we were dealing with a more methodical killer. The murders were three days apart. Both were staged in abandoned buildings out by the airport. They were strapped to old baggage carts, shot in the left shoulder, and left to bleed out. A patrol car on a routine check noticed the burning, black candles in the windows of the empty buildings hours after each crime had been committed. No prints. No DNA evidence. No evidence of any kind, except the dust on the floor."

Hank looked up from his salad. "Ash?"

"Ash. The candle in the window at the second crime scene could have been the work of a copycat; it was mentioned in every newspaper article. Not the ash. We deliberately withheld that from the media. It was our way to identify any future victims of these guys and have them think we just didn't notice."

"Guys? Like in two?"

Hank finished his salad and went back to work on the peanuts. Flynn was happy taking a small bite here and there and pushing the croutons around with her fork as she related the facts of the old case. Rebecca reappeared right on time to remove the empty soup bowls and plates, replacing them with their entrées. Flynn opted to hold onto her salad plate, remarking she liked to pick at it while eating her entrée.

"Yes, two, but I'll get to that in a few minutes," Flynn replied. "It took a little digging, but we found a connection between the first two victims on a social media site the following Monday. Both had been volunteers at a fundraising event at Chicago General two weeks prior to the first murder. By that evening we had collected up the names and contacted all the volunteers at the event except for two. One of them, Dr. Samuel Kaminski, disappeared on his way home from work. The other, Marsha Steele, a finance officer with Lowery and Campbell, we missed by about an hour. A neighbor remembered seeing her with a handsome man Monday evening getting into a cab together. Early Tuesday morning her body was discovered at an abandoned canning facility near O'Hare. Same deal as the first two victims, on a metal cart, shot in the left arm, a dusting of ash around the body. She bled out before officers on routine patrol noticed the candle in the window."

Hank listened intently, paying very little attention to his burger. "And the man she was seen with the night before?"

"He fit the description of Kaminski, but he also fit the description of Calder."

"Calder? Well that's a little suspicious."

"Believe me, we took a good look at Calder. We even brought the neighbor in for a line-up. It wasn't him."

"What about the taxi?"

"Dead end. He dropped them off at Chicago General. No one there remembers seeing them in the hospital."

Hank rested back in his chair. A mouthful of burger puffed out his right cheek, but he managed to squeak a question out from the left corner of his mouth. "So Calder was just chasing down the story like he said?"

"That's right. He started poking around the station for information after the first murder. He was a pain in the ass then, and he still is. He started shadowing my partner and me once we were assigned to the case. I was against it, but our captain thought we could use all the positive news about our investigation we could get. It was part of the deal. Calder was first on the scene with us giving him the scoop over the other papers, for which he would commend our efforts in the articles in bringing this killer to justice. PR crap, pure and simple."

Hank stopped chewing, looked up at Flynn, and raised his eyebrows. "Were you two—"

"No." Sheriff Flynn couldn't stop that thought fast enough. "And unless you want to be on school safety patrol for a month, you better get that idea out of your head."

Hank laughed, returning to his burger.

"I'm not saying Calder didn't have that on his mind. He's not a bad looking guy, and I was attracted to him at first, but he's a little too shady for me. A fading, front-page reporter looking for that one story to throw him back in the spotlight? I don't think so. It was all my partner and I could do to keep him from making shit up. Eventually, he did just that, claiming he was getting anonymous tips about the killers from the killers. My partner and I made a deal with him. Calder would get exclusive access to our investigation and the killer after he was captured if he would stop filling his articles with speculation about a pair of serial killers loose in Chicago. He swore up and down he wasn't making anything up, but he couldn't prove anything about his source. We threatened to cut him off, so he finally agreed. We fed him enough information during the investigation to keep his stories out in front of the other papers. That made him happy.

"Despite the reputation he was getting with us for fabricating facts, it was Calder who told us about the two-week timeline. He said there were similar murders in Seattle six months prior to the first Chicago killing. Four people murdered over the course of two weeks. We checked with the Seattle police. There were actually seven murders during the two-week period Calder mentioned. Only four of them were suspiciously similar in style to the Chicago murders. The cops got a tip after the last murder. They arrived at the scene and immediately came under fire. It didn't last long. When the shooting stopped, they entered the building. The suspect was lying on the cement in a pool of blood. They found his car around back. The fourth victim was in the trunk with a plastic bag over her head, just like the three others. They also found an open case of black candles in the back seat. As far as they were concerned, they got their man. Case closed. They didn't look any further."

"Calder didn't buy it?"

Flynn pushed her plate away and stirred the remains of her iced tea. "He did at first, once he made the connection with the victims and the suspected killer. It all made sense until six months later when he read about Jack Morton. The black candle mentioned in the article got his attention. Next thing I know, he's in the squad room and my new best friend. The facts around the Seattle case were all over the Internet. Any killer-wannabe went out and purchased a case of black candles. They were showing up everywhere."

"So how did you figure out there were two of them?"

"How about coffee?" asked Rebecca, taking their plates and putting them into the gray bin being held by a young, pimple-faced busboy next to her. Flynn nodded her head, but Hank held up his empty iced tea glass and shook it like a bell. "One coffee and another iced tea. Be right back."

"This is that chance I took that bit me in the ass. I got a call from one of Kaminski's neighbors. She said she could hear some-one in his apartment. Calder was with me at the time. Williams, my partner, was down at the courthouse testifying on another case. Reluctantly, I took Calder with me. When we got to the apartment, whoever was in there was gone. Took off in a cab. We caught a break though; the neighbor got the number off the cab.

"As I was talking to the cab company, Calder got a call from his editor. He was pissed about the latest article Calder filed. He insisted Calder get to the office right away or he was going to kill the story and any chance Calder had of ever getting another front-page headline. Everything's a blur after that. I got the address from the cab company for where he dropped the fare. It was out by the airport. The old cargo warehouses they were going to tear down to make room for the new runway. Calder makes me swear not to go there until I have backup. I agree at first, then decide to go anyway. I figured it was just another dead end. One foot into the building, and I'm wacked over the head. Next thing I know, I'm strapped to a metal cart with a burlap bag over my head. I can smell the bitter scent of ash in it. I'm groggy, but I can make out what sounds like two men arguing behind me. At least I think it was two men. The only part of the conversation I made out was someone laughing, saying he'll take care of that damn reporter another time. I heard the siren outside. The same deep, gritty voice yelled out, 'Shoot her.' A moment later, I felt the barrel of a gun pushed into my shoulder. The last thing I heard was that gritty voice through the bag by my left ear, 'Good-bye, Detective.'

That's all I remember until I woke up in the hospital. I found out later it was Calder who called Williams and told him where I was."

"Calder? That was a lucky break."

"Yeah, that's why I can't be too angry at the little shit. Luckily, the jackass figured I would go out there anyway, so he tracked down Williams and told him what was going on. I'm just glad Williams got there in time. The murders stopped and Dr. Kaminski was never heard from again. That's the last I heard from Calder, too, until he showed up here."

"So you think one of the guys that grabbed you was Dr. Kaminski?"

"That's what the conjecture was."

"And the other guy?"

Flynn shrugged her shoulders. "'What other guy?' That's what they kept saying. Said I was under duress. Not thinking straight."

"But you still think there were two?"

Flynn drew her brow down over a determined stare. "I don't think anything, I know there were two."

Hank nodded. "Okay. Does Calder know those guys intend to deal with him at some point?"

Flynn relaxed. "If Calder worried about everybody who threatened to kill him, he'd never leave his house."

"Wow." Hank was wide-eyed. He needed a minute to process the info. "So that was two years ago?"

"Yeah. I went through rehab and weekly visits with a shrink, but things just weren't the same. They didn't kill me that day, but they killed something inside me. I was having real confidence issues. Laura Dearing, my shrink and my friend, suggested I come to Auburn Notch. Our families used to vacation here years ago."

"Oh yeah? How long ago?"

Flynn smiled. "Let's just say you were in short pants. I loved the place. It was familiar, and she thought the good memories would help me heal. She was right. I was a different person from the moment I stepped foot in town. That first month I was here I met Councilwoman Alice Johnson. You know how she is, she wanted to know everything about me."

"And did you tell her?"

"I only gave her the basic highlights. Detective in Chicago. Shot in the line of duty. Here in Auburn Notch to recuperate. She decided she had to introduce me to the mayor. He's a nice guy. I actually met him when I was young; he was a lifeguard out at the lake. We spoke a few times the first week after I arrived and were soon meeting regularly for breakfast Saturday mornings, chitchatting about small-town crime and the old days. It was Alice's idea for me to take over the sheriff position after Thom Dunn passed away. She kept poking the mayor until he agreed. I said no at first. I didn't want to be a cop anymore. I was still having severe headaches and wrestling with a few demons that followed me here. I wasn't sure the change of scenery was going to be enough. Then one morning I woke up and decided I was tired of being afraid. I called the mayor and accepted the position that same day. It was the last time I thought about what happened in Chicago. Even the headaches went away."

"So you think these two guys are here now?"

"I'm afraid so, and Calder thinks so, too." Flynn paused, fidgeting with her empty iced tea glass. "MacGregor's not convinced. He says he agrees with me, but I can see in his eyes he still thinks it's the work of a single person. At least he agrees with Calder's concept about the murders in Seattle, Chicago, and New York being related. Two guys moving across the country killing people have to leave some kind of clue behind. They have to. That's what MacGregor is counting on and the best chance we have of identifying these guys. It's a federal case now, so we'll just lend support and let him do his thing. Hopefully he'll catch them before this town has to deal with another murder."

"So we're not going to do anything?" Hank huffed.

Flynn replied through a wry smile, "I didn't say that."

Rebecca returned, placing the coffee down in front of Flynn, removing Hank's glass in the process, and handing him a fresh iced tea.

"I'll take the check," said Hank, reaching into his back pocket for his wallet.

"Don't even try it," replied Flynn to Hank, handing her credit card to Rebecca. "You can get the next one."

Rebecca laughed, handing the credit card back to the sheriff. "I've never seen so many people try to pay a bill in my life. Your check's been taken care of, Sheriff." Rebecca turned, pointing at a man sitting at the bar. "He said it was his turn to keep an eye on you."

Flynn and Hank both looked over. Lifting a glass of ginger ale at them was Agent MacGregor. Flynn smiled and waved back. Hank was a little less appreciative, but forced a smile and a wave after being prompted by a kick under the table from Flynn.

"I don't like him just swooping in here and taking over our case," grumbled Hank through clenched teeth. "You're a good cop. He should let us do our jobs."

Flynn looked at Hank wistfully, thinking to herself, I don't think I can deal with all this again by myself. She sat back in her chair and took a deep breath. "Be nice. This might be a good time to ask him for that favor. Besides, he's only taking part of the investigation. We still need to deal with Sam Martin."

"Oh, yeah. Sam Martin. What's the story there?"

"I'm afraid if we don't find Sam Martin soon, he could be the Dr. Kaminski of Auburn Notch. We need to find him."

They both stood up.

"Thanks," remarked Hank as they headed over to where MacGregor was seated.

"For what?"

"For filling in the past and the present."

Flynn patted Hank on his shoulder. "I should have done this sooner."

Hank stopped about half way over to where Mac was. "So, what's the future?"

Flynn leaned in close and whispered, "That would be the name you found in Mark Warren's day-timer—Mr. Habberset."

CHAPTER TWENTY-TWO

The morgue in Chicago was a large, white-tiled room, decorated with the latest medical equipment. What wasn't padded in pale-green vinyl for comfort was clad in stainless steel. Eight autopsy tables ran the length down the center of the room, morbidly referred to as "Death Row" by the staff. A long, stainless hand-washing station ran along the wall at the far end of the room, consisting of six deep sinks with knee-action faucet valves, flanked by automatic doors. At the other end was an arrangement of twelve square, refrigerator doors cut into the tiled wall, three rows high and four columns long. The polished, stainless steel doors were cold to the touch, even colder were those unfortunate enough to be slumbering behind them.

Gang fights, home invasions gone wrong, bar shootings, domestic disturbances, auto fatalities. The results were always the same, only the faces were different. Strangers from every corner of the city who would never be found together in life, now rested beside each other in death. There was something cold and distant about the setting and the victims in Chicago.

Flynn maintained a separation, an antiseptic curtain drawn between her duty and her emotions. Standing two steps back in the shadow of a grieving next of kin, Flynn was just an observer. It made it easier for her to distance herself from the all-too-familiar scene.

The victim's families weren't afforded the same options. The colorless room, the smell, the cold touch of the surfaces would haunt them mercilessly. Like the curtain going up on the next performance, one of the eight tables would be illuminated from a multi-light surgical lamp four feet above the victim. The blue sheet would be drawn back. A deep gasp of breath signaled the change from denial to the reality of the situation. An outpouring of emotion would follow. Flynn had stood witness to this routine many times before, but not in Auburn Notch.

As a rookie, the first few were the tough ones. Not for the criminals who lived by the gun, but for the innocent victims who were unfortunate enough to cross their paths. For them, there was sympathy for their tragic end and compassion for those they left behind. Flynn was quick to identify the drowning effect these emotions could have if not addressed quickly. To bring justice and closure became her focus. As a result, a hard outer shell began to develop. Like the coating on a foreign object irritating an oyster's pallet, hers began to build. Case by case, victim by victim. The questions? The explanations? All the same, day after day, delivered with a thinly veiled coating of sympathy and pathos. Each day another unfamiliar face ended up under a sheet on Death Row. Each day a name was scribbled onto the tab of a blue folder. With each name another layer was added, continuing to temper her outer shell. All that changed the day she was abducted. The realization of how close she came to being one of those faces under the sheet on Death Row delivered a devastating blow to what she believed was impenetrable.

Like paint chipping off a neglected shutter, Flynn's ordeal and subsequent separation from hardcore crime took its toll on the tempered layers of impassiveness she required to stay focused. She found moving to Auburn Notch mentally therapeutic, but there were other effects that weren't immediately visible or expected. Effects centered deep within that would remain dormant until a blue sheet was pulled back to reveal the face of her past instead of a perfect stranger. Her dedication to justice and closure were intact, but a long-forgotten demon was still tugging at her confidence.

The morgue in Auburn Notch was housed in the basement of the State House. It was small, almost what some would consider intimate if it wasn't for its use. Like its larger, big-city counterparts, the white tiled walls were a necessity, as was the high-intensity lamp suspended from the ceiling. A town that size had no need for the long row of autopsy tables. Instead there was a single, marble-topped table on a stationary, wooden base—a relic of the past in pristine condition for lack of use—standing at attention below the lamp. A stainless-steel table on wheels stood ready on the opposite side, with a blue medical cloth covering the instruments. The heavy antiseptic odor remained, hitting you square in the face as you came through the automatic doors. If the reason for being there wasn't enough, the 20-degree drop in temperature could raise goose pimples on even the toughest souls.

Pleasantries and condolences were softly exchanged as Dr. Abrams opened one of two square refrigerator doors on the tiled wall near the service elevator. His hands shook as he gripped the handles on the edge of the drawer. He had stood by the side of death for many years, but this was different. This wasn't a natural cause he could rationalize. This wasn't the result of a childish prank gone terribly wrong. This wasn't the inevitable end of a long life that could be mourned by family and friends. This was something you read about happening in those other cities while sipping your morning coffee. This was a young woman taken from her family and friends without reason or warning. This was a senseless murder. With one smooth motion, he drew out the stainless-steel drawer from within. The blue sheet draped over the body hinted at the female form below. Sheriff Flynn stood next to Mrs. Newcomb, her arm around the sobbing woman's shoulder. She could feel her tremble. Dr. Abrams slowly pulled back the sheet.

"My precious, little girl," Mrs. Newcomb whispered through the lace handkerchief she held to her lips. She ran her hand over her daughter's hair, tucking the curls behind her ear. She leaned over and kissed her forehead. "My precious, little girl."

A single tear rolled down over Flynn's cheek.

CHAPTER TWENTY-THREE

"Please, have a seat, Mrs. Newcomb."

Sheriff Flynn pointed at a chair facing her desk. She walked behind the desk and took her seat. There was no reason to talk just yet.

Mrs. Carol Newcomb was a tall, statuesque woman, with shoulder-length, blond hair, slightly graying at the temples. Expensive clothes. Expensive jewelry. Expensive attitude. She was a determined woman, known in her circle to be razor sharp at sizing up any situation at a glance. She was a woman with a fierce grip on every aspect of her life, but not today. Today, her light-brown eyes were lost, surrounded by the redness of grief, and drenched in the sorrow only a mother can feel for the loss of a child. She sat quietly, her hands folded in her lap, composing herself and her thoughts.

"We argued, you know," Mrs. Newcomb stated quietly. She sat upright, her head held high as she spoke. "She was determined to take this opportunity, despite my objections. Something wasn't right. I told her it wasn't right, and now she's—"

"An opportunity?"

"Yes. She was offered a position with a real estate development company." Mrs. Newcomb paused, dabbing at her eyes with her handkerchief. She looked away, focusing her thoughts elsewhere. Anywhere but there for the moment.

"I understand how difficult this is, but it would be—"

"Do you have children?" Mrs. Newcomb interrupted.

"Well, no, but—"

"No. Then you really have no idea how difficult this is, do you?"

Flynn waited, ignoring the sharp rebuke. The sudden outburst didn't surprise her. She understood all too well the grieving process and how it could affect even the strongest will. She gave it a few more minutes, making an excuse to speak with the officer in the outer office to give Mrs. Newcomb a few minutes of privacy to get herself together.

Flynn returned, closing the door to her office and sitting back down. "I don't have children," she said softly, "but I understand the depth of the pain you're dealing with. I've consoled more parents than any one person should ever have to. I've seen what that pain can do to a family. Each time it chipped away a small piece of my heart. Each time I walked away determined to do something to ease their pain. There isn't anything I can do to bring your daughter back, but I'm hoping when we find and bring her killer to justice, it will give you solace. I wish there was more I could offer."

The stern façade was gone. Mrs. Newcomb was sobbing uncontrollably. This was good. This was needed. There will be many more days of crying ahead, but this was the important one. If you are ever to heal, you must allow yourself to grieve. Flynn stepped around from behind her desk, taking the seat next to Mrs. Newcomb. She held her hand in hers.

Mrs. Newcomb looked up into Flynn's eyes. "I'm sorry, its just . . . its just so—"

"I know. We don't need to talk about this right now. It's more important that you take care of getting your daughter back home."

"No." Mrs. Newcomb wiped her eyes dry, patted Flynn's hand, and sat back in her chair. "I'll make those arrangements when we're done here. What's important now is what can I do to help you? Whoever this monster is, I want him found and punished."

Flynn kept her seat, only reaching across her desk for a pad and pen. "It would be extremely helpful if you could fill in the details of the time leading up to your daughter's disappearance."

Mrs. Newcomb nodded. "As I mentioned, we had argued that morning about this job opportunity she was excited about. It would require her moving to New England. Despite my protest, she was packed and determined to leave for Boston the next day. It was all so quick. I asked her to reconsider. Something wasn't right about the deal. Jane just thought I was trying to keep her home. Her father and I divorced five years ago. Before then, the three of us did everything together. Once she reached high school, she could see her father and I had grown apart. She blamed me for the divorce, accusing me of smothering her ever since. Not letting her travel. Insisting she go to a local college. Anything to keep her close to me she said. Maybe subconsciously I was, but she was everything to me. I loved her and I just wanted to protect her. I just wanted to protect her." She took a deep breath, holding back another flood of tears as best she could. "I guess I didn't do a very good job."

"Where's her father now?"

Mrs. Newcomb waved her hand in the air, as if shooing a fly away. "Last I heard, Belgium, but that was two years ago. He's made no attempt to contact Jane. He wrote us both off the day he walked out. Jane just didn't want to believe—"

Flynn stood up and walked around her desk. "Okay. Are you sure you want to continue?"

Mrs. Newcomb dabbed at her eyes once more, took a deep breath, and nodded her head.

Flynn reached across her desk, pulling the photo Clayton had left behind from a blue folder. She handed the photo to Mrs. Newcomb. "Jane looks very happy here. I believe this was taken the night before she disappeared?"

Mrs. Newcomb stared at the photo. A smile came to her face. "They were three peas in a pod." She pointed with her finger to the girls in the photo. "That's Mary Armbruster, and that's Jane Whitfield. I referred to them as the Mary Janes. If they weren't out together, they were texting or doing that social network nonsense hour after hour. You never saw one without the other two."

"If they were that close, I'm surprised she would consider moving away for a job."

"That surprised me, too. When I asked her about it, she said she turned the offer down at first. It was a great opportunity, but she wasn't willing to just pack up and leave her friends behind. They were ready with a counter offer on the heels of that refusal. The man making the offer told her once she was settled into her new position, she would be able to hire two assistants. That's when I started to get suspicious."

"I can understand that. Seems a little too accommodating."

"Yes, exactly. I told her I would look into the company and the project. I would track down the specific details. Well, that just lit her fuse. She begged me to stay out of it. Doing that could jeopardize the job offer, she said. Reluctantly, I agreed." She began to cry once more.

"Have you spoken with her two friends?"

Mrs. Newcomb sniffled back the remaining tears. "Yes. I called them first thing Sunday morning when Jane didn't show up at the restaurant. They told me Jane left the bar about an hour before they did the night before. She had more packing to do and was going to get a cab. That was the last they spoke with her."

Flynn took notes during the conversation. "I thought she lived at home?"

"She does . . . did, but it wasn't odd for her to stay at Mary Armbruster's after a night out, she has her own apartment in town. They did that a lot."

"Did Jane or her friends tell you anything at all about this job offer? Who made the offer? The name of the company?"

"No. Well, that's a lie. Jane was very excited at first. She wanted to tell me everything about it, until I raised a note of suspicion. At that point, she withheld any additional information about the company for fear of me meddling into the who and why of this whole business. I did manage to find out a few more details on my own. Jane graduated from NYU. She was an architect, but also had her real estate license. She was in between jobs, so she spent most of her time renting dingy lofts to artist-types. She had a passion for multiuse property development. Jane met one of the principals of the company who made her the offer quite by chance. She was attending a cocktail party at a newly renovated warehouse down by the Seaport area that was going condo. All the local real estate agents were invited to tour the units. An agent representing a large real estate developer struck up a conversation with her during the party. The agent was very secretive at first, worried about driving the prices up if their development plan became public knowledge. He took a liking to Jane. Over a two-week period he met with her a few more times, releasing more information about the planned development and how she might fit in."

"Did she say where they were looking?"

"There were two possible locations. One was the riverfront north of Tenth Street in North Brooklyn. An old, abandoned industrial site. It's been an eyesore for years. The other was a parcel of land here in New Hampshire. It was an old mill they were going to renovate into an upscale apartment complex. The project was exactly what Jane had been hoping for. During those two weeks, she did a little freelance work for the agent. Nothing too time consuming, just chasing down landowners, checking deeds, the usual paperwork when researching a property. From the research she did, the final decision was made for the New Hampshire site. The agent was so impressed with her by the end of the second week, he offered her a position with the company. That's why she was going to Boston, to meet the developer and get the official job offer in writing. They offered her a director position, contingent on her willingness to relocate to New England. She would start out working with him to secure the purchase of the property, eventually managing the day-to-day planning and schedules for the whole project once the deal was finalized. Opportunity of a lifetime, she said."

Mrs. Newcomb needed another minute.

Sheriff Flynn took a bottled water from the small fridge behind her desk and handed it to her. "I'm sorry, we don't have any cups."

"This is fine. Thank you." She opened the water and sipped it.

"Did Jane have a boyfriend?"

"She had been seeing somebody on and off, but not so much recently. Bob Kelly, a nice boy. He's a grad student at NYU. He's been studying in Spain for the last three months. Jane said he was coming home early next month. She was looking forward to seeing him. He'll be devastated."

Mrs. Newcomb gave up any further attempts to suppress her tears.

Sheriff Flynn sat quietly for a few minutes. "Just a couple more questions if you're up to it."

"Yes. I'm sorry."

"You have nothing to be sorry about." Flynn pointed to the picture in Mrs. Newcomb's hand. "Do you recognize anyone else in that photo?"

Mrs. Newcomb studied it carefully. "I'm sorry, no. Should I?"

Flynn shook her head. "You hired Bob Clayton to look into your daughter's disappearance? Is that right?"

"Yes. I met him at the police station that Sunday. The police were no help at all. They said she wasn't missing long enough to be a missing person. Clayton was there and heard most of the conversation. He saw how upset I was. He introduced himself and said he could help. I said no thanks at first. He was a bit creepy, but I kept his card. By Wednesday I was desperate. The police hadn't turned up anything. I dug the card out and called Mr. Clayton. He said he would look into it for me. I didn't know what else to do. I gave him this photo and a handful of others I printed out from my computer."

"Have you seen him or spoken with him since you arrived in Auburn Notch?"

"No. He's here?"

"Yes. I spoke with him yesterday. He gave me the photo."

"Yes, of course. That makes sense. We spoke a couple times during the week, and I had a missed call from him yesterday. It came in after the police contacted me, so I forgot all about it. I haven't spoken with him directly since I left New York."

"If you do speak with him, would you let me know?"

"Of course." Mrs. Newcomb read a little more into the request than the sheriff had expected. "Is there something you're not telling me?"

"No, not at all. I have a few questions for him, but I'll have my deputy stop out to the motel where he's staying just outside of town. If you don't mind my asking, who took this picture?"

"Jane had a waiter take the photo. She e-mailed it to me that night, saying she was—" She couldn't get the last words out.

Sheriff Flynn knew when enough was enough. "I think I have all the information I need, Mrs. Newcomb. Thank you. I know how difficult this was for you, but the information you provided is invaluable. I will personally keep you posted on our investigation. Are you staying here in town?"

"Yes, I'm at the Fairfield. I'll be there until tomorrow." Mrs. Newcomb stood. "Thank you, Sheriff. Please, catch this monster. Jane didn't deserve this. She was a sweet girl."

Flynn walked around her desk and shook Mrs. Newcomb's hand. "I will. I promise."

Mrs. Newcomb managed a smile, nodding her head in appreciation. She walked toward the door.

"I'm sorry," Sheriff Flynn called out, "did you mention the name of the man who contacted Jane for that developer?"

Mrs. Newcomb thought for a moment. "Habberset. I believe she said his name was Ronald Habberset. Jane said he was a funny, little man, but well spoken."

"Funny? In what way?"

"She said every once in a while she noticed him talking to himself."

CHAPTER TWENTY-FOUR

"Well, Sheriff, what brings you out here? Hank, nice to see you, too."

"I wanted to check in on your guest in Cabin 4. I didn't see his car."

"He was there earlier, I guess." John Mitchell closed up the account book he was working in and continued. "I got a little side tracked. The plumbing in 9 got all stopped up. It was a mess. I went over to Jack's Hardware for a new toilet float assembly. You know, the kind that has that automatic—"

Sheriff Flynn smiled, nodded, and interrupted. She wasn't in the mood for an infomercial on the latest in toilet float assemblies. "This is important, John. How about last night? Was Clayton in his cabin all night or did he go out?"

I saw the lights on in his cabin when I took my walk around. That was about nine thirty. His car was behind the cabin, I think. There was a car there. Yeah, it was his. He must have had a visitor, too."

"What makes you say that?"

"Like I said, I was taking my usual walk around. When I went by his cabin I heard him arguing with someone inside. I was about to knock, when it just stopped."

"Did you hear what they were arguing about?"

"No, but I figured they were related."

Why's that?" asked Hank.

"Well, just when I was about to knock, I heard Mr. Clayton mention something about their father. That's when the argument stopped."

"Did you see another car?" asked Sheriff Flynn.

"Nope, just his."

"Was it there all night?"

"It was there when Martha and I went out to dinner." John smiled proudly. "We always go out Saturday night. Been doing it since before we were married."

"What time was that?" asked Hank.

"Oh, I'd say about five, five thirty maybe?"

Sheriff Flynn walked over to the window, pulling back the curtain for a view of the parking area. "So his lights were on in the cabin when you got back from dinner?"

"Yep. It's been kinda slow, you know since the festival ended. I noticed his lights on the minute we rolled into the lot. It was just after eight."

"Did you see his car?"

John Mitchell bit his inside lip, a bit sheepish in his response. "I know I should have been keeping a better eye on him, but—"

Flynn smiled, walked back over, and patted John on the shoulder. "Nonsense. You did just fine."

"His car was parked behind the cabin at nine thirty though. I'll swear to that. I made one last walk around the property before turning in for the night."

"Thanks, John. We're going to go over and have a little talk with Mr. Clayton. Give Martha my best."

"Will do." John Mitchell nodded, shaking Hank's hand. "You know, I did speak to him earlier today if that's important."

"You did?" asked Sheriff Flynn. "What about?"

"He said he was waiting for a package. Asked if anything had come for him. I told him no. Seemed a bit jittery when I asked what it was he was looking for."

"What did he say?"

"Nothing. Just said it was personal and went back to his cabin. Should I continue keeping an eye on him?"

"Yes, but make sure he doesn't spot you doing it. Just keep track of when he comes and goes. That should be enough."

"Will do."

◆ ◆ ◆

"That's that damn sh–sheriff's car. Look. In front of the office. What does sh–she want?"

"Calm down. You start acting suspicious and this whole thing will go to shit."

Bob Clayton shook his head. "You sh–should have taken care of her right in Chicago. This is your f–fault. We're as good as caught."

"Shut up. Just shut up. I've about had it with your whining. I'll take care of her soon enough. For now, just find out what she wants."

Bob Clayton noticed two long shadows come into view between the cabins. "Get down, th–they'll see us."

He waited a moment, allowing Sheriff Flynn and Hank to pass by and out of site.

"Go see what they want."

"Stop p–pushing me," Clayton snarled. "It's that sh–sheriff and her deputy. It's over, and I'm g–glad. I won't d–do this any more. Do you hear m–me? I won't."

"Stop whining. You'll do what I say, and it's over when I say it is. Now, go see what they're up to."

CHAPTER TWENTY-FIVE

Angela's phone rang. UNKOWN CALLER came up on the screen. Normally she would ignore it, assuming it was some telemarketer or local pollster, but something inside her said to answer this one.

"It's me," said the voice at the other end of the line.

Angela recognized the voice right away. "Marty? Where are you?"

"I can't say. It's better you don't know."

"I don't understand. This is really getting out of hand. I think the sheriff believes you had something to do with that girl's death out at the old asylum. Please tell me it's not true."

"It's not. Please believe me, it's not."

"I do, but why won't you turn yourself in to the sheriff?"

Marty paused. He knew he wasn't supposed to say anything to anybody, but this was different. This is Angela. He just blurted it out. "The agent thinks I'm safer being away from town. He thinks this guy will kill me at some point and blame the other murders on me."

"Murders?" Angel asked. "There was another one?"

"Look, I've said more than I should have. Please don't repeat any of this. Don't tell anyone I called. I really want to see you, but I can't. I'll call again as soon as this is over."

The phone went dead.

CHAPTER TWENTY-SIX

"I wonder what it is he's expecting in the mail?" asked Hank.

Hank and Sheriff Flynn had walked down the long row of cabins. Cabin 12 was closest to the office proceeding down in numerical order as they ran parallel with Route 93. Cabins 5 through 1 followed around the curve of the road. The office stood out at a slight angle, allowing a view down the row of cabins until you got to the curve. At that point you could see both windows on the side of cabin 5, but only the side window closest to the front porch on 4. The other three cabins were completely out of view of the office.

As they walked along, they could see the parking areas behind the cabins. They spotted cars parked behind 11 and 6. Rounding the corner, they saw Clayton's rental parked behind Cabin 4. Flynn paused for a moment for a look, and then joined Hank on the porch. A radio could be heard playing inside.

Flynn raised her hand to knock. Her cell phone rang. Before she could utter a greeting, the voice at the other end made it very clear he was in control of what was going to be a brief conversation.

"Yeah, we're out at Mitchel's Motel, why?" As Flynn listened to the voice on the other end of the conversation, her brow lowered and her breathing became short snorts through her nose. She looked around at all the dark places a car could be tucked into, wondering where MacGregor's minions were hiding. "Look Mac, I'm here and I have a few questions for—" The line went dead.

"What did MacGregor want?"

"He wants us to leave."

"Are we?"

Sheriff Flynn turned and knocked on the cabin door. No answer. She knocked again. Same result.

Hank got his answer. He grabbed the doorknob. "It's unlocked," he whispered, starting to turn the knob.

"Can I help you, Sh–Sheriff?"

Sheriff Flynn and Hank turned in the direction of the voice. It was Bob Clayton walking over from around the back of the cabin.

"Sheriff Flynn didn't miss a beat. She held out the small manila envelope she had tucked under her arm. "There you are. I was afraid we missed you. I wanted to return this photo to you before you left town."

Clayton stepped up onto the porch, putting his brown bag down on the table between the two painted Adirondack chairs. His effort to close the top of the bag didn't go unnoticed. "That's very nice of you, Sh–Sheriff, but you didn't have to come all th–the way out here. It's a copy. I sh–should have told you I had another one."

"Not a problem. I also wanted you to know Mrs. Newcomb was in town. She identified her daughter a little earlier. She's a strong woman, but she's taking her daughter's death very hard."

"Will sh–she be in town long?"

"I believe she's leaving tomorrow, so if you want to see her, you better do it tonight."

"No. She p–paid me up front. I have no reason to s–see her again. How are you doing with your case? Any s–suspects yet?"

Flynn sat down in one of the Adirondacks, motioning for Clayton to do the same in the other. "It's a police matter, and I don't really like to comment on open cases."

"Of course, s–sorry. I was just wondering. Idle c–curiosity really."

"You may be able to help though." Sheriff Flynn pointed to the envelope she gave Clayton. "May I?"

"S–sure," he said, handing it back.

Hank stood by quietly, observing the conversation and Clayton's facial expressions. He just smiled at Clayton any time he looked up at him.

Flynn took the photo from inside, putting it down on the table between them. She pointed to a face in the crowded background. "Does this guy look familiar to you?"

Clayton squinted his eyes even more than usual. "N–no, not really. It's hard to say though. Awfully d–dark place. Who is it?"

"His name is Sam Martin. He lives here in Auburn Notch."

Clayton rested back in his chair, an almost relieved look on his face. "Do you th–think he had something to do with th–that girl's death?"

Sheriff Flynn put the photo back in the envelope, leaving it on the table as she got up. "Let's just say I have a few questions for him once we locate him."

"He's m–missing?"

"To be honest with you, yes. He's a person of interest, and we've been unable to locate him."

"He's your only s–suspect?"

Flynn hesitated, looking up at Hank and then back at Clayton. "He's one of two men I'd like to talk to. The other one is related to another case all together."

"Maybe I can help? It d–does seem an awful big coincidence for him and your v–victim to be in the same club in New York the n–night she disappeared. Then she sh–shows up here dead."

"My thoughts exactly. That's really why I came out here. I was just over in the office asking John Mitchell if you were still here. He mentioned you were waiting for a package? Does that mean you'll be staying a few more days?"

"An envelope, r–really. He's just confused. I'm waiting f–for a check from a job I haven't been p–paid for yet. I called the p–person and asked to have it sent here." He smiled. "I could use the c–cash. I'll be here until the ch–check arrives."

"Well, if you want something to do, maybe you could nose around a bit and help us locate Martin?"

"Sure. Beats staring at the f–four walls." He paused, looking from Hank to Flynn. "Don't s–suppose there'll be a f–finder's fee if I locate him?"

Sheriff Flynn laughed. "Under the circumstances, I'm sure I can get the town council to approve a small fee for your services."

Clayton smiled back and stood up. He shook the sheriff's hand and bid them both good-bye. As he was opening the door to his cabin, Sheriff Flynn called out one additional question.

"You wouldn't happen to know anyone by the name of Habberset? Ronald Habberset?"

Clayton shook his head and shrugged his shoulders. His pleasant look deteriorated into a stern stare, his answer sharp and direct. "It d–doesn't sound familiar."

Sheriff Flynn waved. "Never mind. Keep me posted."

Sheriff Flynn and Hank walked back to the squad car in silence. It wasn't until they were out on Route 93 that Hank spoke.

"He's up to something, I'm sure of it. Why didn't you press him more?"

"I shouldn't have done any of that. There's going to be hell to pay when word gets back to MacGregor that we didn't leave. He doesn't want this guy spooked. If Clayton thinks we're on to him, there's no telling what he might do."

"But what if he's our killer? What if he kills again?"

"It's a fine line we're walking. We need to stop them both. Don't forget the other guy."

"Oh yeah, you still think there's two of them involved."

"Yep. I'm pretty sure Clayton is one of them, but I don't think he's the dangerous one. It's the other guy we need to identify. Dragging Clayton in is easy, but by doing it we have no idea what the other guy will do. One wrong move, and we could lose them both. I'll contact Mac when we get back to the office and let him know about our conversation with Clayton. I'll see if I can pry any more information from him about this plan he has in motion. This could go south real fast. I think it's even more urgent now that we locate Sam Martin."

Hank nodded. "Did you see inside the bag?"

"I sure did," replied Flynn.

"What do you suppose he's going to do with those?"

"I don't know, but I think you should do a little Googling when we get back to the office and find out what you *can* do with those other than the obvious."

CHAPTER TWENTY-SEVEN

Bob Clayton stood in the doorway of his cabin, looking out toward Route 93, and giving a slight wave. When he saw the sheriff's car fade down the road into the distance, he turned, walked inside, and slammed the door shut.

"G–God damn it!" he barked. Th–they know about Habberset. Th–they know!

"Will you lower your voice? They don't know shit. All they have is a name. Just stick to the plan, and we're out of here. The only way we'll get caught is if you do something stupid. Do we understand each other?"

Bob Clayton looked around the cabin. "Wh–what if they'd walked in here? Well? Look at all this s–stuff. That sheriff ain't st–stupid. We need to l–leave right now. R–right now!"

"We leave now, we might as well leave a note admitting everything. No. We stay and finish the job."

"Oh yeah, j–just like you finished the j–job in Chicago?"

"That was *your* mistake. Don't think I didn't know what you were doing. If you had shot her in the heart, we wouldn't be in this situation. You screwed this up, but I intend to fix it before we leave this somber, little town. He looked in the mirror and smiled. Besides, they're going to pay you to help them catch their killer. They didn't say he had to be alive."

"S–so, what do we do now?"

"We'll do just what the sheriff wants us to do, arrange for her to capture her killer."

"S–so, no more k–killings?"

"I didn't say that. There has to be two more, you know that."

"I s–suppose you want me to lure th–them in again?"

"It's what you do best."

Bob Clayton walked around the small room, pacing back and forth in front of the drawn front curtains. He snorted out a final question. "Who th–this time?"

"I'll let you decide. Angela Pierce or Alice Johnson? Or maybe both if you want to get this over with quicker."

CHAPTER TWENTY-EIGHT

Angela tossed and turned most of the night. She couldn't get her brain to turn off about the conversation she had with Marty. Her thoughts shot out in every direction. Leaving town just makes him look guilty. What was he thinking? To hell with what Agent MacGregor thinks. She should have argued. She should have insisted Marty contact the sheriff and explain everything. Once Sheriff Flynn knows the FBI doesn't suspect Marty, she can protect him just as well as that FBI agent. Even better, really. Agent MacGregor will be gone after the killer is caught, but the sheriff will still be here. The sheriff can set those cackling hens in town straight about what really happened and how Marty had nothing to do with it. God knows what the town knows and what they're thinking about him? Even after the real killer is brought in, the idea he was a suspect will taint his reputation in town forever. Once these people make up their minds, he's done. They remember what they want to remember.

At some point, deep in the darkness before Sunday morning broke, Angela managed a few hours of sleep. She awoke to a gray, overcast morning, determined to do something about this mess Marty was caught up in. If he wasn't going to help himself, she was going to do it for him. As she pulled on her jeans and an NYU sweatshirt, she contemplated her next move. Maybe if she talked to MacGregor she could make him understand the harm he was doing by hiding Marty. All he was doing was hanging a guilty sign around his neck. She grabbed a pair of socks from her dresser. This is the way the FBI conducts an investigation? This isn't accomplishing anything. The more Angela thought about it, the more her concern for Marty turned to anger for Agent MacGregor. With a last tug on the shoelace of her ankle boot, it was settled. Someone needs to set him straight. Where did he say he was staying? The Fairfield? Yes, the Fairfield.

Angela owned a small, two-bedroom house at the edge of town on Oak Lane. New England white, with black shutters and a slate roof just like the postcards in town. The porch ran along the front. It was just long enough and wide enough for two rocking chairs separated by a brightly painted, flea-market-find table at one end. At the other was a black enamel front door with four small windows along the top. Below the windows hung a grapevine wreath with plastic ivy and thistle intertwined within the loose wrappings. A small, detached garage sat at the end of a thin, gravel driveway that ran along the right side separating her house from Mrs. Parker's next door. The garage door was old and heavy, something she intended to replace one of these days with a lighter vinyl door on a remote opener. For the time being, she just parked her pale-green Beetle in the driveway.

The wood trim on the inside of the house needed a little paint, the carpets had seen better days, and the wallpaper was out of a 1960s sitcom. None of that mattered to Angela. It was her proudest day when she signed the papers and Mark Warren handed her the keys. Her dad supervised the move, directing her two younger brothers with the furniture and boxes being unloaded from their respective pick-up trucks. The furnishings were sparse at the beginning, but she and her mom made frequent trips out to the barns and white, clapboard buildings along Route 10 where the best antique furniture deals were found. A table from one place, an Eastlake rocker from another, a brass fire screen for the living room. It wasn't long before her little cottage had the same warmth and feel of the family home she left behind. A hot cup of tea and homemade cookies fresh from the oven on a chilly evening completed the transformation.

Angela reserved Sunday mornings for coffee and fresh-baked Pillsbury Cinnamon Buns while she caught up with friends on Facebook. She walked into the kitchen. There was a quick glance at the laptop waiting patiently for her on the kitchen table and then over to the coffeemaker. She just shook her head, ignoring the ritual, and grabbed her handbag and keys. With a determined step, she was out the door and in the car without a second thought. She tossed her purse on the passenger seat, pointed her Beetle in the direction of town, and sped off down the street.

It was early. Seven thirty-one according to the radio. Probably not a time when you should be banging on an FBI agent's hotel room door unannounced. She eased off the gas pedal a bit. Angela didn't want to admit it, but the ride into town was spilling the wind from her sails. Her determination to right the wrong she got herself all worked up about was now looking more like the knee-jerk reaction of a love-struck schoolgirl. There were merits to what she was doing, but there could also be consequences to interfering with an official investigation. Coffee in town was the better approach, she thought to herself, and then we'll see if approaching Agent MacGregor was still the best way to help Marty. It sounded like a good idea in her head, but everything sounds like a good idea when you're rubbing the sleep from your eyes. Better to sift it through a cup of coffee, maybe a couple eggs, too, and then make a decision.

Angela parked behind the Starlight. The lot was empty. Ahead of her, between the buildings, she could see the Rocket Café. The neon sign of the cafe lit up the alley, its bright colors reflecting in the puddles accumulating from the light rain that had started. As she made her way down the alley between Jack's Hardware and the bowling alley, sidestepping the puddles, a man called to her from behind.

"Excuse me," he called out in a pleasant voice. "Excuse me. Are you Angela P–Pierce?"

Angela turned with a start. "I'm sorry, do I know you?"

A curious, little man in a rumpled trench coat was walking at a quick pace towards her. He stopped a third of the way down the alley, picking up something from underneath a collapsed cardboard box. A moment later he was facing her, holding something close to his chest, his one hand tucked into his coat.

"Are you Angela P–Pierce?" he repeated.

She looked over at the Rocket. There were small groups of people sitting at the tables in the front windows. Some faces were familiar. They continued buttering their rye toast and conversations, not noticing the two people in the alley across the street. Angela waved, not at anyone in particular, just waved to give the impression she had singled out someone at the cafe. "Yes, I am. I'm in a bit of a hurry. Someone's waiting for me. What can I do for you?"

"M–my name is Bob Clayton." He fumbled in his pocket for a business card without the luck of retrieving one. As he did so, the wet face of a shivering, black kitten peaked out from his coat over his other hand. "S–sorry, I thought I had m–more cards with me. I'm a p–private detective from Brooklyn. I'm here about th–that girl they found out at the old asylum. No m–matter. I have a m–message from Marty."

"You do?" Angela blurted out. She thought for a moment, tempering her response as she continued. "You know Marty?"

"Well, n–no. I met him out at th–the asylum about an hour ago."

"The asylum? What in the world were you doing out there?"

"Mrs. N–Newcomb, that poor girl's m–mother, hired me to find her. That's what b–brought me here to town. My j–job is done, and

I'm l–leaving later today." He paused. "I know it's a bit m–morbid, but I just wanted to see where they f–found her."

"You're right, it is a bit morbid. Look, I'm really busy. Just tell me what all this has to do with Marty and—"

"I'm sorry. Like I said, I w–went out to the old asylum. P–pretty spooky place, especially on a rainy m–morning like this. I was poking around the s–second floor when this guy jumps out. He was w–waving an old, rusty p–pipe. Scared the sh—crap out of me. When I t–told him who I was, he calmed d–down a bit. He was s–scared though. I could tell. Just pacing back and f–forth while he spoke waving that pipe around. He made me p–promise not to tell anyone I saw him, especially the sh–sheriff."

Clayton took a handkerchief from his pocket and rubbed it gently over the kitten's head.

The genuineness of his concern for the stray kitten caught Angela's attention, but she wasn't completely convinced about the innocence of his story. There was still a sharp edge to her response. "So why tell me?"

"Look, I'm j–just relaying the message. I'm on my way b–back to Brooklyn, that's what I told your f–friend. He was m–making me nervous with that pipe, so I backed away sayin' I was sorry f–for trespassing. That's when he r–realized I wasn't there to hurt him. He p–put the pipe down and asked if I would do him a f–favor. He said his ph–phone was dead and he wanted to t–talk to you. I t–told him I would relay a message. He g–gave me your name and address. I was coming to your house to g–give you the message when I saw you p–pull out of your driveway. I followed you here. I'm h–harmless, miss. I'm s–sorry if I scared you. I'm just trying to help th–the kid out."

"You just surprised me, that's all." Angela was warming to the idea Clayton might be on the level. "What was he wearing?"

Clayton continued drying the kitten, thinking for a moment. "Well, it was kind of d–dark in there, but I think he had a b–blue tee shirt on and a canvas j–jacket. Jeans, too, I think."

Angela relaxed her pose. That's what he had on yesterday when she saw him. "Did he say anything else?"

"No, j–just that he wanted to t–talk to you. He made me swear not to t–tell anyone else." Clayton paused. "L–look, I don't know what's going on here, but m–my job is done. I'm going back to Brooklyn. The kid l–looked scared, so I figured it was the l–least I could do. Nice meeting you, m–miss. I hope everything w–works out okay." Before he walked away he made one more gesture, pointing back to a wet pile of boxes at the other end of the alley and handing the kitten to Angela. "Would you l–look after him p–please? I f–found him under one of th–those boxes back there. He won't last l–long like that. I th–think he's hungry, too."

Without a moments thought to the bizarre request, Angela took the kitten from his hands. She lightly stroked the purring kitten's back as she watched Clayton walk back through the light drizzle to his car. He was around the corner of the building and gone from sight when she made up her mind. "Well, that's it," she murmured to herself, directing the conversation to the wet ball of fur in her arms. "I'm going to put an end to this cloak-and-dagger shit. The hell with what Agent MacGregor thinks. If Marty doesn't have enough sense to come in out of the cold, we'll just go out and drag him back to town ourselves."

"Mr. Thurlow," the nurse said, bending down close to his ear. "Your son called. He said he was unable to visit with you today. He'll come by next week."

The nurse stood up, waiting for an acknowledgement. She repeated the message, louder this time.

"He's retired now. Fishes most days." Mr. Thurlow was staring straight ahead, pointing towards the large glass windows along the front of the lobby. The building was purposely situated on a hill with a commanding view of the valley. The bluish-gray, muted silhouette of the White Mountains rose up in their entire splendor beyond the distant tree line. "Used to take him there as a boy. Camping with his brother. Always caught a fish for dinner."

The nurse leaned down close again. "Would you like me to take you back to your room?"

Mr. Thurlow looked up at the nurse through wistful eyes. "Always late as a boy. I can wait. I'll just wait here for Tom."

"I'm sorry, Mr. Thurlow, but your son said he wasn't able to visit with you today. He said he was sorry. Why don't I take you back to your room?"

Mr. Thurlow smiled and looked back out the windows. "He still fishes, you know. Probably just held up in traffic. I'll wait here. He won't be long. Always late as a boy."

The nurse patted Mr. Thurlow on his shoulder. "I'll get you a glass of juice in case you get thirsty while you wait."

CHAPTER TWENTY-NINE

It was a little past twelve-thirty in the afternoon when council-woman Johnson found herself at a gas pump on Route 16, about three miles outside of town, grumbling over the idea of having to pump her own gas. Through the window of the mini-mart she watched the clerk inside flirt with some young girl at the counter. She ground her teeth with each giggle and strand of hair the young girl wrapped around her finger.

Councilwoman Alice Johnson was a sturdy woman, with heavy limbs and a smile any dentist worth his floss would be proud to lay claim to. Though she appreciated and often commented on the abundance of colors throughout the town, she dressed only in various shades of black. Light black. Dark black. Medium black. On those special occasions—a spring outing or afternoon wedding requiring something more festive—a gradated black to white, pleated dress hung ready in her closet. Bright, blue eyes peeked out from behind puffy, pink cheeks. She had a reputation of being direct to a fault, and determined to have her opinion heard on whatever subject she currently fancied. If your intent was to ignore her, you better have a note from the coroner; it's the only excuse she'll accept.

Councilwoman Johnson shook her head and turned her attention back to the gas pump. She was determined to touch the gas filler nozzle as little as possible, holding it at arms length with a substantial wad of complimentary windshield wipes wrapped around the trigger as she topped off her tank. This wasn't the first time she was faced with pumping her own gas. She was a creature of habit and had a regular Sunday morning ritual—go to church, pick up cinnamon buns at the Rocket Café, top off her gas tank for the week. It wasn't at all odd for her to travel upwards of fifteen miles to find the cheapest price for gas. Most times, like that day, the savings came with an additional irritation. Stations located in town in Auburn Notch are all repair and inspection centers. They hire local kids as attendants to pump gas, fix tires, and give directions. It gives the mechanics the interruption-free time they need to concentrate on repairs. Not so much when you get outside of town. The stations along the main roads leading in and out of town are combined with mini-marts, so you're on your own at the pumps.

As she continued to grumble and reflect on ways to have the state's self-service gas station amendment repealed, a man standing out by the highway caught her attention. He had a map in hand, turning it in a few different directions as he gazed up and down the highway. He turned and saw Councilwoman Johnson looking in his direction. She waved him over with an inviting smile, afterwards replacing the nozzle in the holder on the pump and disposing of the wipes.

"Excuse me, but are you f–from around here?" he asked, quite frustrated with the breeze and the unwieldy map.

Seeing every face, whether recognized or not, as a potential vote, Alice Johnson smiled and brightly answered. "I'm quite proud to say I'm a long-time resident of Auburn Notch." She extended her hand. "I'm Councilwoman Alice Johnson, how can I help you?"

"I'm afraid I'm a bit l–lost. I'm looking for Warren Lane? I was t–told it was off Route 16, but I can't f–find it."

Alice Johnson shook her head. "It's actually off Oak Lane. *That's* off Route 16." She pointed down the road. "Go toward town. You'll cross over Route 93. About a mile further you'll see Oak Lane. Turn right, and Warren Lane will be on your left."

The man looked at his map. "I don't s–see it here. Is it new?"

Alice Johnson gave an indignant snort. "Not so much new as private. It's the driveway of a local realtor in town. It used to be a graveled fire access road to the lake. When Warren bought the property it sat on he bullied the council into paving the road. Gave them some story about how he would continue to allow them access to the lake when needed if they did. When he built a home at the end of the road, it became a very convenient driveway. It was before I became a councilwoman." She tapped her finger on the map. "I can assure you he wouldn't get away with nonsense like that with me."

He smiled and looked down the road. "That way, you s–say? Cross over 93 and a r–right on Oak Lane?"

"Yes. You shouldn't have any trouble finding it." She paused, the location sinking in. "Forgive my nosiness, but may I ask why you're going there?"

"I'm sorry. I r–represent a gentleman interested in p–purchasing a property Mark Warren holds the listing for. I'm not r–really at liberty to divulge the d–details, only to say it's imperative our intensions n–not become public knowledge until after the deal is signed. The man I r–represent, and I'll just call him Mr. Smith, has been in negotiations w–with Mark Warren. We came to a final agreement last w–week. The only thing left to do was sign the papers. We were to meet first th–thing this morning at our hotel in Sanford, Maine. Mr. Smith became concerned when Mr. Warren didn't sh–show up, and we couldn't reach him by phone. I've been calling all morning, but without any l–luck. I'm hoping to catch up with him at his home. We're very concerned. It's been a m–miserable morning."

"You don't know, do you?"

"Know what?"

"Mark Warren was found murdered at his home yesterday morning. It's a terrible thing. Home invasion gone wrong the police are saying."

"Oh my, that p–poor man." He looked back down the road, folding the map as best he could and stuffing it back in his pocket. "This is just terrible. Not to sound insensitive, but Mr. Smith w–was hoping to close the deal before anyone caught wind of our intentions for th–the property. We've put so much time and tr–trouble in finding just the right location. We've spent a few th–thousand dollars with our engineers just to be sure the main building is structurally s–sound for our needs. We've made arrangements with contractors. I know how insensitive I m–must sound. This is just terrible. You have my utmost sympathy for this tr–tragic, tragic turn of events, but we've made financial commitments b–based on getting all the work done at that old mill before the end of next year. This is terrible. I don't know wh–what we'll do now."

The *old mill* caught Alice's attention. "You don't sound insensitive at all, this is business. The police will sort out what happened to Mr. Warren, and perhaps I can be of some help with the dilemma you are now faced with as a result of this tragedy? You mean the old Willis Mill #4? The one outside of town? Why don't we go over here and talk about this?"

Alice Johnson took the man by the arm and led him over to where a couple white, round tables with benches were on the side of the mini-mart. She brushed off the benches with a handkerchief and the two sat down.

"M–murdered, you say? No wonder I couldn't reach him. The gentleman I r–represent was so afraid the seller had changed his mind, that's why he had me m–make the trip over here. It never occurred to us it was s–something like this."

"Yes, it's tragic, but not at all reflective of the business-friendly and family structure Auburn Notch is noted for. You say you intend to purchase the old mill? I don't believe Mr. Warren mentioned anything to council about a pending sale on that property."

"I'm afraid I'm at f–fault for that. We insisted the particulars of the deal be held in s–secret until the last moment. Mr. Warren was supposed to take c–care of filing the p–paperwork late yesterday, with the actual signing of the papers to take place this morning. He was apprehensive at f–first, but we convinced him it had to be done this way. When he didn't show up, we thought something might have happened. I met with him at the l–location about a week ago. We had a preliminary deal in p–place. It was a handshake, but he seemed honest enough. We were w–waiting for the report from our engineers. I got that yesterday. It gave the l–location a positive assessment; so I called Mr. Warren first thing so we c–could get the ball rolling on the paperwork. I tried all day to reach him, but no r–response. So here I am. Mr. Warren told me about his pl–place on the lake, and I remembered the name of the road. I've been looking for it for almost t–two hours now."

Alice Johnson was like a bulldog latched onto a trouser leg when she was focused on something. "Yes, it is a bit off the beaten track. This isn't the first time Warren sidestepped council, God rest his soul. As I said, the police will take care of that investigation so we shouldn't let it affect your plans for that old mill. I assume you're still interested in purchasing it? I'm very familiar with the property. My seat on council can open doors for you and the man you represent. I can tell you it's a bit of an eyesore now, but with a little loving care, it could shine again like the jewel it once was. Just what are your plans for it?"

Alice Johnson's smile and the direction of the conversation was all that was needed to brush away the dark cloud that had been hanging above the gentleman's head all morning. There was a renewed hope, evident in the smile he directed back at his new friend.

"I'm so fortunate that I r–ran into you. You'll forgive me, but I'm r–really not at liberty to go into the details, except to say we pr–pride ourselves in civic renewal. An abandoned mill, repurposed for a c–contemporary use, is a perfect fit for our business model. Mr. Warren was very helpful in n–not only introducing us to the Willis Mill, but also in getting us aligned with investors willing to undertake such a pr–project. That money is waiting in escrow." The gentleman moved a bit closer to

Councilwoman Johnson, continuing in a whisper. "Between you and I, and I believe I can trust you, our intent is to m–make it a center for seminars and classes for a variety of subjects related to wr–writing and the arts. It would be open to the public and staffed by t–teachers from the surrounding colleges and universities. Part of it would be offered as a b–business conference venue, complete with catering."

Alice Johnson's eyes were like saucers. "What an exceptional use for such a historic building, not to mention the revenue such a place would generate for the fine businesses in Auburn Notch. Well, we certainly can't let this opportunity wither on the vine. I'm sure I can get this transaction back on the rails within a few hours. Why don't you follow me into town? I'll call an emergency meeting of the council, and we'll get the ball rolling on the paperwork."

"Would you mind if we drove to the Willis Mill first? The gentleman I r–represent is on the verge of pulling the plug on this deal. He was more c–concerned than I was when we couldn't reach Mr. Warren. He suggested we abandon this l–location and move on to the secondary location he liked near Nashua. You have a l–lovely town here. I wasn't about to give up on this property without a f–fight. It would mean a lot if I c–could take a few additional photos inside and out and e-mail them to Mr. Smith. I can tell him of our m–meeting and your intensions to c–complete this deal within our timeframe. It will put his m–mind at ease and give me something to do while you get the paperwork in order."

"Well, we certainly can't lose this opportunity to Nashua. Of course, we'll drive over to the mill first, and then back to town. If you have no pressing plans, I would like to extend an invitation for you to stay overnight in Auburn Notch . . . at our expense, of course. It will give me a chance to show you what our little town has to offer your future clientele."

"This is very exciting. I can't tell you how m–much it means to me meeting you. I thought all was l–lost."

The two stood up. Alice Johnson extended her hand. "It's *my* pleasure meeting you. Do you want to follow me? Better yet, we'll take my car." She winked. "I can expense the gas that way."

"An excellent idea. No s–sense taking two cars. I have my c–camera and lights in a bag in the trunk of my c–car. I'll just grab that. I'm parked around back. Why don't you m–meet me there, and we'll go."

CHAPTER THIRTY

The light rain quickly gained a more determined attitude. Angela stopped in front of the gates to the Willis Asylum. She found the chain securing the gates on the ground, glistening in the lights of her Beetle. She hesitated, thinking how odd it was for the place not to be secure. She quickly assured herself it made perfect sense since Marty was inside.

The old place felt even creepier than she remembered. Most of the glass in the windows had been broken out. Rusted window bars dangled precariously from the facade where the bolts securing them had long rusted away, a single bolt remaining here and there to hold them in place. There wasn't much holding the old place up. Even the holly attached to the brick seemed to be pulling the structure back down into the depths of the dirt and granite it rose up from.

Angela looked around. There was no sign of Marty. There was no sign of anyone. Maybe he didn't hear the car pull up because of the storm? It's a big place; maybe he was in one of the interior rooms away from the weather pouring in through the gaping holes in the roof over the front rooms? She was about to blow her horn, but stopped. What if MacGregor was there, too? Her attempt to help Marty could just as easily get them both in trouble. Suddenly her idea to drag Marty back to town wasn't sounding as good as it had earlier.

She turned off her engine and thought for a few minutes. The whole idea of going inside, unaware of whether Marty was in there or not, was becoming a bit frightening now that the building was staring back at her. It was raining pretty hard at that point. There was a good twenty yards of wet gravel and puddles between the gates and the front steps of the building. Going inside frightened is one thing; going inside frightened, wet, and cold was something else. The smart thing was to leave and wait to hear from Marty, but that idea quickly faded remembering what Clayton had said about his phone being dead. She put caution aside, determined not to leave without at least trying to convince him to return with her.

Before she could change her mind, Angela leaped out of the car, splashing her way to the moss-stained, marble steps ahead. She shook herself off at the top of the steps under the portico that sheltered the front entrance. One of the large, oak doors was still in place, the corroded vestige of a once-ornate knocker remained in the center panel. The other door had been ripped from its hinges long ago, left lying on the floor inside the foyer. Angela looked back at her car, then into the wide, dark foyer that led to the stairs. Safety was assured in one direction, uncertainty in the other. The wind picked up suddenly, helping her to make up her mind by pushing her into the asylum.

Rain, dripping from a thousand holes above in the domed ceiling onto the wooden floor and metal carcasses of the abandoned equipment, created a barrage of noise. Like the flash of a camera attempting to capture the spirit of long-forgotten residents, lightning illuminated the abandoned rooms she passed on either side of the foyer as she made her way to the stairs. Grotesque shadows were caught from the corners of her eyes, quickly dissolving into the peeling paint and mold on the walls when she turned for a closer look. Rodents scurried about behind her, darting from one dark corner to another, pausing only long enough for a glance at their visitor.

"Marty?" Angela called out when she reached the bottom of the stairs. She paused, waiting for a response, but only received the muffled echo from deep within the asylum. She tried again. The result was unchanged.

She was confronted again with two options, neither of which had a safety factor this time. Next to the stairs, through two swinging doors, a tiled hallway led deep into the asylum. Peering through an opening where only shards of glass remained around the edges, she could see piles of rubbish strewn as far down the hall as the limited light would allow her to see. She reasoned with herself that if she were unlikely to venture down that dilapidated hall, Marty would probably come to the same conclusion. Occasional flashes of lightning revealed beams that had broken through portions of the ceiling, hardening her resolve to move on to the second option—the stairs.

Angela called out once more. Still no response.

A dark pool of water had accumulated at the base of the staircase. Water cascaded down over the worn, marble stairs in streams from the hall above. With careful placement of each footstep, Angela slowly started up the wide staircase. One tug on the ornamental, iron railing proved it unworthy of any stability.

She moved to the center, taking one step at a time. With each step she paused, hoping a friendly face would peer out from one of the dark corners above. A sudden flash and a crack of thunder startled her. She reached for the railing, catching herself before throwing any weight onto it. She was half way up the staircase. Her heart pounded. This wasn't such a good idea at all. She looked back toward the door. Making a run for the car wasn't even an option any more. Water created a slippery surface on the marble stairs—anything more than a cautious step would surely result in an injury.

Angela took a deep breath and continued up the few remaining steps. The wooden floor creaked beneath her foot as she reached the top.

White, double doors on each side of an octagon reception area divided the second floor into two wards. On the far wall a large window, surprisingly intact, looked out over an interior courtyard. Through the double doors were wide halls, tiled three quarters of the way up, and stained a pale green from the moss clinging to the grout. Above the tile a foamy residue covered the surface of the plaster walls, the long forgotten color of paint chipped away by time collected in piles along the floor. The outer rooms of each ward looked out onto the grounds along the outside, forming the square shape of the asylum. The manicured lawns and gardens that once marked the perimeter were now nothing more than overgrown thickets of wild rose and ivy. The rooms on the interior looked down into the courtyard. It was a confined outdoor space perfectly suited for the unstable mental patients housed within its walls to enjoy fresh air and the warmth of the sun's rays on their faces. The crumbling remains of the imported Italian fountain Dr. Willis had placed in the center were all but recognizable, overgrown with weeds and despair.

Angela looked to the left. A large mass of rusted, metal gurneys and cane-backed wheelchairs blocked the doorway. WOMEN'S WARD could barely be made out on the rusted enamel sign above the double doors. To the right, things were somewhat more orderly. One door was missing, but the other was propped open with a heavy, oak chair. Just beyond was the pile of rubbish pictured in Marty's photograph. A chill went up her spine. She took a few steps further down the hall stopping in front of a doorway. She peered into the room where they found that young girl's body. The yellow police tape had been torn away from the door, dangling from the hinge it was tied to.

She took a few steps into the room. The gurney Jane Newcomb had been bound to still remained in the center. The small table stood by the window, but the police had taken the black candle and plate away. A foreboding wind rushed in through the broken panes of glass. It whooshed by Angela, tousling her hair, the dust sweeping up into her eyes. It was cold on her cheek. She squinted, holding her hand up in front of her eyes.

"Who's there?" she said, jerking her head around to a sound she heard in the hall.

The floorboards creaked. It was the same sound she heard when she gained the top of the stairs. "Marty, is that you?" She gave a start.

A dark figure blocked the doorway.

CHAPTER THIRTY-ONE

The faded, wooden sign over the door said, WILLIS WOOLEN MILL #4. It defiantly remained standing, the last of six mills that once stood in proud testimony to a thriving, woolen business. It had a frame of steel, with a pitched, glass roof. The sides were brick with large banks of steel-framed windows. Unlike other abandoned structures tucked away in the rolling hills of New England, this one was relatively untouched by the harsh grip of winter or the hands of the local vandals.

The weathered remains of a waterwheel were attached to the north side of the building. Through the dirt-encrusted windows you could see the shadow of the upper curve of the wheel once the sun peeked over the top at midday. The small river that had been diverted years ago still flowed beneath the deteriorated cedar paddles. For years it was the main source of power from spring to fall, turning the giant wheel, ever ready at a moments notice to power up the now-silent looms when needed.

Professor Jack Steedle was an art teacher at the local university. He was born and raised in Effingham, the next town over. The mill sat along the border of the two towns, close to Jack's home and a favorite spot of his growing up. He spent much of his youth exploring every inch of it, affording him ample fodder for his artistic development along with the assorted cuts and bruises that go along with poking around an abandoned factory. He often told his students how it was the driving force behind him becoming an artist. Through the years he filled one sketchbook after another with drawings of the old mill. After college he taught for a few years at the high school in town, finally taking a position with the university after getting his doctorate in art history. He made the mill part of his curriculum, taking groups of students out during each semester to do watercolor sketches. It quickly became the highlight of the class for his students and himself.

His students found him curiously particular about the time and setting of the excursions, opting for stormy days over bright sunny ones. On the day of such an outing, as they waited outside the main entrance to the mill for the last of his students to arrive, he detailed the contrast possible between the shadows cast by a violent sky as opposed to a bright-blue sky over inanimate objects, referring back to his own sketches and years of collected photos he used in class for examples. With great passion and a slight thespian flare, he would explain how they were about to step into a setting that will produce a dramatic visual sense of space combined with an inner feeling of uncertainty. The conflict between what your eyes see verses what your psyche has twisted the images before you into can have a defining impact on an artist's style. Painting in bright sunlight will produce a pleasant painting he would scoff, miming extravagant brushstrokes on an invisible canvas to the amusement of his students. Painting in the shadows of dubiety gives the artist and the painting's meaning a sharper edge. With the limited lighting of iridescent purples and deep oranges, an artist is left to rely on his inner artist and talent alone. Such an evening sky after a storm will last only ten to twenty minutes, so urgency adds one more level of difficulty. In what feels like the blink on an eye, it's finished. The brushes and paint are packed away, the sketchbook closed. He would insist the images ferment overnight, not allowing the true essence of the work to reveal itself until it is brought into the light of the classroom the following day. Only then will the artists understand their creations.

With the last two of his group of fourteen students arriving late, playfully chided by the others for missing Steedle's soliloquy on the inner artist, Jack took a key from his pocket and unlocked the chain wrapped around the thick, metal door handles. Years ago he purchased the chain and lock to secure the building. To his surprise, no one ever questioned or removed it, or even cared that he took ownership of the building's well-being by attaching them to the entrance doors.

The earlier storm had blown past, leaving behind a pale, gray sky gradating into a deep orange at the horizon as a reminder of its presence. Pools of water dotted the parking area like giant stepping-stones of color. The double doors creaked on their hinges, groaning from the weight as they swung open. The bank of windows along the east side and the glass roof high above the mill floor allowed enough light in to illuminate the interior. Long, trapezoid shadows from the steel framing stretched out along the deep-purple cement floor, disappearing into the odd corners and dark, secret places. Evening wasn't too far off, maybe an hour before they would find themselves in the dark. Jack instructed his group of students to find a place to set up as quickly as possible and create.

With tote bags filled with art supplies, and a couple students with folding easels resting on their shoulders, the group followed behind Jack like obedient ducklings. As large as it looked standing outside the building, it was cavernous inside. The metal bones of a dozen weaving machines ran down each side of the vast space. Above was a catwalk that crisscrossed the room, connecting different processes in the mill along elevated mezzanines running down the north and south walls. Long shafts, driven by the power generated from the waterwheel, ran beneath the catwalks. Wide, leather straps, now tattered and hanging limp from the transfer wheels above each station, transferred power to each of the weaving looms in the years past.

The Willis Mill, like most factories of this type in the early stages of the industrial revolution, ran on the gravity principal. The washing, picking, carding, and roving were done on the upper level. The wooden bobbins full of yarn were dropped down to the next level where the spinning, winding, and finishing took place. The paper cones of yarn were then dropped down to the weaving machines on the main floor. At the far end of the mill were two service elevators, flanked by large, roll-up doors with faded and chipped signs over them indicating SHIPPING and RECEIVING respectively. Looking down the length of the room, eerie, dark forms from the piles of carts, industrial bobbins, machinery, and furniture rose up from the wet floor. It was a blistered, rusted patch of forgotten prosperity. Animals, to soften their otherwise hard winter dens, had carried off whatever soft material might have been left behind after the mill's final days. What they now saw before them, as explained by Professor Steedle, was the debris field from more than a hundred and fifty years of history waiting to be captured by the artists' eyes.

Following his final suggestion to look for the untypical subject, he dispersed the group. By his calculations they had an hour of working time, ". . . or until the long rays of vibrant color were drawn back into the somber clouds from whence they burst forth," he remarked with a grand sweeping motion of his hand toward the heavens beyond the glass ceiling above.

Their assignment was to complete a rough watercolor study of any subject of their choosing. Each headed off in a different direction. Steedle, himself, took a familiar spot above on the catwalk facing the side entrance. It also gave him a pretty good vantage point to keep an eye on his students. He had no reason to expect they would run into any trouble, but they were in an abandoned building, so anything was possible. They were in his care, and he took that responsibility very seriously.

Lucy Anderson, a junior and part of the group Jack Steedle brought out to the mill, found it difficult to contain her enthusiasm about being there. She was a little more adventurous than some of the others. She opted to explore the lower level, venturing into the darker recesses of the mill. With her excitement leading the way, and her boyfriend Justin in tow, they quietly slipped away from the others. They made their way through grotesque metallic forms and deep purple shadows to the stairs between the dying vats. A flight of metal stairs snaked around in both directions—up to the catwalks and mezzanines or down to the boiler room.

"That's curious," Lucy whispered, squeezing her boyfriend's arm at the bottom of the stairs.

"What?"

"Look. Over there." Lucy pointed to the far end of the boiler room. "Doesn't that seem bright to you?"

"It's nothing, just a reflection of light from outside. I'll bet Steedle left his car lights on again. He's a great teacher, but a bit of a dork."

To the left of the staircase two wood-stoked boilers were encased in brick. Stoked and fired up when the river froze, they were the main source of power for the mill through the harsh winters. The immense drums of the Babcock and Wilcox boilers stood proud from the oxidized, cast-iron front plates. Below each were two fireboxes, their doors left agape after being cleaned out years ago for the last time. Winters continued to come, but another load of wood was never to be. With blackened steel stacks leading upward from the top of the boilers, they gave the appearance of locomotives bursting through the brick and mortar wall.

Cast-iron piping from the boilers ran overhead to a Rollins steam engine opposite the boilers. The scrap of a wide strip of leather remained draped over the top of the twelve-foot flywheel, the remaining pieces scattered on the dusty floor. Because of its size, a third of the flywheel disappeared below floor level allowing it to clear the rafters above by inches. The whole of the engine was encased in a rusty cloak of neglect. Only slight traces of green paint were evident on the pipe railing marking out the safety boundary, and the cross-head and connecting rod.

A rusted, narrow gauge track was embedded in the floor between the steam engine and the boilers. A small, steel hopper car rested on the tracks in front of Boiler #2. At the north end of the track a raised, granite platform ran parallel to the lower track, protruding out from the wall eight feet or so. The platform had the same gauge track mounted on top with a bumping post at the near end. At the far end of the platform, stored in a sheltered area beyond a heavy, steel door suspended on rollers, train loads of wood for the boilers were dumped and remained dry until needed. Rust dissolved most of the black enamel on the door, leaving only traces of the color on the frame around the dirt-encrusted window. The door was partially open, revealing beyond it the hopper used to transfer wood from the woodpile into the boiler room. The upper hopper would be filled in the wood room, pushed into the boiler room, and dumped into the lower hopper. The lower hopper would then be pushed and unloaded in front of the boilers. It was hard, dirty work and an endless daylong cycle. But on a frostbitten February day in New England, it was the warmest place in the mill, so I doubt anyone complained much.

Along the east side of the mill ran a railroad siding to service the shipping docks at the north end. A spur led to the sheltered overhang in front of the boiler room, allowing for train cars of wood to be dumped within easy access to the men working the boilers. The walls of the boiler room were part of the stone foundation, leaving it partially below ground level. There were two windows at eye level looking out into the sheltered area. The windows were towards the open end of the overhang, affording a view of the tracks and down the access road leading up to the mill.

Once Lucy's eyes adjusted to the dim condition of the room, she noticed where the additional light was coming from. It wasn't at all from outside. There was a black candle lit on the window ledge to the right of the sliding door. She put her tote bag down and carefully walked up the three worn, granite steps to the top of the platform.

"Be careful," Justin called out. "Don't fall off the edge. I'm not about to carry you up those stairs if you do."

"It's a candle," Lucy replied excitedly. "A lit candle." She waved her hand franticly for Justin to join her.

"What?"

"Get over here," she barked. "I'll bet Steedle set this up to spook us. Dork."

Lucy was so mesmerized by the candle, she hadn't noticed the solitary form laid out on a steel plate on top of the hopper on the platform behind her.

"What's that?" asked Justin, pointing toward the hopper as he climbed the steps.

Lucy turned, leaning in the direction Justin was pointing. She couldn't quite make out what it was, her body was blocking the light. She took a few steps closer, moving to the side as she did. The light from the candle fell across the form. In an instant Lucy knew what they were looking at. An instant later, and she knew *who* they were looking at.

A horrifying scream echoed up the stairs.

Steedle jumped to his feet before a second scream sliced through the darkness, racing down the staircase from his perch. He recognized the voice. "Lucy!" Steedle called out desperately. "Lucy! Where are you?"

A few of the other students were already standing by the staircase on the main level, too scared to venture any further. They clung tightly to each other, leaning over the rail, looking down into the boiler room. Steedle waved them away from the stairs as he darted past them, following the beam from his flashlight as he continued down to the lower level and the source of the screams. At the bottom he aimed his flashlight into the center of the room, the light reflecting off the wet surfaces, finally falling across Justin. He had his arm around Lucy. They were running towards him. Lucy was crying uncontrollably, her head buried in Justin's sweater.

"Over there," Justin panted, pointing in the direction of the light. "She's dead. I think she's dead."

CHAPTER THIRTY-TWO

All remnants of the brilliant hues of orange and purple left in the wake of the earlier rain had dissolved by the time the sun set behind the tree line defining the rise on the edge of Miller's field. It was a large parcel of land on the opposite side of the stream from the Willis Mill. The dim light from the stars and the moon peeking out through the wispy trail of clouds reflected on top of the gently moving water, gradating from black to a star-cluttered blue.

The students were clustered close together in front of where their cars were parked just passed the first set of windows. Jack Steedle was talking with Lucy, who was sitting on the hood of his car, when he noticed the lights of the sheriff's SUV coming around the bend.

Sheriff Flynn and Hank made their way up the access road to the mill, stopping by the entrance to the main building. Jack walked over as Sheriff Flynn got out of the patrol car.

"Is everybody in your group okay, Jack?" asked Flynn, looking over at the group huddled by the cars. Flynn understood Steedle's attachment with the old mill, but she's never been a fan of him bringing students there.

Jack nodded, shaking the sheriff's hand. "I think so. Lucy's caught the worst of it, I'm afraid. She's pretty shook up. It's not a pretty sight down there. I'd like to take her home if it's okay with you?"

"Sure." Sheriff Flynn glanced down the gravel road, then back at Jack. "This place is going to be crawling with FBI agents soon. They can be a little intimidating if not downright insensitive. There's no reason for Lucy or any of your group to be subjected to their questions in the state they're in. I'll assure the agents your group had nothing to do with this, just wrong place at the wrong time. I can catch up with Lucy at the Rocket tomorrow if I need to. Why don't you get your group out of here?"

"Thanks, Sheriff."

Jack turned to walk back to his students.

"You know," said Flynn taking his arm, "it's one thing you being in that old mill, but taking those kids in—"

155

"I know," Jack interrupted, shame-faced. "It's just that—"

Sheriff Flynn released his arm. Her official stare eased into a forgiving smile. "I know, all in the name of art, right? Before you go, did you or any of the kids see anything unusual? Were there any other vehicles around when you pulled up?"

Jack started to shake his head, but stopped. "Now that you mention it, I passed a car out on Rt. 4. Late-model, foreign car, I think. I didn't pay it any mind until I turned onto the access road to the mill."

"Why's that?"

"The dust was all stirred up as if a car just came down the road. Shit, do you think it was the murderer?"

"Probably just the wind," Hank said, joining them. He handed Sheriff Flynn one of the flashlights he pulled from the trunk. The look in each other's eyes confirmed they both knew it wasn't the wind.

"I'm sure Hank's right," added Flynn. "Don't let it bother you. Anything else you can think of?"

Jack was preoccupied looking down the access road. It took a minute before he answered. He turned and pointed towards the side of the building. "There was a light. I saw a light in the window over there. I guess it was the candle? I thought it was the reflection from my headlights as we pulled up. That poor woman. I should have done—"

"There's nothing you could have done," cautioned Flynn, intercepting his unwarranted guilt. "Be thankful you didn't arrive earlier. No telling what these guys are capable of."

Steedle nodded. "I should go."

"You said on the phone she's in the boiler room?" Hank confirmed.

"Yes. Lower level. Take the stairs by the dying vats."

Sheriff Flynn nodded toward the group of students. "Go on, get out of here, and get those kids home. You've all been through enough tonight. If you remember anything else, just make a note of it. I'll have Hank find you tomorrow to get a full statement."

Jack Steedle nodded and walked away. Lucy appeared much calmer, or at least she had stopped crying. Jack hustled the kids into their cars. The small caravan made its way down the gravel road back towards the highway and the normalness of town.

"Late model, foreign?" said Hank as they watched the cars disappear around the bend. "Councilwoman Johnson has a Mercedes."

"Yeah, I think Jack was right. I'm just glad they got here after the murder. This could have been a lot worse. A lot worse."

"You know, MacGregor isn't going to be happy you let those kids go before he could talk to them."

"It won't be the first time I've caught flack from the feds." Flynn gave Hank's arm a nudge with her elbow, turned, and started toward the door of the mill. "Besides, who said there were any kids here? Let's take a look inside."

"This place is nasty," said Hank, shining his flashlight from one dark form to the next as he and Flynn walked through the doors. "Dirt. Cobwebs. I don't know what that is. What kind of art can you get from this?"

Flynn laughed. "That's why we're cops, not artists. Over there. Those must be the stairs."

"Should we call MacGregor?"

"He has a way of just showing up at our crime scenes. Let's take a look first, then we'll call Mac if he isn't here by then."

Hank and the sheriff walked carefully down the stairs leading to the boiler room. Across the room they could see the candle. It remained lit. Someone had used their hand or sleeve to clean off the dirt in the center of the pane. It's why the candle was so visible from the access road. The flame flickered in the slight breeze their movements produced, reflecting back into the room, casting an amber glow on Councilwoman Johnson's blond hair.

"This is just getting nastier by the minute," mumbled Hank, stepping onto the wet, cement floor, following behind Flynn. He moved towards the platform. Reaching up, he wedged his flashlight between two pipes, shining the beam down on the body. "These guys are sick."

Councilwoman Johnson's eyes were open, staring up toward the flashlight. Her mouth was agape, the final plea for mercy frozen in her expression. There was a bluish hue to her cheeks, and her light-blue eyes added to her ghostly appearance. A dark streak of blood stained the curled hair behind her left ear, the result of a blow to the back of the head like the other two victims. Unlike Jane Newcomb and Mark Warren, there were ligature marks on her wrists and ankles. She must have regained consciousness at some point and struggled to free herself. This was not a pleasant death by any means. Alice Johnson did not go quietly.

Flynn walked up the stairs onto the platform, scanning the area beneath the hopper with her flashlight. She pushed the dust around with the toe of her boot. No need to taste it, she was certain it was ash. The beam caught a shiny object on the floor below next to the platform. It was in one of the recessed tracks.

"What's that?" asked Flynn, pointing with her flashlight.

Hank followed the beam of light down. With his latex gloves on, he cautiously picked the object out of the recess. "It's a clamp. One of those spring clamps you get at the hardware store. Looks pretty new."

Flynn held her hand up for silence, turning her attention to a sound she heard coming from the floor above. She looked back at Hank. "Can you get a quick picture of that with your phone?"

"Sure."

"No flash. Just put it in the light and get the shot."

No sooner had Hank taken the picture and returned the clamp to its resting place when a stampede of agents thundered down the stairs. Leading the charge was MacGregor.

"This is your fault," Flynn barked, not giving MacGregor a minute to assess the situation. She jumped down from the platform, stormed over to MacGregor, and began tapping her finger into his chest. "You did this. That poor woman is lying there because you dragged your feet with this investigation. She was a friend. She didn't deserve this."

Hank and Macgregor drew the same look of surprise over the outburst; the difference being, inwardly, Hank was cheering his boss on.

"Calm down, Sheriff. Calm down." MacGregor looked around to his agents. "Can you give the sheriff and I a few minutes please? Get our ME out here right away. The rest of you check the first floor and the grounds for tire tracks and any signs of Clayton."

"I knew it. You knew it was—"

MacGregor raised his hand and a pugnacious stare, cutting off her tirade. He pointed at Hank and jerked his thumb in the direction of the agents moving up the stairs.

Hank looked over at the sheriff.

Flynn shook her head and turned towards MacGregor. "He stays. I don't care what kind of weight your badge can throw around here, I'm done letting you boss us around."

"Fine," MacGregor griped. "You two want in? You're in." He walked over to Promise, took her by the arm, and leaned in close to her ear. "I'm just trying to protect you. I know what happened to you in Chicago. If it comes to it, I need to know you won't freeze."

Flynn yanked her arm free, taking a step back. "I don't need you running interference for me. I'm fine." Flynn had more to say on the subject, but MacGregor wasn't in the mood. He threw up both of his hands, turned, and walked up the few stairs to the granite platform where the body of Councilwoman Johnson lay motionless atop the hopper.

Sheriff Flynn followed behind, not about to be dismissed so callously. She took her place around the opposite side of the body from MacGregor. Hank was content to lean on the railing leading up the stairs—never step between two snarling dogs.

"I wasn't finished," Flynn bitched.

MacGregor didn't respond.

"You knew it was Clayton behind this all along, didn't you?" Flynn asked looking across the body at MacGregor. Her chiseled brow held her eyes in a determined stare. "You knew all along Clayton was one of them and did nothing."

There was no putting this off. "That's not true, Sheriff. There are other circumstances I've had to take into consideration. Despite what feelings you may harbor to the contrary, I'm as surprised and upset about this woman's death as you are."

"Well, that's not doing her much good now, is it?"

MacGregor didn't have an answer for that. Instead, he posed a question of his own. "Aren't you the least bit curious how my men and I ended up here?"

It was Flynn's turn not to answer. The two were locked in a staring contest, and Flynn wasn't about to blink first.

"I am," Hank responded, cautiously breaking the silence.

MacGregor blinked first. He began pacing in front of the hopper, finally walking over and leaning against the steel door. "We've been following Clayton since last night. I'm certain he's one of the two men we're looking for. Bringing in one without the other doesn't stop this. We need them both, otherwise who's to say his partner won't just strike out on his own?"

"Wait a minute," Sheriff Flynn interrupted. "Now you believe there are two of them?"

MacGregor thought for a minute. "A few days ago I would have said no, but in light of the recent circumstances I think it's highly probable. Clayton's a stooge. I don't believe he's capable of masterminding all these murders. Someone else is pulling the strings."

"Well, at least we finally agree on something," replied Flynn, the Irish beginning to drain from her face.

Mac's stern countenance softened. "I don't want to take a chance and arrest Clayton unless we're absolutely sure he isn't working with someone else. If he is, and we spook him, this other guy will just get another chump and start again in some other city. I know we both want this to be over."

Flynn looked over at Alice's body and shook her head. "At what cost?"

"Believe me, I'm sorry about Councilwoman Johnson. I never thought this—"

"I know," Flynn replied softly. She took a deep breath. "Okay. Tell me how you figured out something was going on here."

"Like I said, I've had a man on Clayton since last night. We saw him talking to Angela Pierce this morning, and then he went back to the motel."

"Angela? I hope you—"

"Yes, yes. I've had a man on her since they talked. She's perfectly safe."

Flynn wasn't overly convinced, but she accepted his assurance for the time being.

MacGregor continued. "Clayton parked his car in front of the cabin and went inside. About eleven thirty he got in the car and headed back towards town. I told my man to wait at the motel and I'd have another agent pick him up at the crossroad. Clayton came into town, went into the hardware store, came out with a small bag, and just sat in his car reading a newspaper."

Hank shined his light down on the spring clamp in the recess of the tracks. "I don't suppose he bought a few of those?"

MacGregor nodded his head. "Yes, the clerk at the counter said he purchased six clamps and a plastic tarp. We figured they were getting ready to strike again."

"That's what we thought, too," Hank chimed him. "Clayton had two CO_2 fire extinguishers in a bag back at the motel."

"What do they have to do with anything?" MacGregor argued, but was quickly stopped by Flynn's raised hand.

"It's how these guys are making their dry ice," Hank smugly continued. "If you discharge those extinguishers into a canvas bag, the resulting effect is the formation of dry ice. It has the consistency of snow, but just as lethal if you have enough. You put it in a confined space with your unconscious victim and that's it. It dissipates quickly, so it makes sense they're making it at the crime scenes. It leaves no residue either."

Flynn smiled, like a proud parent. "That explains the fire extinguisher in the pile of rubble at the asylum. I just thought it was from putting out fires those kids were starting on the second floor. Good work, Hank."

"You've gotta love Google."

"That's pretty good police work, son," MacGregor remarked, jotting down a note in his book. "I'll send an agent over to the asylum. If that extinguisher is still there, maybe we can tie it to Clayton or his accomplice." He put his notebook away.

"You still didn't explain how you got here," said Flynn.

"I had an agent in town watching Clayton. Clayton sat on the bench in front of the bowling alley reading a paper for an hour. Without warning, Clayton put the newspaper down, went down the alley to his car, and started out of town. That was just after noon. My agent followed him to Rt. 93 where he made a left. He radioed to the agent we had stationed at the motel that Clayton was on the way. He never made it there. Best we can figure is he spotted the tail, doubled back after the first agent dropped off. It was only about an hour ago we found his car behind the minimart out on 16. The clerk inside said a guy fitting Clayton's description was sitting at the table talking with a 'fat woman' and then they left together in her car." MacGregor gave a nod towards the body. "We got the name from her charge slip. One of my men tracked down her assistant, Lori Sterns. Apparently, at some point Johnson called Sterns all excited about a deal on this property. Said she was coming out here with a Mr. Habberset and would call her when she got back to town. That was the last she heard from her. She gave us a description of her car. Look, Sheriff, we came out here hoping to be in time. I didn't want any of this to happen."

"Well," remarked Flynn, "he knows we're on to him now. That's not going to help Sam Martin at all. We still haven't located him, and they have no use for a fall guy any more. He may already be dead."

"Well, I can give you some good news there," said MacGregor through a calm sigh. "The agent I put on Angela followed her to the old asylum. It seems Sam Martin was also following her, despite the orders he was given to stay out of sight by FBI Agent MacGregor."

"*You* had him hidden?" Flynn's Irish was beginning to rise again.

"Take it easy, Promise. It was either Clayton or his partner masquerading as me. He gave Martin some story to get him out of town and out of sight. I presume until they finished with the forth victim. Fall guy, remember? They had to keep him alive, they were setting him up for the murders. Lucky for us he's in love with that girl. It was a bit touchy there for a moment. My agent almost shot him when he jumped out of the shadows at the old asylum. He thought my agent was there to harm her. Fortunately, Miss Pierce shouted out his name. They're both at Angela's house with two of my best agents."

"We still have a big problem," Hank chimed in. "Just because we think they know we're on to them, doesn't mean they'll stop. This woman is number three, and we're no closer to how they choose their victims. If they're just random, number four could be anybody."

"I don't think so," replied Flynn. "I think Clayton was waiting in town for Councilwoman Johnson to go by. That's why he was just sitting there reading the paper. I think they knew exactly who their victims were going to be before they even got to town. I just don't know the how or why yet."

The conversation was sidelined by the sound of heavy footfalls coming down the metal stairs. It was a tall man with a medical bag in one hand and a flashlight in the other illuminating the stair treads in front of him as he walked down.

MacGregor waved his hand. "Over here, Walsh. I'll get some of the boys to bring lights down for you." He looked at Flynn, giving a nod it was time to leave the scene to the ME. "Why don't you, I, and your deputy continue this conversation over at that motel on 93. I don't think Clayton or his partner will be going back there, so we might as well see what he left behind. Maybe we can get an insight into who the forth victim is. I'll be honest, at this point I'm not holding out much hope. I've gotten almost this close before and lost them."

"Yes, but you have a name now and a description of at least one of them," Flynn argued. "Any anonymity they were able to hide behind before is gone. You think there's any chance they'll forget the fourth victim and leave?"

"Smart money said they should have done that instead of this." MacGregor pointed to the body. "I have to assume they'll stick to their previous agenda, take care of the next victim quickly, and get as far away from here as possible. We need to find them before that happens."

Flynn looked around. Hank was gone.

"Hank?" Flynn called out into the darkness. "You out there?"

There was silence for a moment. A dark silhouette emerged from behind the staircase. "There's two of them," Hank called out.

"Two of what?" said MacGregor and Flynn in unison, squinting to get a better look at what Hank was holding in his hands.

"Fire extinguishers! They tossed them under the stairs. This is a break."

"How so?" replied MacGregor.

Hank put the extinguishers down on the platform next to the hopper. "These look like the ones we saw in the bag back at the motel. They used both of these on Mrs. Johnson. That means they have to get another one before they can kill the next victim. It might buy us some time."

MacGregor patted Hank on his shoulder. "Let's just hope you're right."

"Why don't we get out to the motel?" suggested Flynn. "There has to be something there."

Mac paused for a moment, looking over at the body. "I changed my mind. I think I'm going to stick around here for a while. I'll call my agent out at the motel and let him know you're on the way. Keep me posted. I still want my men to go over the cabin, but you take a look and see if there is anything that makes any sense of all this. I'll dedicate my resources to locating that Mercedes and processing this place. I'll also stop and check in on Angela and Sam when we're done here. I was actually on my way there when all this hit the fan. We can touch base later back in your office?"

Sheriff Flynn shook her head, nodding toward the stairs for Hank to follow.

"Sheriff?" MacGregor said before Flynn stepped away. "You didn't say what you were doing here."

Sheriff Flynn smiled. "No, I didn't. I'll see you back at the office."

CHAPTER THIRTY-THREE

The Manchester Airport has been enjoying a steady growth for some time. Twenty-five years ago it was nothing more than a regional landing field without a tower. Local pilots used it on bright, summer weekend days, keeping their planes tethered in the grassy field next to the asphalt runway, or in the handful of rickety, wooden hangers that lined the north side. A sky once filled with the humming of single engine Beachcrafts and Cessnas has been replaced with the roar of regional jets. A recent renovation added a third runway and doubled the terminal space. Four multi-story car parks were built in line across from the terminal, housing the usual car rental booths and rows of assorted rental cars at ground level. Four car parks were ambitious and in consideration of future growth, but were largely unused above the second level for the time being.

Five cars were spread out between seven spaces half way down the aisle on level three. Bob Clayton looked around from between two of them. Satisfied they were alone, he yanked the Slim Jim up to unlock the car, he couldn't help reflecting on how different the place looked from the last time he was there. He was in a constant struggle to forget everything about New England, but he carried with him a constant reminder of the tragic events that brought him there so many years ago. With the door open, he pushed the button for the trunk.

"I don't like th–this," he grumbled. "I don't like this one b–bit. You're going to g–get us both caught, and for what? Just so you can s–say you outwitted that sheriff?" His discomfort with the situation went unacknowledged. He brushed off his coat and closed the door. "Th–this has gotten out of hand. I w–won't do it any more. Do you hear me? I'm th–through."

"Who are you talking to, dude?"

Clayton had walked around to the back of the car. He was about to toss the Slim Jim into the trunk when a pimply voice from behind startled him. He turned. A young man with a backpack over one shoulder stood ten feet away from him, balancing on his toes, attempting to get a look inside the trunk.

Clayton quickly slammed the trunk shut. The nervousness left his face, dissolving into a determined stare. "My brother," he replied, his voice inviting but course and tinged with a purpose. "He thinks I should trade this old car in. Too many problems." Clayton slipped his hand into his pocket, gripping the neoprene handle of the knife he had with him. "He's right over there. Would you like to meet him?"

Clayton took a step forward. Just then a car honked. The appearance of a white minivan startled him. It had pulled out of a space near the ramp. A second honk followed. A woman in the driver's seat waved out the window.

"You're creepy, dude," the teen mumbled, running off and hopping into the van.

Clayton watched as the minivan turned onto the spiral ramp leading down to the lower levels and the exit. He closed his eyes tightly, rubbing his temples roughly with the tips of his fingers. Beads of sweat were running off his furrowed brow and down the sides of his face. His usual nervousness was elevated up a notch. It reached a point of obvious disturbance. His breathing was deep, his heart pounding. He leaned against the car, catching his breath. "Y–you were going to k–kill that boy, weren't you?"

No response.

Clayton looked over the tops of the cars making sure no one else was lurking around. He reached into the car once again, pushing the button for the trunk. After one last glance around the level, Clayton cautiously opened the trunk half way. He walked over to Alice Johnson's Mercedes they had parked in the next space and opened the trunk. Inside, bound with duck tape, was an unconscious Hugh Calder. He shoved his arms under Calder's armpits, yanking him up and out of the trunk. In one fluid motion, he flung him into the trunk of the other car, tossing the Slim Jim in afterwards and slamming the trunk shut. He walked around and was about to get into the drivers seat, but stopped. Something in the reflection in the side window of the car caught his attention.

"I'll drive. You need to get a grip on the situation. We have one thing left to do, and I'm not going to let you screw this up for me. Between that damn stutter and the look of guilt on your face, we wouldn't have a chance if the cops stopped us now."

Clayton looked back towards the trunk. "Wh–what about him?"

"We'll take care of him when we're done and move on. I promise."

CHAPTER THIRTY-FOUR

Sheriff Flynn knocked on the door of Cabin 4. No answer. She tried the door handle. It was unlocked. Both she and Hank had a hand on their revolvers standing on opposite sides of the doorway. Flynn gave a nod, and with a single motion she turned the handle and swung the door open. They waited a few seconds and then both peered inside.

The drawers in the dresser were open and empty, same for the small closet. The bedspread and sheets were disheveled. A pillow and blanket were stacked neatly on the small settee across from it. The rest of the room looked as if there had been a struggle of some sort. Nothing broken, just copies of the photos Clayton had showed Flynn earlier strewn about on the floor. One of the two chairs by the table near the window had been overturned. The trashcan by the bed had been knocked over, its contents spilled out onto the rug.

"What do you think?" asked Flynn as they entered.

"It looks like they left in a hurry."

Flynn walked over to the bathroom to have a look. The door was slightly ajar. She had her gun drawn, pointed towards the door. With her left hand she carefully pushed the door open. It creaked on its hinges as it swung into the room. The light above the mirror over the small porcelain sink washed over the pink, plastic tiles on the walls. A rhythmic drip from the faucet echoed her heartbeat. On the counter by the sink was a bottle of Pepto Bismol on its side, the remaining contents puddled beneath it, a few crumpled photo printouts, and the torn wrapper from the Irish Spring hand soap. A couple towels and a face cloth were in a ball on the vinyl-tile floor, with the empty box from a fresh tube of toothpaste. The trashcan was empty. She pulled back the shower curtain. Her breath was instantly snatched away by a few words scrawled on the tile with a red Sharpie.

Hank's attention had been focused on the front room. "Hey, Sheriff," Hank called out. "Take a look at this."

No answer.

"Sheriff?" Hank called out again. Nothing. He stood up and walked over to the bathroom doorway. "What is it?"

Hank peered over Flynn's shoulder. He could see the tile wall in the shower. Written across the tiles were the words: NICE TO SEE YOU AGAIN, DETECTIVE.

Sheriff Flynn yanked the shower curtain closed, turned, and walked out to the main room.

"Looks like you were right," said Hank quietly, following behind Flynn.

Flynn holstered her revolver, sat down on the end of the bed, and rubbed her shoulder.

"Are you alright?" asked Hank after a minute or two of silence.

Flynn stood up and gave Hank a nod. "I will be. What's that? Have you found something?"

Hank held out a crumpled printout he had pulled from under the bed. "It's a screen grab of Sam Martin's Facebook page. There's a mention here about his upcoming trip to New York. The time stamp on the bottom shows it was from two weeks before Jane Newcomb disappeared."

As Flynn looked over the print out, they heard footsteps at the cabin door. In an instant their hands were back on the grips of their revolvers as they turned.

"Whoa, Sheriff, don't shoot."

John Mitchell peered in through the open door, almost dropping the black laptop he was holding.

"Sorry, John," Flynn exhaled. "What is it?"

John looked around the room. His expression was suggestive of an attempt to answer, but he couldn't get past the condition of the cabin to get a word out.

"John?" repeated Flynn. "What do you have there?"

He looked over with a blank stare for a second. "Sorry. I found this . . . well my son found this in the dumpster a little while ago. I don't know if it's important, but I thought I should give it to you."

Hank took the laptop from John. "Thanks. If we get lucky, maybe it belongs to Clayton."

Hank put the laptop down on the table and opened it.

"I think it does," said John. "My son said he saw the guy in Cabin 4 toss it into the dumpster from his car as he came around the back of the office. He just told me a few minutes ago. When I saw you and Hank here pull up, I figured you would want it."

Flynn smiled and gave a nod of appreciation. "Good work, John." She looked over at Hank who was concentrating on the laptop. "Well? Does it work?"

"It's dead, but it doesn't look like anything harmful was done to it. I'll take it home, charge it up, and see what's on it. Maybe we'll get lucky."

"Well, I'll get back to the office. Just lock up when you're done." John took one more look around the room and shook his head.

"Don't worry, John," Sheriff Flynn replied to the disappointed look on his face, "I'll ask Agent MacGregor to make sure his agents take special care and not damage the cabin when they process it. I'll let you know when they're done. Afterwards, get the place cleaned and give me the bill. I'll see that the FBI picks up the tab."

That wiped away the concern and brought the semblance of a smile back to John Mitchell's face. "I appreciate it, Sheriff."

"One more thing, John. Did your son notice if anyone else was in the car with Clayton?"

John thought for a moment, and then shook his head. "Well, he didn't say he saw anybody else, but I'll ask him. How's that?"

"Real good. Let me know one way or the other."

"Sure will, Sheriff." John left, closing the door behind him.

Hank closed the laptop. "He's either incredibly stupid, or he wants to get caught."

The sheriff had to think for a minute. "Oh, you mean Clayton. Yes, it doesn't make sense to go through all this trouble to arrange these murders and then leave your laptop behind in a dumpster where it could be found."

"Maybe he's looking to put an end to this. Maybe he's being forced to commit these crimes? He seemed pretty harmless that day he came into the office. More like a doofus, not a criminal mastermind."

"That's what I thought at first. He doesn't seem to fit the profile, at least not from what I remember from Chicago. That's really what's driving my belief there's two of them at work here." As she spoke, she caught a glimmer of something shiny sticking out from under one of the pillows. "What's that?"

Hank looked over in the direction of Flynn's fixed stare. He squinted his eyes trying to see what apparently the sheriff saw that he didn't. "Oh, I see it."

Hank reached over and pulled an FBI badge from under the pillow. He took a quick look, and then held it up for the sheriff to see.

"How about that. That's our boy Clayton on the ID card and Mac's name under it." Flynn took the leather wallet from Hank.

She walked over to the window for a little more light, taking a few minutes to study the photo. "It's Clayton alright, but there's something different about him. Look at the eyes."

Flynn handed the badge back to Hank. He looked again and confirmed the observation. "None of this is making any sense. These guys killed how many? Fifteen according to MacGregor? They're in and out of town in two weeks, lay low for six months, then move on to the next town and four more victims? All this is too well thought out. They set up a fall guy to keep the local cops busy. Change up their MO in each town so the murders don't seem linked to the murders in the other cities. No trace evidence, so none of the cops have any clue who they are. They do all this then suddenly get sloppy? I'm not buying it."

"You see it, too?"

"Yep. There has to be a link here somewhere that we're missing. There has to be something that ties Auburn Notch with Seattle, Chicago, and New York."

Sheriff Flynn rubbed her shoulder as she looked around the room. "I think you're right. I think we've been so focused on the victims here in town that we're missing the big picture."

"Exactly," replied Hank. He tapped on the laptop. "And with any luck the answer is in here."

Sheriff Flynn smiled. "And I know you're going to get to the bottom of it."

Hank shared the smile for a moment, but then a dark concern fell over his expression. He waved his hand out over the room. "What if all this was staged for our benefit? In each of the other cities they've had the cops chasing their tales. What if all this is just to send us off in the wrong direction?"

"It doesn't matter. We're not going to let anyone lead us around. You just take that laptop and see what it has to say."

"What are you going to do?"

"I'm going to call an old friend and cash in a favor."

Hank wasn't sure he understood, but nodded anyway.

"I'll also check in with Mac," Flynn continued, "and tell him what we found here. Once we get Clayton's picture out to the media, he won't have anywhere to hide."

"Do you think MacGregor will let you release his picture?"

"Screw MacGregor. By now those art students have tweeted every gory detail of that crime scene at the mill. I don't care if Mac has a problem with me releasing the picture. As far as the Auburn Notch Police Department is concerned, Clayton is a person of interest in the murder of Councilwoman Alice Johnson."

"Well, when you put it like that." Hank winked and thought for a moment. His countenance turned to a serious side. "You know, I didn't mean anything by it. I was just mad."

Flynn smiled. She had no problem figuring out what he was referring to. "I would be too if some nobody from out of town came in and took my job." She assumed a stern look, raised an eyebrow, placed her hands on her hips, and slowly drew out each of the following five words, "Burned-out, big-city detective?"

"Yeah, I'm sorry about that, too. I just—"

Flynn laughed, letting him off the hook. "Hey, I've been called worse. Now, let's get that picture of Clayton out and get this case wrapped up."

Hank nodded like a child offered a second lollipop. "Do we have a picture of him?"

Sheriff Flynn held up the FBI badge. "We do now."

Hank kicked something as he turned towards Flynn. He leaned down, pulling a small cardboard box from under the spindle-legged table next to the bed. He held it up, showing Flynn the printed label.

CANDLES, BLACK, QTY. 6

"Would you like another cup of coffee, Agent MacGregor?" asked Angela, getting up from the sofa.

"I'm fine, thanks. Please, relax and sit down. Call me Mac."

Angela smiled, agreeing to do just that. "I still can't believe all this. Not here. Not in Auburn Notch."

"I can't believe you went out to that asylum alone," Marty chimed in. "What were you thinking? This guy's a murderer. I couldn't live with myself if something had happened to you because of me."

"Me? You're the jackass that's been holed up in that creepy, old place instead of telling the sheriff everything that was going on."

Mac shook his head, amused by the arms-length profession of mutual love he was witnessing. "True love can be mightier than any known force in nature. You two should be glad you have each other and fess up to the feelings."

Both Angela and Sam turned red-faced to each other, and then at Mac.

"You can sort out the details later," Mac continued with a slight laugh, "for now I'm just glad I had an agent following you, Angela, and you're both safe. Sam, anything else you can tell me about the *other* Agent MacGregor?"

"I was getting a little suspicious about the guy. Something didn't seem right, especially for an FBI agent."

"In what way?"

Marty pulled something from his pocket. "For one thing, this crappy flip phone. What kind of an agent would use this?"

Mac laughed, taking the phone from Marty. "You're right about that. I'll have my people see if they can get anything from it. What else?"

"He brought me a couple sandwiches and a big bottle of Coke this morning. I watched out the back window of the asylum when he pulled around back. I thought he was coming right in, but he just sat in the car for about ten minutes."

"What was he doing?"

"Looked like he was arguing with somebody."

"Was anyone else in the car?"

"Not that I could see. I just figured he was talking to someone on his cell phone. When he came in, I asked him about it. You know, joking around about sitting in the car talking to himself. His face got real red, like he was mad. He calmed down pretty quickly and made a joke about it, but something didn't seem right."

"That was this morning? Are you sure?"

"Yeah. Around seven o'clock. Why?"

"No reason." MacGregor stood up. "What kind of car was it?"

"An Audi. Pretty sharp too."

"Did you get a plate number?"

Marty shook his head.

"Well, no matter. I'm going to leave an agent in the front and back tonight."

Angela took a quick breath. "Do you think he'll—?"

MacGregor raised his hand, and shook his head. "I don't believe you two have anything to worry about. Sam, it's going to be better if you stay here tonight and easier for my agents to keep an eye on you both. I'm leaving the agents here just as a precaution, that's all. We hope to have all this wrapped up and suspects in custody soon."

"Is that okay?" Sam asked Angela.

"Well, if it will keep us both safe I guess I can live with it."

Sam gave an appreciative nod, and then glanced back at MacGregor with a raised brow. "You said suspects? There's more than one?"

"This other Agent MacGregor," Mac replied. "What did he sound like?"

"Nothing special. Kind of a you're-in-trouble-with-the-principal voice."

"Did he stutter?"

"Stutter? No, why?"

"No reason." Mac tossed the flip phone up in the air a few times like it was a ball, then stuffed it into his pocket. "You know, son, Angela's right, you should have contacted the sheriff right away and told her what was going on. She's not going to be too happy with you."

"I was going to, but that agent said he would take care of her personally."

Mac's expression froze. "I've got to go. As soon as I have something I'll let you both know." He left them sitting on the sofa and walked away, pausing at the door and looking back. He could sense the confusion his abruptness caused. He softened his look. "Meantime, maybe you two should figure those feelings out before I get back?"

Mac whispered a final instruction to his agent at the door, gave Angela and Marty a nod, and closed the door as he left.

"Jeez, so that guy in the alley this morning was the guy impersonating agent MacGregor?" asked Angela, choosing not to focus on her feelings for the moment.

"I guess so," Marty responded, taking Angela's hand in his. "I don't even want to think about what he was up to. I'm just glad you're safe."

CHAPTER THIRTY-FIVE

Sheriff Flynn looked up from her breakfast to see Hank popping his head up and around the people standing at the counter at the Rocket Café. It was crowded, as it is most mornings, with people picking up breakfast orders and Danish trays. She waved, getting his attention.

"What's up?" Sheriff Flynn asked, as Hank sat down across from her in the small booth at the end of the aisle. He was a bit more animated than usual, so it was evident something got his attention. "What's going on?"

Hank had Clayton's laptop with him, and part of the Sunday Auburn Notch Monitor. He placed the folded newspaper down in front of Flynn, pointing to an article half way down the page. "Read that."

Flynn put her sausage and egg sandwich down and tilted the paper up. The headline and article read thus:

"Noted school official found dead in his home. Dr. William Fortnum, Head Master at the Owens Boarding School, an exclusive, private school just over the Acton, Maine, border from Sanford, was attacked and killed in his home early Friday. A concerned associate of Dr. Fortnum called the local Sanford, Maine, police to investigate his uncharacteristic absence from an important meeting on Saturday morning. His home, located on a small access road just off Hanson Ridge Road, showed no signs of forced entry.

"Sargent Kenny Hill, the investigating officer, stated the home had not been ransacked. It's believed Dr. Fortnum surprised a burglar in his home early Saturday morning. A search of the property produced evidence of blood and marks on the carpet consistent with a body being dragged. It appeared Dr. Fortnum was struck from behind with a bronze figurine in his kitchen, dragged to a leather chair in the study, where he was eventually strangled. A length of cord was found next to the chair.

"The late model Audi Dr. Fortnum was known to drive was also missing from the garage. An APB has been issued in the tri-state area in an attempt to locate the vehicle.

"Dr. Fortnum was a widower, having lost his wife, Anne, ten years earlier. They had no children . . ."

Flynn put the paper down, looking over at Hank. "Judging by the way you're fidgeting in your seat, there must be more to this story than I'm reading here?"

Hank tapped on the laptop. "It's all in here, every bit of it. It took a little bit to figure out his password, but once I did, you won't believe what I found."

"Hold that thought." Flynn waved over at Lucy who was at the counter with her father. "Mac's on his way here. Why don't you order something and wait until he gets here and fill us both in. It will also give me a chance to fill both you in on what I've dug up."

"Would you like more coffee, Sheriff?" asked Lucy. She had a bright expression, but there were still traces of what happened the previous day in her voice. Her father didn't want her back at work so quickly, but she insisted working at the café would help keep her mind off it.

"Yes, please. Hank, what would you like?" Flynn asked.

"Nothing, thanks, I ate earlier. I'm just on my way into the station to verify one last detail. If it's okay, I'll meet you and Mac back there and we can compare notes."

Lucy topped off Flynn's coffee and walked back over to the counter.

"Is she okay?" asked Hank.

"A lot braver than I was at her age. It'll take a little time, but I think she'll get over it. I spoke with Mac first thing this morning. He doesn't see any reason to question her about any of that business out at the mill. I told Burt, and he was relieved. He's going to keep a close eye on her."

"Well, that's a plus."

As Hank was getting up from his seat, MacGregor came walking down the aisle. He had a blue folder in his hand and a manila envelope. "Please, Deputy, sit back down, you'll want to hear this, too."

"If it's all the same, I've got a few things to follow up on. Shouldn't take long, so I told the sheriff I'd meet you both back at the station."

Mac gave a nod and slid into the booth. He held out the envelope. "Here. It's that information you asked me about the other day."

Hank took the envelope, gave an appreciative nod, and left.

"He's a good man, your deputy," said Mac, waving at Lucy.

Mac ordered the special with coffee. He went over the arrangements he had made concerning Sam and Angela's safety overnight as he waited for his breakfast. He touched on finding Councilwoman Johnson's car abandoned about a mile away from the old mill. His men found it late the night before stashed behind a road sign out on 16. They found a length of rope in the trunk with blood on it, and a canvas bag. The bag appeared to have been filled with soot or ash of some sort. Everything, including the evidence collected out at the old mill, was sent back to the field office in Manchester for analysis. Mac expected to have a preliminary report back by noon.

Lucy returned, placing the oval plate of eggs, sausage, and toast down in front of Mac.

"Thank you," Mac said through a bright smile.

Lucy returned the smile, picking up Flynn's empty plate.

Mac waited until she walked away. There was a fatherly look to his expression. "That's a terrible sight for a young girl to see. You think she'll be okay?"

Flynn looked back towards the counter, then at Mac. "So, the hard-nosed FBI agent has a gooey center. Don't worry, Lucy comes from good, New England stock. I'm sure she'll be just fine. Thanks again for keeping her out of your investigation."

"Not a problem, Promise." Mac pushed the blue folder towards Flynn. She finished putting cream and sugar in her coffee and took a quick glance in the folder as Mac continued. "Now, that's a rundown of all the victims we believe Clayton is responsible for. We think Seattle was the start, we just don't know why. Chicago came next, which I'm sure I don't need to tell you about. New York followed, and now here we are in Auburn Notch. There's also a report in there my people put together on Robert Clayton. He bounced from job to job for ten years before becoming a private eye. He did mostly keyhole peeping on cheating husbands, some bail-jumping work, and the usual young-girl-runs-off-with-the-shady-boyfriend missing person work. My people came up with one very interesting fact about Mr. Clayton. Bob Clayton had a connection to Auburn Notch."

"He did? That can't be a coincidence."

"That's what we thought." Mac took a few more bites, and then rested back into the booth as he continued. "Clayton's brother, John—or I should say his stepbrother—was once a resident of the Willis Asylum. It was twenty-seven years ago. His last name was Stevens, from his mother's first marriage. Not much else is known. Shortly before the asylum closed, about twenty-five years ago, there was a fire. All the records were lost, so any additional information about Stevens and the asylum went up in flames. Three months later there's a report about a suicide in Vermont. John Stevens hung himself, leaving a note behind about the murders at the asylum. The handwriting was a match."

Sheriff Flynn sat quietly for a few moments, digesting the facts with a couple swallows of coffee. "Anything in that file to indicate who Bob Clayton might be working with?"

"Not that we found."

Flynn could sense MacGregor was starting to ease back into his theory that Clayton has been working alone, but she still didn't buy it. "Think what you want, I know what I heard." Flynn pulled the leather ID wallet from her pocket and handed it to Mac. "Here, we found this in Clayton's hotel room along with the laptop you saw Hank holding."

Mac took the wallet, opened it, and shook his head. It confirmed something else, something he wasn't ready to tell Flynn. "This is a pretty good fake. You can get just about anything on the Internet these days. We shut one operation down, and two more open up." Mac tucked the wallet into his pocket.

"Angela and Sam? They're okay?"

"I saw them last night. I've got a couple agents watching over them until this is over."

"You think they're still in danger?"

"Nope, but I'd rather err on the cautious side." Mac stuffed a couple more bites into his mouth. "They really make a great breakfast here. I can see why this place is so popular."

Flynn agreed, sipping her coffee, watching Mac over the top of the cup she held in front of her with both hands. She knew Mac was beating around the bush about something, but was content to wait. He would get around to it soon enough. She was sure of that.

"So, how are you holding up, Promise?"

Mac only used her first name when delivering bad news. She answered between sips of coffee. "I'm good."

"How are those demons?"

Flynn put her cup down with a thud. "Come on, Mac, out with it."

MacGregor wiped his mouth with a napkin and settled back in the booth. "I've been chasing this guy—or these guys, as you believe—for a couple years now. Mostly off-book, but with my field manager's knowledge. I've been pretty accommodating allowing you and your deputy first shot at the evidence, but it's time for you to take a few steps back from the investigation. I saw the message on the tile in that shower. We'll take it from here. It's for your own safety."

"I don't understand," replied Flynn. She ignored the last remark. "Yesterday we're working together, today you sideline us. So someone leaves me a note. So what?

"Dr. Kaminski."

"Dr. Kaminski? The guy we were looking for in Chicago?"

"That's the one. I got a call this morning after we talked. A couple of joggers found his body bobbing in the water under the Randolph Street Bridge. From the agents on the scene, I'm told they believe he was weighted down with something. His ankles were tied together with a length of rope. They believe he's been in the water a long time. I mean a *long* time. We'll know more later, our ME has the body now."

"That's it?" Flynn huffed. "You're shutting us out of the investigation because you found a body in the Chicago River? There's lots of bodies in the Chicago River. What does that have to do with my safety?"

"Nothing." Mac looked around at the diners. These are good, strong people, but you can see in their faces the concern the events of the last two days have raised in them. You can hear in their whispers they know something is very wrong. So far the local newspaper was treating the deaths of Jane Newcomb and Mark Warren as separate incidents. That could all change once the details about Alice Johnson's death goes to print. These people weren't in a visible panic yet, but Mac knew that wasn't going to last too much longer once they realize there is a menacing threat tearing at the fabric of their town. "There's more to it than that, but why don't we go into it later at the office?"

Mac reached for his check, but Flynn was quick to snap it up and put it with hers. She pulled a twenty from her pocket and put it down on top of them. "You got the last one. Forget later. If you're done, why don't we go back over to the station now and get this all out in the open? Hank says he found something on Clayton's laptop. He was pretty excited about it. At least listen to what Hank found before you pull us off the investigation."

Mac didn't answer.

Flynn stood up. "You owe me that much."

Mac took another look around the room. "I'll listen, but don't get your hopes up."

CHAPTER THIRTY-SIX

Sheriff Flynn was settled in behind her desk, with MacGregor seated in one of the chairs on the opposite side. Flynn was still steaming about Mac's abrupt change in plans, but turned her attention to Hank. Mac sat quietly with his hands folded, waiting to hear what Hank was about to disclose.

Next to the desk Hank had rolled over a white board he dragged out of the meeting room where the borough council meets. There was a large printout of the photo of Bob Clayton taped top center. Below it, where a name would appear, was a length of wide, blue painter's tape. Next to the photo were a plus sign and a question mark in a circle drawn with a marker. The question mark was crossed out with red marker. Like an organizational chart, a line dropped down from Clayton to a picture of the Willis Asylum. Another line dropped down from there to a horizontal line, further dividing into four subsections. The subsections were labeled with the city names—SEATTLE, CHICAGO, NEW YORK, and AUBURN NOTCH. On the edge of the desk there was a pile of additional printouts and the open laptop from the motel. Hank was still unaware of what had transpired between the sheriff and Mac at the Rocket Café, and for the time being that's how Flynn wanted it.

"Looks like you've been busy, son," said Mac, looking over the board. "Let's see what you got."

Flynn gave Hank a nod.

Hank took a deep breath and started.

"The one thing that kept bothering me was there had to be some kind of a connection to all this. I thought maybe the victims, or the cities. Something had to tie this all together. Then I found it." Hank tapped on the photo of the Willis Asylum with the knuckle of his curled index finger. "This is the connection. It all comes back to the Willis Asylum twenty-five years ago."

"So you're saying our fifteen victims all had a connection to the asylum?" said Mac, a little disappointed in the direction of Hank's explanation. "Jane Newcomb was an infant at the time, son. I can't see how—"

"Let him finish," interrupted Flynn. "I think I see where he's going with this."

Mac conceded, raising both hands and resting back in his chair. "My mistake. Continue please, Deputy."

"It's not the victims, the fifteen people Clayton murdered—" Hank paused looking over at the sheriff. "You would have been sixteen, but . . . well, that doesn't matter. It's the three people who disappeared after the murders I looked at. The people the police were convinced committed the crimes in each of the cities. These people weren't random at all. They were Clayton's actual targets. By committing the other four murders in each city, then framing a specific individual in that city, he sent the police on a wild goose chase looking for them while he moved on to his next target."

Hank had a full head of steam and both Flynn and MacGregor's full attention.

Hank pulled a photo from the pile, taping it below SEATTLE. "This is Margaret Thompson. The Seattle police believe she murdered four people, and then took her own life. The details of the case say she was upset about being passed over for a promotion at the hospital where she worked. She blasted the hospital and the victims on her Facebook page the day the police found the fourth victim. When the police went to question her, they found her dead, hung herself from a doorway in her apartment. Along with information found on her computer, the police found pictures in her apartment and a note explaining why she did it. It was an open-and-shut case. They looked into her background, but the police decided it didn't mean a thing at the time. If you look at her previous employment record and put it together with the backgrounds of the other three victims, it means everything."

"Three victims?" Mac interrupted. "What do you mean three? Who's the—"

"Shut up, Mac," Flynn snarled. "Go ahead, Hank, continue."

Hank got right back into it. "Margaret Thompson started her career as a nurse at the Willis Asylum. She was there when Clayton's brother was a resident. She and John Stevens shared duties once he became a trustee and an orderly. It must have started out okay, but she became increasingly suspicious of injuries and bruises on the patients in their care. Margaret Thompson came forward when Stevens was named as a suspect in three suspicious deaths. An investigation was opened, but Stevens disappeared before the police could question him. Streak ahead twenty-some years. This woman had no previous record or signs of hostilities toward the people she worked with. She did post her disappointment about not getting the promotion a few weeks before the murders, but that was it. I believe the note they found in her apartment and the social media posts of that same day were planted by the killer to frame her."

Mac sat forward. Suddenly Hank's presentation was taking on a whole new meaning. He had his notebook out, jotting down quick notes as Hank continued.

Hank pulled a second photo from the pile, taping it below CHICAGO. He looked over at the sheriff, once again tapping the photo with his knuckle. "This is Dr. Samuel Kaminski. He was your main suspect in the Chicago murders. You even tied him to one of the murder scenes with an eyewitness."

"That's correct," Flynn interjected. "Someone saw his car parked close to where we found the third victim. They got his plate number."

"Correct," Hank continued. "The police found photos and assorted notes about the victims at his home in Oak Park, but he was long gone. They also found a medical report on his desk. He had been diagnosed with a brain tumor a few weeks earlier. They think that's what set him off. He had a regular daily routine at the local gym that kept him pretty fit. There was a note in the police report that all of the victim's were members of the same gym at some point. He was well known there—a miserable, old man to be around, most of the other members interviewed by the police said. A few even mentioned him having at least one run in with each of the victims, except one." Hank paused, looking over at Sheriff Flynn. She was lost in thought.

"Of course," Flynn mumbled under her breath. "I knew his face looked familiar at the time. That's why I knew the name." She looked at Mac. "I went to that same gym on a regular basis for a while. There were pictures of me on the bulletin board, and I mentioned the place a few times on my Facebook page. It had to be six months before the murders. I kind of remember Kaminski, but never spoke to him. Clayton must have figured that out and decided they better do something about me before I put the pieces together."

"I think you're right," agreed Hank. "At least that's what I think someone wanted the police to believe. I don't know whether the police told you, but they found a few pictures of you along with the other victims' photos in Kaminski's apartment. Those photos made you less random and more targeted like the others."

"I found that out later, after I got out of the hospital. I sat down one night with my partner and went over the facts. I kept insisting there were two men involved, but he said all the evidence pointed to Kaminski acting alone. He was certain the whack on the head and the trauma of the event was playing tricks on me. The murders just stopped, and they never found Kaminski. At that point, I was more concerned with putting the whole ordeal behind me and moving forward."

"Understandably," said Mac. He looked back at Hank. "By the way, we found Kaminski . . . or what's left of him. I told the sheriff over at the cafe, she'll fill you in later. Please continue. What's Kaminski's connection with the asylum?"

"Dr. Samuel Kaminski was the director of the asylum at the time John Stevens was there. Kaminski was the one responsible for starting the investigation into the suspicious deaths at the asylum. It was his investigation that pointed the finger at a specific person—a patient who Kaminski made a trustee and eventually hired on as an orderly. That patient was John Stevens. By the time the police were called in, Stevens must have figured out what was going on and just disappeared. It was three months later they found Stevens. He had hung himself in a cheap motel room in Vermont. There was a note detailing the murders, ending in his confession of the crimes. John's only family member was his stepbrother, Bob Clayton. Clayton identified the body for the police. It gets real interesting here, but I'll get back to that in a minute."

Hank pulled another photo from the pile, taping it below New York. "This is Roy Barnes, the missing suspect in the New York murders. Like the other two up here, he has a direct connection to the asylum also. At the time of the investigation into the suspicious deaths, he was a cook at the asylum. It was information and evidence he furnished to Kaminski that pointed him towards Stevens. About a week after Stevens disappeared, Barnes resigned and moved out of state. According to city records, about a year later Barnes shows up in New York City and opens a shop on 23rd Street. Streak ahead twenty-some years again. A series of murders take place in New York, and Barnes becomes a suspect. The police questioned Barnes because a neighbor in his building told police of his argument with one of the victims. They let him go because they had nothing solid to hold him on. They continue digging. Once the police connected the other victims with Barnes and his shop, the evidence against him was pretty convincing. They even got an anonymous tip about his possible involvement in the suspicious deaths at the Willis Asylum years earlier. Once again, the main suspect disappeared." Hank looked over at MacGregor. "There was a mention in the report about an FBI agent connecting the New York murders with murders in Chicago and Seattle, but when they couldn't place Barnes in either city at the times of the murders, it was dismissed. The police were convinced Barnes was their man, and he was acting alone. Then Hugh Calder jumps in and stirs the pot. Calder's not convinced at all Barnes had anything to do with the murders. He wrote a speculative article tying the New York murders with the Chicago and Seattle crimes. It was pretty scathing, pointing out the flaws in the NYPD's investigative skills. Calder was chastised for it in the media. Even his editor accused him of inciting a panic. It all but ruined him. Barnes never surfaced, and the case is still open."

Mac sat back in his chair, staring at the pictures on the board. "That's right. The big problem was Calder only had conjecture, and no tangible facts or leads. Everything he had came down to the black candles at the crime scenes. The Seattle, Chicago, and New York police found connections between their respective groups of victims and their killers, but nothing that would tie the three groups together. As far as they were concerned, they had each identified their respective killers, and that was that. The murders stopped. Even my people at the bureau thought I was wasting time chasing a ghost. I went off-book and started following up leads on my own time. You say all this is on that laptop?"

"Most of it, or at least the background on these three victims. There's years of data on that computer. All of this was well thought out. The way I see it, all three of these suspects share a similar background and are conveniently dead or missing. You can't get any more connected than that."

"And that last spot on the board, Auburn Notch?" said MacGregor pointing.

Hank pulled another picture from the pile and taped it in place. The action caught both MacGregor and Flynn by surprise.

Flynn bit her inside cheek, shaking her head. "I thought it was Sam Martin he was setting up for these murders? What does Calder have to do with the asylum?"

"For that matter," MacGregor chimed in, "what's Sam Martin have to do with the old asylum? He wasn't even born when Stevens was there."

"That's what was bothering me, too," replied Hank. "My theory is Sam Martin was just a victim of convenience. I think Auburn

Notch was the killer's final stop. He went to a lot of trouble to find the right person and coordinate his appearance at the bar where Jane Newcomb was last seen. I think Martin was originally the intended suspect for this group of murders, but things changed."

"In what way?" asked MacGregor.

"Sheriff Flynn changed everything," said Hank. "I think Clayton was genuinely surprised to find out his forth victim in Chicago was alive and well, and here in Auburn Notch. I think it completely threw his plans off. I also think for the first time since he started these revenge killings, he's realizing he's losing control of the situation. As a result, he no longer cares about Sam Martin. He knows we're on to him, so he has to scramble if he's going to finish what he started."

"And you really think this is his last group of killings?" asked MacGregor.

Hank nodded. He took an enlarged copy of the photo of Jane Newcomb and her friends in the bar Clayton left behind and handed it to Sheriff Flynn. He pulled this copy from the original he found on Clayton's computer. It wasn't cropped, so there was more background image. There was a face in the background just visible in the shadows. Hank had circled it with a grease pencil. "Who does that look like?"

"I'll be damned," said Flynn. She studied the photo for a minute and handed it to MacGregor.

"That's your boy, Calder." MacGregor handed the photo back to Hank. "What was he doing there? And, better still, why didn't he say anything?"

"Anything to protect his story," Flynn grimaced. "His showing up in Auburn Notch wasn't by chance, he knew there was something here."

Hank pulled a handful of copies of newspaper articles from the pile. "I'm not sure how it all sticks together, but Calder's articles show a pretty intimate knowledge of all the crime scenes in these cities."

MacGregor smiled. "That's pretty good police work, son. I tried to put Calder together with these murders a while ago, I just can't—"

"That's crazy," Flynn uttered with a snort. "You think he's Clayton's partner in all this? He's a bit slimy, but I don't make him for these murders." She thought for a moment. "You two think he's the guy pulling Clayton's strings?"

"I don't think he had anything to do with the murders," said Hank. He tapped his finger on the pile of articles. "I think he's being used to chronicle the events. Calder's been putting the pieces together, speculating as he's gone along. I think Calder's Chicago articles brought him to the attention of the real killer. It was Calder who proposed the idea of their being two men involved with the murders." Hank looked over at Sheriff Flynn. "It was Calder's article that said you were dead."

"He based the second-person theory on my account of my abduction. And his article said the fourth victim died of her wounds. There was no mention of me by name, or even that the victim was a police officer. That was the department's idea."

"That was done on my request," MacGregor interjected. "The police were closing in on Kaminski at the time. I wasn't completely convinced about his guilt, but I wanted the murders to stop. It was also the perfect opportunity to see if Calder's theory held water. If Calder was right, the fourth victim would be the last victim in Chicago, and the killer would move on. He did, so that's when I started to take a closer look at the suspects to see if there was some kind of a connection. I still couldn't put them or the cities together."

Hank nodded. "That's what I thought at first. If you look at the dates on Calder's articles about the Seattle murders, they were published *after* the Chicago murders. Someone had been using him to plant the seed of there being a serial tie to all the murders. That person gave him just enough information to keep the theory alive, the theory about there being two perps."

"So how did Sam Martin get pulled into all this?" asked Flynn.

Hank pulled a green folder from the bottom of the pile, handing it to Flynn. "Our killer's been stalking social media pages for the last year. From what I found, he did quite a bit of research before pinpointing the final two. Like I said, I believe Auburn Notch wasn't a random choice at all. He picked this place specifically. Once he found Sam Martin, it was settled. Next he needed to tie him together with Jane Newcomb with a little cyber stalking. There are screen grabs in that folder from Sam Martin and Jane Newcomb's social media pages and on-line calendars. From those postings, and postings their friends made, the killer was able to coordinate putting Jane Newcomb, Sam Martin, and Hugh Calder in Brooklyn, in the same place, at the same time. It was genius, really . . . but in a sick kinda way. I believe the job offer from Habberset was used to lure in Jane Newcomb. You can track a dozen separate postings between Sam Martin and his friend and Jane Newcomb and her friends that indicate they would probably be at the same bar in the city on the same night.

I'm sure Habberset's insistence on Jane Newcomb leaving immediately for the job prompted the farewell party at the bar. Once again, from a posting he knew the place was a favorite of Jane and her friends. He already knew Martin would be there from his friend's posting a week prior to the game of his intent to 'down a few cold ones,' at the same place after the game. We need to ask Calder how he ended up there. I'd put money on it being from another anonymous tip."

"It does corroborate Calder's account of why I found him in Brooklyn after the New York murders," Mac mumbled. "Wow, what's the odds of getting all three of them there at the same time? I wouldn't think that was even possible."

"Oh, it's possible," replied Hank, "especially when you consider all the events leading up to it were probably carefully coordinated by the killer."

"And you think Clayton did all this alone?" said Flynn.

Hank reluctantly nodded his head; not at all happy about having to dispute the one fact about the case Flynn has been clinging to. "But before I get to that, let me tell you what I just found out about Dr. Fortnum."

"Dr. Fortnum?" asked MacGregor.

Hank handed him the newspaper he had shown Flynn at the Rocket. "He was found dead yesterday afternoon in Sanford, Maine. It's not that far from here, so I thought it worth a quick conversation with the Sanford police. One lead they were following up on was an appointment Dr. Fortnum had with a commercial real estate developer on Friday morning. They found a notation in his daily planner on his desk with the name of the realtor. What was odd, there was a question mark in red next to the name."

"Let me guess," remarked Flynn. "Ronald Habberset?"

"Exactly. I told Sanford about our investigation. They'll keep us posted on any new developments they come up with."

MacGregor stood up. He recognized Habberset's name. He paced back and forth between Flynn and the white board. "So, you're saying this Fortnum has some kind of connection to the asylum and our deranged friend?"

"It wasn't Fortnum," replied Hank, "it was his wife, Mary. She was the activities director at the asylum. She also filed a complaint against John Stevens, believing he had something to do with a suspicious death. She was single then, Mary Henderson."

"So none of this is by chance? He's here to finish off the last person he blames for his brother's death?"

"Yep. It's possible Clayton didn't know about the death of Fortnum's wife until he confronted him. I don't know why he killed Fortnum. Maybe just angry he was cheated out of his last kill. It also makes it more important that we find him as soon as possible. I went through everything on that computer. There's no other connections between Clayton and any previous asylum employees at the time Stevens was there. I believe Mary Henderson was the last victim. Our bigger problem is he knows we're close. There's a good chance he'll just tie up lose ends and disappear again."

"Lose ends?" said Flynn.

Hank tapped on the picture of Calder on the board. "If this is it, he doesn't need a reporter any more."

Flynn took her mobile out and dialed a number. Calder's name came up on the screen. It rang, but went straight to voice mail. "No answer. He's a bit of a shit, but we need to find Calder and warn him."

"I agree," added MacGregor.

"Well, maybe we'll get lucky and they'll find the car," Flynn added.

"Oh, they found the car," Hank interjected. "It was in the long-term parking garage at Manchester Airport. Some woman called airport security. She said some guy was there acting suspicious."

"Did they find anything?"

"They found traces of blood in the trunk."

"I can't believe Clayton is capable of all this," MacGregor pondered. "He never seemed that sharp to me."

"It's not Clayton." Hank turned and pulled the blue tape from beneath the picture of Clayton. There was a name scribbled underneath, but it wasn't what Flynn and MacGregor expected.

"That's not possible," MacGregor insisted. "He's dead."

"That's what I thought, too," responded Hank. "They found someone dead in that motel room, and I believe it was Bob Clayton. I went back through the police report. The identification of Stevens was based on the handwriting match from the note and his stepbrother's identification of the body. The police had no reason to believe it wasn't him."

"So, what makes you think otherwise?" said MacGregor.

Hank pulled another photo from the folder and taped it up on the board next to the picture of Clayton. It was an enlargement of a picture of two men sitting on a bench in front of the Willis Asylum. Hank pointed to one of the men in the photo. He was wearing a Willis Asylum coat with a name stitched over the pocket. "This is the last known photo of John Stevens."

Mac and Promise instantly saw the resemblance. He was a little younger and a little thinner, but there was no mistaking the face. It was Bob Clayton.

"Where did you get that?" asked MacGregor.

Hank pointed over at the laptop. "It was in a folder with a bunch of other photos."

MacGregor could feel Flynn's eyes burning a hole in his temple. He casually glanced over at her. "What?"

Flynn rested back in her chair. "Hank, would you mind stepping out and closing the door behind you, please? I need to speak with MacGregor in private for a moment."

Hank nodded and started for the door.

MacGregor stopped him. "That's great work, son. When all this is over I just might steal you away from this town. I'm going to send a few agents over to see you. Would you mind going through this with them?"

"Sure." Hank looked over at Flynn. He took the manila envelope he had sitting by the laptop and handed it to Flynn. "You'll want to take a look at that."

She gave him a nod and watched as he left the office. After the door closed, Flynn looked over at Mac. "That boy just tied your case up in a nice little package. If you think I'm going to let you cut him out of this investigation you're crazy. I don't know what's going on, Mac, but—"

Mac raised his hand. "It's not Hank I'm worried about, it's you."

"Me?" Flynn's face tightened up, the Irish rising, her nostrils flaring.

"Hold on a minute before you bite my head off. This all goes back to something Sam Martin said last night."

"What did he say?"

"I was asking him why he didn't just come to you with what was going on. He said the other Agent MacGregor told him he was going to take care of you *personally*." Mac settled back in the chair. "You understand now why I'm taking you out of the equation?"

It took a minute, but her angry, drawn lips curled right up at the edges. She shook her head. "Soft, gooey center. Are all you FBI guys sentimental jerks, or just the ones in charge?"

"This isn't funny, Promise. After what you went through—"

"You know, Mac, I'm so tired of hearing that. Yes, it affected me. Pretty badly to tell you the truth, but I'm over it. The worse part wasn't what he did, it was not knowing *who* did it. Not having a face to put with that voice in my ear. I know who it is now. I know we can catch him." She leaned over the desk and pushed the intercom button on the phone. "Hank, can you get back in here please?" Flynn waited a moment.

Hank opened the door. "You want me?"

Flynn waved him in and over to the chair next to Mac. "Agent MacGregor thinks my life's in danger. He thinks I should be removed until he catches this guy. What do you think?"

Hank looked from one to the other, hoping it was rhetorical.

Mac let him off the hook. "Fine. I guess we've come this far together, no sense breaking up the band now. There's one stipulation, I want him alive."

Flynn and Hank shook their heads in agreement.

Flynn leaned in close over the desk. "Okay, Mac, what's our next move?"

CHAPTER THIRTY-SEVEN

"G–get out," Clayton said, stepping back from the car. He pointed his gun toward the trunk.

"You know, you won't get away with this, Clayton." Calder's hands were bound with duct tape behind his back, but his feet were free. He swung his legs out over the edge of the trunk. "If you expect me to get out of this trunk, you're going to have to help."

Clayton stretched his arm out, grabbing Calder by his shirt collar. He gave a yank and got him on his feet, then took a couple steps back.

Calder looked around. They were standing on the gravel driveway behind the old asylum. He shook his head and gave a nervous laugh. "I should have known a weasel like you had no imagination whatsoever. This is it? You kill me here, and then what?"

"Shut up. J–just shut up."

"You know, MacGregor and Flynn have this all figured out. There isn't anywhere you can hide. Why don't you just give yourself up? Well? What do you say, asshole? By now they know I'm missing, and this is the first place they'll look." Calder looked up at the asylum. "What a shit hole. I'm not going in there. I'll bet they're already on their way."

Calder felt a sudden crack on the back of his head. Everything went black as he dropped to the ground.

"No, Mr. Calder, they're not on their way here yet . . . but they will be as soon as I take care of a few minor details."

CHAPTER THIRTY-EIGHT

"You know, Promise, I've been more than tolerant with you about all this." Mayor Olson paced back and forth in front of Sheriff Flynn's desk, flailing his arms about as he mounted his protest. "This town wants answers, and they are looking to me to get to the bottom of all this. I don't care what that FBI agent says." He stopped, placing one hand on her desk and pointing to the headline on the newspaper in front of her. "Councilwoman Johnson, Promise! He killed Alice. The good people of Auburn Notch are scared. I'm scared. What are you doing about all this?"

"Please, Bob, have a seat." Sheriff Flynn waved him toward a chair behind him. "I've kept the newspapers up to date with as much information as I'm able to give them. The FBI is here in town looking into all this. We're working together, but it's their show. We've got leads, but nothing we can share without jeopardizing the investigation. We're close. Real close. I just need you to work with me and keep this town calm. I don't believe anyone else in town is in danger."

Mayor Olson slumped back into a chair, not hearing half of Promise's reassuring words. His eyes were red, fighting back tears. "He killed Alice, Promise," he quietly repeated. "My wife's best friend. She didn't deserve that."

"I know, Bob. Alice was my friend, too. We're dealing with a mentally unstable individual. I know what he's capable of. He's terrifying."

"You know who this monster is?"

"I'm afraid I do. And, what's worse, he knows me."

"What do you mean?" The mayor sat forward, almost slipping off the edge of the seat.

Before Flynn could answer, her mobile phone rang. She read the name on the screen and abruptly cut the mayor off. "I'm sorry, Bob, but I have to take this. When this is all over, I'll tell you the whole story." She tapped her phone and put it to her ear. "Hold on, Chuck."

The mayor settled back into his chair, not about to be dismissed without an answer.

"I'm sorry, Bob, we have to continue this later." Flynn pointed toward the door. "This is important, and it's a police matter."

"I don't give a shit about your phone call. The people in this town are what's important to me. They have a right—"

Sheriff Flynn was quick to cut the mayor off. She tapped the mute button on her phone, placing it down on the desk in front of her. "These people are important to me, too. And whether you give a shit or not, I'm taking this call. You say or do the wrong thing, and it could get someone killed. That'll be on your consciences. I told you before, I don't believe anyone else in Auburn Notch is in danger. Let it go. Get your emotions under control, and get out there and reassure your voters we're doing everything possible. You can fire my ass later, but right now I'm taking this call."

Mayor Bob Olson hasn't been scolded like that since grade school, a point he drove home with the stern look he shot back at Flynn as he stood up. "This isn't over, Sheriff, but your career here could be. I'll expect you in my office before the end of the day with a full account of what's been going on."

"I was coming over to see you anyway, Bob," replied Flynn, tossing the manila folder at him. "I had Hank pick up your buddy Carl a little while ago. He had some very interesting things to say about your term as president of the swim club."

All the color drained from Bob Olson's face as he pulled the report out of the envelope. He staggered back a few steps, dropping the report on the floor.

"I suggest you get your affairs in order. Think about coming clean on your own. I owe you that much."

Bob Olson didn't respond. He lowered his head, turned, and walked to the door.

Sheriff Flynn waited until the mayor closed the door behind him on his way out before picking up the phone. She tapped the mute button once more. "Okay, Chuck, what've you got?"

CHAPTER THIRTY-NINE

"MacGregor, is that you?" Flynn called out when she heard the station door close. Hank walked through the door of Flynn's office, plopping down in his usual seat across from her. "Just me. What's up? New developments?"

"You were right about who they found dead in that motel in Vermont years ago, and I was right about there being two of them involved with these murders."

Hank was surprised, as his expression revealed. "I was gone for an hour and a half, what did I miss?"

"Last night, after we left Clayton's cabin, I called my old partner in Chicago. I gave him a quick update on what was happening here and how we thought it tied together with what happened in Chicago. Something's been nagging at me about the Vermont suicide. I asked him to run down a few things for me. He was reluctant at first to get involved, thinking it was going to do me more harm than good. He remembers how that affected me. Since Kaminski's body surfaced, it tilted the argument in my favor. We left it at that he would think about it. He called me back about an hour ago."

"An hour ago?" Hank thought about the time for a moment. "When the mayor came in? I heard he walked out pale as a ghost. I take it he knows we picked up Carl?"

"He sure does. Hopefully he'll do the right thing and save himself the embarrassment of being escorted down here in cuffs."

"You think he will?"

Flynn shrugged her shoulders and breezed right into what she found out. "I had Williams dig through Kaminski's files that had been archived. When you said John Stevens was a patient of his, I figured the doc had to have some kind of file on him. Williams found it. It was pretty extensive. There was a picture in the file, along with detailed notes about his sessions with Stevens and employment at the asylum." Flynn handed Hank her phone. "He sent me this."

Hank took the phone, looking at the image on the screen. "Hey, that's Clayton . . . I mean Stevens. So I was right?"

"It looks that way. Flip to the next picture."

Hank followed along. The next picture was badly faded, but you could make out the features. "This looks a little like Stevens, too . . . but he also looks dead. Who is it?"

"That's Robert Clayton." The look on Hank's face brought a smile to Flynn's. "Confusing, isn't it? There's a pretty good family resemblance. It explains how he's been able to get away with impersonating him all these years. That photo is from the files at the Coroner's Office in Vermont. They dug it out at Williams's request and e-mailed the photo to him. It certainly clears up one murder. John Stevens killed his stepbrother and wrote the note confessing to the suspicious deaths at the asylum. It confirms your theory why the handwriting matched."

"So John Stevens is alive and well, and the real Bob Clayton has been dead for years?"

"That's about right."

Hank sat quietly for a moment, flipping back and forth between the two pictures. "Amazing. Kind of sloppy police work, wasn't it?"

"Remember, this was twenty-five years ago. No computers. No DNA matching. The crimes might have been the same back then, but solving them was a lot tougher. You get a confession and a positive ID on a suicide, what's left to investigate?"

"I didn't think of it like that." Hank handed the phone back to Flynn. "So they found Kaminski floating in the river. That just leaves Barnes. Any word on him?"

"I have a few thoughts on that," replied Flynn, settling back into her chair. "Before I forget, MacGregor called. He's on the way here and was pretty excited about something. While we wait, I'll give you a couple thoughts to chew on about Barnes. My whole theory revolves around Barnes and Stevens working together at the asylum. I think one or both were stealing from the patients. The ones who caught on suspiciously died before they could report them. Williams is chasing down family members of the patients to find out if anything was ever reported stolen. Boy, I'm going to owe him big time when this is done. We figure it's a long shot, but we'll see what he finds out. Until then, I've made a few inquiries myself, and I've started connecting the dots. You ready?"

"I'm all ears."

"We'll start back at the Willis Asylum twenty-five years ago. Here's what the police concluded based on the facts present at the time. There's a series of suspicious deaths at the asylum. Dr. Kaminski, acting on information from Mary Henderson and

Margaret Thompson, opens an investigation into the deaths. Everything points to John Stevens, a patient-turned-trustee at the asylum. When Kaminski gets the police involved, Stevens gets nervous and disappears. Over the next two months, Mary Henderson marries Fortnum and resigns, Margaret Thompson leaves to care for her ailing mother in Seattle, and Roy Barnes decides to leave for no apparent reason. The investigation escalates, with the asylum eventually closing as a result. One month later, the Vermont police find the dead body of John Stevens in a motel room, an apparent suicide. He leaves a note behind confessing to the crimes at the asylum and a number where his stepbrother can be reached. The police contact his stepbrother, who we now know was actually John Stevens. He gives a positive ID of the body. Case closed. Are you with me so far."

"So far, so good. So where does this go off the rails?"

"I think this story jumps the tracks from the point where John Stevens disappears from the asylum. Knowing the police are closing in, he goes into hiding with the help of his stepbrother. My instincts tell me Clayton knew all about the thefts and suspicious deaths at the asylum, but it would be tough to prove that now. Anyway, Stevens arranges to meet his stepbrother at that motel in Vermont. He kills him, writes the confession, and stages the would-be suicide. Stevens, now masquerading as Bob Clayton, the grieving stepbrother, identifies the body. Whether Barnes was in on it or not is something only Barnes can confirm. It just seems very coincidental they both show up in New York City. The new Bob Clayton, a quiet, timid man, becomes a private eye in Brooklyn, and Roy Barnes opens a health-food store in Manhattan.

"Fast forward twenty-three years. Margaret Thompson is in New York City for a medical convention. Williams ran her credit card history. Besides the hotel receipt, he found a receipt for an assortment of snacks from a natural foods store . . . wait for it . . . owned by Roy Barnes. Margaret Thompson had a peanut allergy."

"So you figure she recognized him? That's why he killed her?"

"It's hard to say for sure. I figure if she recognized him, she would have said something right away. It was almost eight months later she went on her alleged killing spree and took her own life. What I think is more probable is Barnes tells Stevens about Thompson, and something snapped inside him. I think that's when the other personality took over, and that's when all the murders started."

"Other personality?"

"According to Kaminski's records, he was treating Stevens for severe depression, but wasn't totally convinced that's all it was. With medication, he got it under control. I think that's why he made him a trustee and finally an employee. It gave him a chance to study Stevens more closely and on a daily basis. Stevens was there almost six years without incident. Then something changed. Kaminski's notes indicated Stevens had multiple episodes where he would lose awareness of hours and even days at a time. Then there was the stuttering. Kaminski continued regular sessions with Stevens. During the sessions, he documented two distinct personalities evolving. There was a timid Stevens who developed a stutter, and an aggressive Stevens who was calculated, articulate, and stutter free. The doctor's final notes indicated Kaminski was convinced Stevens suffered from DID. There was a note on one of the final pages in Stevens's file. Kaminski wrote and underlined —'Potential for homicidal acts.'"

"DID?"

"Dissociative identity disorder. It became a relatively popular diagnosis at the time for patients exhibiting multiple personalities. Somewhere inside John Stevens lurks a very dangerous alter identity. I believe Kaminski put that together with the suspicious deaths at the asylum and concluded Stevens unknowingly was committing attacks on fellow patients and finally murder. By then it was too late, Stevens disappears. The investigation continued, uncovering thefts, abuse, all sorts of terrible things I'm sure you've heard repeated over the years since you grew up here. The town was shocked and wanted to know how something like that could go on undetected. They got their answers once the police informed Kaminski and the board of Stevens's confession and his suicide. The investigation was closed, but the asylum never reopened."

"Unbelievable," muttered Hank, thinking aloud. "It would account for the two voices you heard. It makes sense, I guess. The only person not accounted for is Roy Barnes?"

"That's a mystery we'll save for another day. Right now, we have bigger issues."

"Like what happened during the twenty-some years between Stevens and Barnes returning to Brooklyn and the day Margaret Thompson walks into Barnes's shop?"

"Yep, that's one of them. Williams is passing this info on to the NYPD, suggesting they look into any unsolved disappearances in the general area of where Barnes had his shop and where Clayton lived. We're both convinced they're going to be able to solve a few of those cases."

"What else?"

Flynn picked up her phone, hitting the redial button. She put the phone on speaker.

This is Hugh Calder. Leave your message. If I think it's worth my time, I'll call you back.

Hank shook his head. "What a jackass."

"Jackass or not, we still need to do everything possible to locate him." Sheriff Flynn tapped the red disconnect button. "He's a reporter. Reporters always answer their phones. This isn't a good sign."

"I stopped over at the hotel earlier. His rental car is gone. I have the state boys looking for it. I had the maid open his room. His luggage is there, but no sign of him."

Flynn tapped her finger on the desk, staring off in thought. "We must be missing something. Stevens has no reason to continue this charade of framing someone else for the murders he's committing. He knows we're on to him. He'd be a fool to stick around here any longer than he absolutely had to. If he grabbed Calder, it has to be for a reason, but why?"

"You there, Promise?" a familiar voice called from the outer office.

"In here, Mac."

MacGregor walked in, waved his hand to indicate they were to follow him. "Come on, I've got someone you need to meet. He's outside." MacGregor started toward the door, with Hank and the sheriff right behind him. "Funny sort. He refuses to come inside. Said it reminds him too much of being here years ago."

"Who is it?" asked Flynn.

"My agents located and spoke with a patient who was in the asylum when John Stevens was there. He's been living in an assisted living facility in Concord for the last twenty years. They specialize in depression. Many of the Willis patients were transferred there when the asylum closed."

The three found themselves out on the sidewalk in front of the police station. It was a particularly bright, cloudless day. There was a park bench beneath the window of the station with one of MacGregor's agents standing a few feet away. Next to him was a female nurse. A very frail, older man sat quietly in the middle of the bench looking around, up and down the street. He had a worn, wool coat on, cinched up around his neck with one hand, dark trousers and plain, black loafers that were remarkably polished to a military shine. A frayed, white cuff peeked out from the sleeve of his coat. Wisps of thin, white hair rippled in the cool, afternoon breeze.

"Mr. Thurlow," MacGregor said softly, leaning down close to the man's face, "this is Sheriff Flynn and Deputy Harris. Would you mind telling them what you told my agent, please?"

Mr. Thurlow looked up at the sheriff, taking a labored breath. A slight smile came to his drawn face, fading back to an expressionless, pale gray stare as he exhaled. He looked back down the street and pointed toward the church steeple piercing the tree line above the rooftops. "They used to bring us to town on Sunday," he started, taking short, labored breaths between each sentence. "We sat in the back of the church. No sound. No sound at all. That was the rule. They gave us juice out back." He lowered his head. "Killed his brother. That's what he said. Killed him dead. Killed those others, too. Said it was almost over."

Sheriff Flynn sat down on the bench next to the old man. She took his free hand in hers and softly asked her question. "Who killed them? Who killed those others?"

The old man looked up at Hank then turned back towards Flynn, leaning close to her ear. "The orderly. He killed them."

"John Stevens?" Flynn whispered, leaning back to see his eyes.

The old man nodded. "Stevens. He killed them. Said only one left."

"Only one left?" replied Flynn patting his hand. "Who's left? Who did he say was left?"

The old man looked up into Flynn's eyes, his stare continued past her, disappearing into a time long gone. "No name. Said you would know."

Flynn gave his hand a final pat and went to stand up. The old man clutched her arm, pulling her back down. "He said you made his brother angry. Be careful."

The remark surprised Flynn and Hank. She looked up at MacGregor who nodded his head, and then looked back at the old man. "How do you know I made him angry?"

The old man leaned in close again, pulling something from his pocket as he spoke. "He gave me this. Said it was yours." He put the object in Flynn's hand. "Said I should give it to you. Only you. Said he tried to stop him. Said he was sorry." The old man paused, pointing at the Rocket Café. "Bought my shoes there. Nice people. Polish them every morning."

Flynn looked down at the object in her hand with surprise. "When did he give you this?"

"I keep them polished."

Flynn stroked the sleeve of the man's coarse, wool coat. "Thank you. I'll be careful. I promise."

The old man's smile returned once more, fading just as quickly behind a shallow exhale.

MacGregor nodded at his agent and the nurse.

As the nurse helped Mr. Thurlow to his feet, she looked over at Sheriff Flynn. "Yesterday. I think someone gave it to him yesterday."

"Thank you," Flynn replied, taking Mr. Thurlow's other arm as he stood.

Hank and MacGregor watched as they put Mr. Thurlow into the car waiting at the curb. As the car pulled away, Sheriff Flynn's attention returned to the object in her hand.

"What did he give you?" asked Hank.

Flynn opened her hand, revealing the tarnished object she held. "My badge. It's the badge I had on me the day I was abducted in Chicago."

CHAPTER FORTY

"So that means John Stevens was at the assisted living home in Concord yesterday," said Flynn, leaning back in her chair. "But why?"

"I've got agents over there now," replied MacGregor. He leaned forward, turning on the desk lamp. The bright, sunny day they had been enjoying less than an hour ago had suddenly been enveloped in a dark blanket of clouds. "So far everyone is accounted for, patients and employees. The receptionist remembers seeing Stevens in the lobby. He didn't ask for anyone, just said he was waiting for a family member. He just sat reading a magazine for a while. She said it was the first time she saw him. The receptionist walked away for a few minutes to get coffee. When she came back, John Stevens was gone."

"Any surveillance cameras?"

"They have cameras in the lobby and most of the hallways. The lobby camera has John Stevens entering around noon. He sits in the lobby for about ten minutes reading. Old man Thurlow is on the other end of the sofa. He doesn't say a word to the old man until the receptionist walks away. Then he moves down to the end, pulls something from his pocket, puts it in the old man's hand, whispers in his ear, and gets up and leaves."

"That's it?"

"Yep. A half hour later an orderly comes to collect the old man and walks him back to his room."

"So how did you end up bringing him here?"

"When the orderly got the old man back to his room, he noticed the badge. When he asked him about it, he just kept repeating 'Detective Flynn. Return to Detective Flynn.' The director at the home called the police, they called your precinct in Chicago, and they called me. I sent a couple agents over to talk to Mr. Thurlow. Once he told us what happened in the home, I had the agents bring him here."

"And there was nothing else out of the ordinary over there?"

"Nothing." MacGregor waited, watching Flynn check her phone for the third time since they came back into the office. "So where did you're deputy get off to?"

Flynn looked up. It took a moment before the question sunk in. "Calder's hotel. I sent him over to have another look around the room to see if there was any clue to where he might be."

"Well, let's not give up hope yet. I know you're concerned, but he's pretty resourceful and—"

"He's pretty irritating," Flynn interrupted. She wasn't doing a very good job hiding her true concern. "I told him that mouth would get him killed some day. That day just might have arrived."

"Let's not go there yet."

Flynn nodded, shifting the conversation. "Have you found out anything else about Stevens or his stepbrother? I don't think the Bob Clayton personality is a willing participant in all this . . . at least not in a mortal sense. Hell, I think he's trying to stop him."

MacGregor nodded, understanding where she was coming from and indicating his willingness to consider the idea. "If what you're saying about this multiple personality thing going on in Stevens is true, I'd have to agree. It doesn't make him any less guilty though."

Flynn tapped the redial on her phone. Same result.

Mac continued. "I had our forensic accounting team go back through Clayton's records for the past twenty-five years. He's regular as clockwork, doing PI work in Brooklyn. Pays his taxes. No extravagances. Nothing out of the ordinary. Not even a late notice on any of his credit cards. Then, about two years ago his habits change. Suddenly he's taking trips—you'll never guess where—car rentals, hotels stays.

"My guys found the online purchase receipt for the laptop the kid found in the dumpster behind the motel. You can't imagine the data they pulled off the hard drive. The computer he used to track these people and order the instruments of their death is the same computer that's going to hang him. We have enough now to indict and convict him for the murders in all four states. According to the data, even the three victims here in Auburn Notch were specifically targeted. They're chasing down the last of the data, some motel in North Carolina. We think it might have something to do with Barnes, but it's a stretch."

"That's great, but you know this is going to go down the insanity plea avenue."

"Insane or not, he's going to stand trial for all those murders."

Flynn leaned forward, her elbows on the desk, her fingers intertwined. "If Kaminski's diagnosis was correct, Stevens is the cold, calculated killer and some distorted version of his stepbrother becomes his stuttering conscience. Do you really think they're going to convict him of anything?"

"Our job is to catch him. It's up to the courts to sort out the particulars."

"That's just it. Even if we catch him—" Flynn's phone rang, interrupting her thought. "It's him." She hit the speaker button. "Calder? Where the hell have you been?"

"I–I'm sorry to d–disappoint you, Sheriff. Mr. Calder is n–not able to come t–to the phone."

"Listen, Stevens—" MacGregor was in no mood for games, but Flynn raised her hand cutting off whatever MacGregor was about to say.

"Is he alive, Bob?" Sheriff Flynn asked calmly.

There was a short pause. "Y–yes, but he's going to k–kill him. I can't s–stop him. I don't l–like this place."

Flynn tapped the mute button, stopping MacGregor from highjacking the conversation. He was angry, but threw his hands up allowing Flynn to continue. She tapped the mute button again.

"Tell me where you are, and I'll come get you both." Flynn paused for an answer, but there was only silence on the other end. "Bob? Are you still there? Tell me where you are. I'll come get you."

There was breathing on the phone, no other sound. Just slow, deliberate breaths.

Flynn leaned down close to the phone. "Bob? You don't have to do this. Tell me where you are."

"You're starting to sound just like him," a distinctly coarse, determined voice answered. A chill shot up Flynn's spine. She knew that voice. The voice she heard in her ear just before she was shot. "I would expect that level of incompetency from your FBI friend there, but you disappoint me, Detective. Think about it. You know exactly where he can be found. I just hope you're not too late. You should have figured out by now we'd come back here."

The phone went dead.

MacGregor pounded his fist down on the desk, but Flynn just ignored it. She closed her eyes, mouthing the final words before the phone went dead. MacGregor was quick to react, picking up his phone and telling whomever at the other end to trace the last incoming call to Sheriff Flynn's phone. Sheriff Flynn remained frozen, her eyes closed, still mouthing the words. MacGregor was barking orders, but none were getting through. She opened her eyes, looking right through him. He started at the beginning again. She continued to stare. Before he got the first sentence out, Flynn jumped to her feet.

"The asylum! They're at the asylum."

That got MacGregor's attention. "Are you sure?"

"Positive."

"Why would Stevens go back there?"

"He didn't go back there, Clayton did. Stevens had no say in the matter. That's why Clayton called. He's there, and he's trying to put a stop to all this. He wants to get caught."

"I sure hope you're right," said MacGregor, following behind Flynn.

CHAPTER FORTY-ONE

A flash of lightning lit up the overgrown and dilapidated interior of the second-floor observation room. The long shadow from the candle in the window sliced through the dirt and dried leaves, disappearing into the pile of rubbish in the hallway outside the door. The crack of thunder following echoed down the stairs, rattling the exposed pipes and piles of glass shards along the way.

Calder was conscious, very much aware of his situation, but remained perfectly still. Leather straps held him down tightly against the cold steel of the metal gurney. He wiggled his hand slowly, hoping for a week point in the straps. He tried desperately not to jump with each crack of thunder. With one eye slightly open, he tried to get a bearing on who else was in the room. A flash of lightning exposed the thin, steel framework over the upper portion of his body. A plastic tarp was pulled partially back. On his chest was an enameled tray. He could hear a whooshing sound behind him, like something under pressure being released.

"I–I'm going as fast as I c–can," a voice from near the windows stated. A man was hunched down in front of the window, a canvas bag taped over the nozzle of a fire extinguisher he was holding with thick, woolen gloves, "Th–this is your f–fault. Playing with that sh–sheriff is dangerous. Sh–she knows everything. Stop y–yelling at me!"

"Who's there?" Calder finally spoke up. "Who's there? Enough of this shit." Calder tried kicking, but the restraints were too tight. He could sense someone had walked over and was standing next to him. A flash of lightning was enough to reveal the familiar face. Calder began to kick again and pulling at the restraints on his wrist. "Oh, it's you, Clayton. If I get free I'm going to kick your ass."

"I'm afraid my stepbrother is a bit busy, Mr. Calder. We haven't met. I'm John Stevens." He lightly ran the heavy glove over Calder's arm, the cold causing him to tense up. "It will do you no good to struggle. I can assure you those leather straps are more than enough to keep you restrained."

"Stevens? Are you nuts, Clayton? I know it's you. Undo these straps." Calder continued to kick, but to no avail. He was certain it was Bob Clayton he was talking to, but there was something unnatural in his eyes. "Come back here!" he shouted out as the shadow of the man standing next to him faded back into the darkness.

It was quiet for a few minutes; only the sound of rain tapping on the peeling, neglected windowsills filled the silence.

"S–stop yelling at me! I'm almost d–done. That o–one extinguisher is empty. This sh–should be enough. Lets just f–finish this and get out of here. Do you hear that? Th–they're coming. They're coming, and we're s–still here. All right! All right. S–stop yelling at m–me."

Again there was silence.

"It's time."

In the distance a muffled siren could be heard through the dense pine forest lining each side of the road. It was faint. Four miles away, maybe five.

Calder was straining every muscle in his neck trying to get a look out the window. The flame on a candle flickering in the window caught his attention. The realization of what was happening to him was setting in. He struggled trying to break free from the leather straps binding his wrists. A metallic whine rose up above the rattle of the gurney he was strapped to. They're coming, he thought to himself. They must be coming. It was getting closer. It was a siren. Calder closed his eyes and drew his head back around. A shadow fell across his face. It was Clayton, standing next to him and holding something in his hands. Calder watched as he put an enameled tray on the gurney next to his chest and dumped the contents of a canvas bag into it.

"Jesus, that's cold. What are you doing? What is that?"

The siren was getting closer. There were flashes of red and blue piercing the darkness.

Calder continued to struggle; continued to shout out questions; continued to hurl profanities, but to no end. He felt the strap around his chest tighten. A flash of lightning piercing the stagnant air, reflecting off the damp walls, conveyed the final direction of his fate. A plastic tarp was being pulled forward over his head. He heard the snap of each clamp as it secured the plastic around the edges of the gurney. He struggled to keep his eyes open. His breaths grew shorter. Through the frosted plastic he could see a blurred image of a face close to his.

"I'm s–sorry, Mr. Calder. I t–tried to s–stop him. It'll all be over s–soon."

CHAPTER FORTY-TWO

The road out to asylum was treacherous on a clear day, narrow and without guardrails most of the way. Only the sharp curves near the top had any type of protection. MacGregor ignored it all, including the driving rain and the potential for a mudslide as he slid around each curve on his way to the top. Two other cars were following close behind, keeping pace with Mac's suicidal climb up the mountain.

A flash of lightning pasted the silhouette of the asylum against a wrathful, gray sky in front of them. There were still two miles between them. Two miles of treacherous curves. It didn't matter. It didn't slow MacGregor down.

"Did you get a hold of Hank?" MacGregor asked trying to distract Flynn enough to get her white knuckles back to a normal flesh tone.

"Yes. I told him what was going on when you were bringing the car around. He'll meet us there. Careful. There is a bad curve just before the entrance to the asylum." A slight fishtail around a curve brought on a short breath and a kneejerk reaction to stomp the nonexistent pedal beneath Flynn's right foot. "That's assuming we make it that far."

MacGregor looked over and smiled. "Don't worry, they train us to drive like this."

"Does the road know that?" Flynn looked back through the rear window. Above the vehicles behind them she could see the flashing lights on a parade of emergency vehicles darting out between the swaying branches, reflecting off the wet leaves like so many colored diamonds. She turned back. "I hope we're in time. Slow down, Mac, that curve is coming up."

A huge explosion ahead of them caught their breaths. MacGregor stomped on the brake, the car sliding to a stop on the gravel shoulder. Deep orange and yellow flames unfurled up into the rain above the trees, made more intense by a dense cloud of gray smoke expanding out against the black sky.

The last curve before the entrance to the asylum was just ahead. Slowly returning to the roadbed and moving forward, he and Flynn approached the curve. The wooden guardrail was busted through; splinters and chunks of wood were strewn all over the road. Three of the five wooden police barricades Flynn had put in place at Alice Johnson's request were in pieces. The flames, shooting up from the steep slope below the roadbed as high as the surrounding pine trees, illuminated the scene. MacGregor rolled to a stop. Flynn was the first one out of the car. The open gate to the asylum was twenty feet ahead of them. She looked up, pointing MacGregor's attention to the candle visible in the second-story window.

"I'll take my men up there," he called out, shielding his eyes from the driving rain. "See who's in the car." He pointed at the flames and smoke. Repeating his instructions over the sounds of the storm and sirens. "See who's in the car. See—who's—in—the —car."

Flynn nodded. She watched MacGregor with two of his agents head for the gate. All three men drew their guns. With two long strides they were up the marble steps and through the open door of the asylum. Flynn turned. A patrol car pulled up along side her. Hank hopped out and ran over to the embankment. The intense heat from the flames pushed him back. He looked back at Sheriff Flynn. She was splitting her attention between the fire in front of her and any sign from MacGregor that Calder was inside and alive.

"I called for the fire department when I saw the fireball," Hank called out, making a second attempt to see down the embankment. "Who is it? Do we know?"

Sheriff Flynn just shook her head.

The heat was still too intense to get close enough to the edge of the road. Hank walked down past where the cars were parked hoping to get a better vantage point. He could make out a car about twenty yards down the embankment, its front end wedged between two stout, pine trunks. He stepped over the guardrail onto the lose rocks. With a firm grip of the steel support beam with one hand he leaned forward, craning his neck for a better view. He slipped once. Digging his heel into the soft ground below the rocks, Hank tried once more to get a glimpse inside the car. The smoke and driving rain were relentless, pushing him back over the guardrail.

Pumper # 2 pulled past Flynn, coming to a stop in front of the gates to the asylum. Within minutes they had two hoses dowsing the flames that enveloped the car. A second engine pulled up where Hank stood. They concentrated on the flame working its way up the trunks of the pine trees.

Hank walked back to where Flynn was standing and shook his head. "I can't make out a thing. It's up to the fire department now." His attention shifted to the flames and smoke billowing up from the embankment.

Flynn turned back towards the asylum, still looking for some indication from MacGregor. She could see a figure in the doorway. She raised her arm over her eyes, blocking the rain for a better view. It was Mac.

CHAPTER FORTY-THREE

"I see they gave you a room with a better view this time," said Sheriff Flynn from the doorway of the hospital room.

Hugh Calder pushed himself up a bit more, resting back on the extra pillows he had requested earlier. His head was bandaged like before, but the outline of an additional bandage was visible through the front of his hospital gown. "If I didn't know better, MacGregor, I would say she's genuinely concerned about me."

MacGregor laughed. "You could be right. She seemed very upset over the thought of you being at the bottom of that fireball. It wouldn't surprise me—"

"If you two comedians are done," Sheriff Flynn grumbled rolling her eyes as she slid a chair over next to MacGregor, "why don't we go over what happened."

Calder wiggled around a bit, looking to settle into just the right spot as he began. "Like I said in the ambulance, I was going out to my car when I got whacked over the head. The next thing I know, I woke up inside the trunk of a car." He paused, looking from one to the other. "He's crazy, you know. Clayton is certifiable. I could here him arguing with himself as we were driving."

"Yeah, yeah, we know," MacGregor interrupted. "What happened then?"

"He opened the trunk and pulled me out. It was a parking garage. The airport, I think. The next car over had the trunk open —an old, blue skylark. It had antique plates on it. 7 3 5 were the last three digits I think. The asshole tosses me from one trunk to the other. He put a cloth over my mouth. Chloroform, I think. I passed out."

Flynn looked over at MacGregor and nodded.

"What?" Calder asked, moving around a bit more.

"There wasn't much of the car left after the fire," MacGregor offered, pulling out a note pad and flipping to a specific page, "but that confirms the license plate. The VIN number from the engine block shows the car was a '68 Buick Skylark. It was registered to a Mr. Aaron Westville of Effingham. He was away visiting family and left the car in long-term parking at the airport. He'll be back later today to confirm the theft and identify what's left of the car."

"Good luck with that," replied Calder. "I saw that blast before I passed out. The whole place shook. I thought it was lightning, but it was yellow. I remember the plastic turning yellow. I made one last attempt to break free. The next thing I knew I saw Mac here standing over me. I was never so glad to see anyone in my life."

MacGregor smiled. "You managed to push the enamel tray to the edge of the gurney. It must have tipped over spilling the dry ice onto the plastic. It burned right through. The tray was on the floor next to the gurney when my men and I got to you. Otherwise . . . well, this might have had a very different ending."

"Tell me about it," Calder responded with a grunt. "That shit Clayton. If he wasn't dead I'd—"

"So you saw Stevens get into the car," asked Flynn.

"Stevens? Who the hell is Stevens? You mean Clayton? No, he mumbled something after he pulled the plastic up over my head, but I didn't hear what he said. I was a little too busy trying to STAY ALIVE."

Flynn looked over at MacGregor. "So we don't really know who was in the car, do we?"

"Oh, it was Clayton all right," interrupted Calder.

"How do you know?" asked Flynn.

"When I woke up I was strapped to that rusted gurney. I could here him talking behind me. He didn't know I was awake. 'I'm ending it,' he kept repeating. Real loud, like he was arguing with someone, the stuttering fool. 'Th–this is it. We k–kill him and then get in the c–car and end it.' It was pretty surreal. 'We're not done,' a course voice replied. This went on for a few minutes. 'S–stop yelling at me. They're c–coming. They're coming.' Then I heard the sirens. He did, too. 'It's time,' the coarse voice said."

"And you're sure it was Clayton?" asked MacGregor.

"Yep, it was Clayton. It was his voice, even the raspy one—like he had a sore throat. No stutter, either. I called out, telling him to release me. He came over and stood by the gurney. It was that little shit all right, but he had this vacant look in his eyes. Gave me the chills. Pretty strange, uh?"

MacGregor stood up, giving Flynn a jerk of his head for her to follow. "Well, Mr. Calder, I'll send one of my agents back later for a complete account for the record. One last thing." MacGregor took a folded piece of paper from his pocket and tossed it at Calder.

"What's this?" asked Calder, unfolding the paper.

"That's a photo of you in the shadows of the bar behind Jane Newcomb the night she disappeared.

Calder took a hard swallow. "I can explain that."

"I can't wait. If you'll excuse us, I need to speak with the sheriff." MacGregor walked towards the hall.

"It's not what it looks like," Calder shouted.

"You just can't help yourself, can you?" said Flynn.

Calder winked at Sheriff Flynn, a gesture met with a smirk and a shake of her head. "Don't try to hide it," he called out as she left the room. "I know you care."

"That man is exasperating," said Flynn, as she and MacGregor made their way down the hall to the elevator.

MacGregor smiled. "We think he got a call from a burner phone the night Jane Newcomb disappeared. I'm sure it was Stevens setting him up for the next article, but we'll let him sweat for a while. At least he can place Stevens at the scene. We'll need to wait for the ME's report to confirm, but it's looking like Stevens was the man behind the wheel when that car went over the embankment."

"You don't think it's a setup?"

"If it was a normal person we were dealing with, I might be more obliged to agree, but we're dealing with two separate people here. One bent of revenge, the other trying to stop him."

The elevator door closed.

"You really think the Clayton personality was trying to stop the killings?" asked Flynn, pushing the button for the ground floor. "Everything was far too calculated to be suddenly derailed by an attack of conscience on Stevens's part. All those murders in four separate cities? Why now? Why stop it now?"

"You heard the old man, 'Only one left.' Calder was the last lose end. Let's assume it was Margaret Thompson's appearance in Chicago that awoke the dormant, homicidal personality and started the killing spree. If Stevens harbored any guilt at all, it was for killing his stepbrother. According to one of our shrinks, it's probably what evolved into the Clayton personality. As Stevens, he makes his way around the country tracking down those who wronged him in the past. He has a list of four people. One by one he stalks them online, manipulates them into a specific situation, and commits the four killings they will eventually be suspected of. With the police chasing after their suspect, he moves on to the next city, the next four killings, and the next victim on his list. Systematically, he locates and extracts his revenge on the four people he blames for his lot in life.

Fortnum's wife was the last. I'm sure he was quite surprised when he found out she was already dead. At that point, killing Mr. Fortnum was a necessity—he could identify him. As for Calder, he was a means to an end. Whether he died or not wasn't significant to Stevens. The shrink also believes the Clayton personality gained strength with every killing, finally becoming the dominant one. Clayton became determined to stop Stevens, and he needed Calder to get us to the asylum to witness his final act. This is really one for the books."

"What about the candles?" asked Flynn, as the elevator door opened on the ground floor.

"Yes, the candles. One of my agents has been sifting through old microfiche slides of the three local newspapers published around the time Stevens was a patient. He's not too happy with me at this point, but he dug up a few things about the Willis Asylum that made it all worthwhile. It detailed their annual fundraising efforts. They had a woodshop in the basement where Noah's Ark sets and an assortment of painted wooden animals were made. They were sold in shops in town. There was also a candle making facility on site. They relied on donated material to make the candles. They were pillar style candles and known to be of an exceptional quality, but the only coloring they were able to get was black. As a result, sales were light and cases of the candles were locked away in a storeroom in the basement. The same agent found a separate article about the suspicious fire at the asylum. The fire was believed to have started in the candle facility. I gave the agent an extra week vacation for sticking to it."

They made their way out to the parking lot.

"You think Stevens was connected to the candles and the fire?"

"Absolutely." MacGregor opened his car door. "Remember, this was prior to the *World Wide Web*. You could burn your records back then and vanish."

"But why kill his stepbrother?"

"I think Clayton knew what Stevens had been up to. If he confronted Stevens, it could be what sent him over the edge. Like I said, our shrink figured the Clayton personality was the voice of reason before and after death." It was probably strong enough to keep him under control for all those years, then Margaret Thompson shows up, and it all goes to hell. Doesn't matter now, it's over." He paused, noticing the skepticism on her face. "What, you think he's still alive?"

Promise ignored the question. "So, what's next, Mac?"

"Hopefully we'll get some kind of positive ID from the ME, and we can put this whole business behind us." MacGregor got in his car, shut the door, and lowered the window. "Until then. I think I'll get a little fishing in. A pleasure working with you, Promise."

Sheriff Flynn shook his outstretched hand. "See you around, Mac."

As she watched MacGregor pull out onto the main road, his hand waving out the window, Hank pulled up in his police car.

Sheriff Flynn opened the front passenger door, picked up the blue folder on the seat, and got in. "Is this everything?"

"It sure is," replied Hank pulling away. "I'm just not sure what you're going to do with it."

Flynn smiled, fingering through the papers in the thick folder. "It's not what I'm going to do with it, it's what *we're* going to do with it."

Hank glanced over, then back at the road ahead. "And what might that be?"

"We have one loose end, and I want to know what happened to him."

Hank tapped on the file with his finger. "It looks like you were right about Barnes. So, what's next?"

CHAPTER FORTY-FOUR

"So, how long will you be staying with us?"

"Oh, I'm . . . I'm n–not sure," he stammered, fumbling with his coat in an attempt to locate his wallet. His suit coat was wrinkled, the way thin, wool fabric would look after being bunched up during a long car trip. He smiled, finally producing the wallet. "It s–sure is hot out there. You s–said I could have the room by the w–week for $145?"

"Yes, sir," replied the older woman behind the counter. She had a pleasant smile to go along with a genial lilt to her Southern voice. Tight, white curls peeked out from beneath the gingham kerchief she had over her head and tied tightly below a full ponytail. "It's been overcast for some time, but they say fair weather ahead for the next few days. Are you here for the fishing?"

"Two w–weeks, probably," he replied, taking the correct assortment of bills from his wallet and handing them to the woman. "Maybe th–three. Cash is okay?"

"Sure. I just need a credit card for our records and the first week in advance."

He complied with another smile and a few nods, handing her a MasterCard. The woman made a copy of the card and started to fill out the registration form.

The sign on the side of the road said, CLOVER MOTEL. Below was a small neon sign flashing VACANCY, the red of the sign reflecting off the polished, wood counter. It was a family-run motel about twenty-five minutes outside of Charlotte, the long strip type you would see on vintage postcards. At the end was a wooden building, painted white with an unattractive shade of blue trim and shutters. Along side was an old Jeep Cherokee, looking more like an advertisement for an auto museum than the daily mode of transportation it obviously was.

"There we go," the woman stated, turning the form around and holding out a pen. "I'll just need your signature, Mr. Fortnum. You're in number three. We just redecorated, so I'm sure you'll find it very comfortable."

He nodded, took the pen, and signed his name. "Th–thank you. I'm s–sure it will be just fine." He finished signing, receiving a smile, a key, and the credit card in return.

"So, if you're not here for the fishing what brings you to Clover?"

He smiled, stuffing the key and card in his pocket. "I'm m–meeting my brother here. We're h–here to see an old f–friend from the past. I b–believe he opened a health-f–food store in town."

Stevens pulled his car around in front of Cabin 3. He had one suitcase, and a small bag of groceries he had picked up at a convenience store he passed on his way to the motel. Leaving the car door open, he picked up the groceries and fished the key out of his pocket. He opened the screen door and unlocked the room. The door swung open. As he stepped inside, the dark outline of a figure in the room caught him by surprise. It took a minute for his eyes to adjust from the bright sunlight outside. He squinted his eyes trying to bring the figure in focus. Looking back at him was the aged but familiar face of an old friend sitting on the edge of the bed.

"I heard you were looking for me."

"Wh–what are you d–doing here?" said Stevens. Suddenly the contrived nature of finding Barnes waiting for him in his cabin threw him into a panic. His voice changed in a snap. "You saved me the trouble of looking for you, Barnes." He reached into his pocket, taking a firm grip of the .38 he had with him. Before he could pull it from his pocket, he felt the end of a barrel on the back of his neck and the click of a hammer.

"I'll take that," said Hank from behind, reaching into the pocket and taking the gun from Stevens's hand.

Hank handed the gun to Sheriff Flynn who had walked in behind him. Flynn gave a jerk of her head. Let's go, Barnes, you're done here. There's a couple FBI agents outside that would like to have a conversation with you.

Roy Barnes didn't say a word. With his head down, he cautiously walked around Stevens and past Flynn. Two FBI agents met him at the door.

MacGregor looked in. "You bring him along when you're ready, Promise. I'm sure you two have a few things to iron out." He closed the screen door and caught up with the agents who were walking Barnes over to one of the black sedans.

Stevens sat down on the end of the bed. "I'm g–glad it's over," he mumbled softly. "I didn't want to h–hurt those people." He glanced up for only a moment at Sheriff Flynn. "I'm glad he d–didn't kill you. I wanted you to s–stop him. You have to s–stop him. You have t–to."

"It's over, Bob. No more killing."

He was a pathetic sight, slouched in defeat, his head bowed down, his hands shaking slightly.

Bob nodded his head. "How did you f–find us?"

"I got a missing person report from the Concord Police. It seems a gentleman named Thornton went to visit his mother over at the assisted living facility there and never returned. You know the place; it's where you went to visit Mr. Thurlow. You can imagine my surprise when I noticed the description the Concord PD gave me of the missing guy was your same height and build. It didn't take much to put that together with the body we found in the burned-out car by the asylum." The tips of Flynn's lips curled up in satisfaction. "I don't have confirmation yet, but I'm pretty sure the ME will confirm it was Thorton that went through the guardrail in that fireball. You had Calder's car stashed up at the Asylum, didn't you? You found that fire access road."

Bob smiled and nodded his head.

"Hank put the rest together from bits and pieces of info he found on your computer.

"I was hoping you w–would find that. It was all th–there. Everything he made me d–do." He began to tear up. "I didn't want to d–do it. N–none of it. I couldn't stop him. I t–tried. I really t–tried. Those poor—"

"I know," said Sheriff Flynn, "I know." She took out her cuffs and sat down on the bed next to Bob. "I figured out Barnes was probably still alive, and he was the last person on your list. Between what Hank found on the computer and what MacGregor's agents dug up, it lead us right here. It wasn't too difficult to find Barnes. I figured if we could, you probably already did. It made sense you would come here. But now it's over, Bob. You'll have to stand accountable for all those murders, but you should get the help you need."

Bob was gone. Stevens slowly raised his head. Hank was looking through the screen door at the agents outside, watching as they put Barnes in the back of one of their cars. Flynn's attention shifted away for a split second. Stevens pulled a tactical knife from his pocket and leaned in close to Flynn's ear, stating in a course, determined voice, "You're wrong, Detective. You're the last person on my list."

The course whisper took Flynn's breath away. It was a moment before she could react, but not before she heard a click and the blade snap into place. She felt his hand grip her collar. She was yanked backwards. Above her head a tight fist held the knife about to be thrust into her heart. Deep within the dark eyes staring down at her the cold memories of that day in Chicago when she was abducted flashed before her. She raised her hand in defense of what was about to happen. It was all she could do.

A shot rang out. It threw Stevens backwards and off the bed. In a second, the room was filled with blue nylon jackets, their guns drawn. Flynn pulled herself up into a sitting position. The knife was on the rug in front of her. It all happened so fast.

Hank was standing by the door, the last curls of smoke rising from the barrel of his Sig Sauer. "Did I mention I was tops in my class for marksmanship."

Flynn smiled and shook her head. "No, but why don't you mention that at your next why-didn't-I-get-the-job bitching session with the town council."

Hank tucked his revolver away in the holster and smiled back. "I don't think I'll be having any more of those conversations."

ACKNOWLEDGMENTS

An author takes an idea, breaks it down into characters, setting, and plot, and then strings it all together. This is a story in its simplest form. From this, it is an accumulation of the hard work and dedication of others that turn those three things into a book. In acknowledgment of this, the author wishes to thank the following people: Lawrence Knorr, whose belief in the author's ability to tell a story made this book possible; Janice Rhayem, a fabulous editor who took a good story and turned it into a brilliant book; Crystal Devine, for her unique talent to capture the true feeling of the book in her layout and design; Amber Rendon, whose exceptional artistic skills brought the story to life on the cover; and Abby Galardi, for being a creative sounding board during the plotting stages of the book.

ABOUT THE AUTHOR

R. Michael Phillips lives in a historic community is southeastern Pennsylvania with his wife and son. He is a classically trained artist turned mystery writer, and a proud member of Mystery Writers of America and the Crime Writers Association.

Other books by the author:

The Ernie Bisquets Mystery Series

Along Came A Fifer
Rook, Rhyme And Sinker
Passage Of Crime

CPSIA information can be obtained at www.ICGtesting.com
Printed in the USA
BVOW02*1715050216

435552BV00001B/2/P